#2

Dial Meow
for Murder

Bethany
Blake

KENSINGTON BOOKS
http://www.kensingtonbooks.com

KENSINGTON BOOKS are published by

Kensington Publishing Corp.
119 West 40th Street
New York, NY 10018

All Kensington titles, imprints and distributed lines are available at special quantity discounts for bulk purchases for sales promotion, premiums, fund-raising, educational or institutional use. Special book excerpts or customized printings can also be created to fit specific needs. For details, write or phone the office of the Kensington Special Sales Manager: Kensington Publishing Corp., 119 West 40th Street, New York, NY, 10018. Attn. Special Sales Department. Phone: 1-800-221-2647.

ISBN-13: 978-1-4967-0740-6
ISBN-10: 1-4967-0740-0
First Kensington Mass Market Edition: October 2017

eISBN-13: 978-1-4967-0741-3
eISBN-10: 1-4967-0741-9
First Kensington Electronic Edition: October 2017

10 9 8 7 6 5 4 3 2

Printed in the United States of America

For my father, Donald "Butch" Fantaskey,
a gentle soul who loved all creatures,
whether great, small, easygoing or ill-tempered.

Acknowledgments

Like all books, this one is the result of collaboration with and assistance from a lot wonderful people—way more than can be credited here. However, I would like to take some space to thank, in particular, my editor, Wendy McCurdy, whose incredible support and patience were much appreciated over the course of the last year.

Thanks, in fact, to everyone at Kensington Publishing, including Norma Perez-Hernandez, as well as Lauren Jernigan, Karen Auerbach and Kimberly Richardson on the awesome PR and marketing team. I'm also grateful for the guidance of my agent, Helen Breitwieser, who always supports me when I tackle a new project.

In addition, I'd like to acknowledge my friends and family, including my fellow spinners at the gym, the stylish women at the Styling Nook, and everybody in our little town who cheers me on. If I am able to write about a cute, tightly knit community, it's because I am lucky enough to live in one. Speaking of friends, a special thanks to Jackie Kelly, Mary Leo and Marjorie Priceman, who all dwell in the world of publishing and offer encouragement on rough days.

I'd also like to thank my in-laws, George and Elaine Kaszuba, and my sister-in-law, Sandra, all of whom are shameless promoters of my work. And the biggest thanks to my parents, Marjorie and Donald "Butch" Fantaskey, who always encouraged me to be a writer, as well as to my supportive husband, Dave, and my children, Paige, Julia and Hope.

Without all of your help, guidance and good wishes, this book wouldn't be here. Thank you!

Chapter 1

Flynt Mansion sat high upon a hill just outside Sylvan Creek, Pennsylvania, its twin turrets stabbing at a huge October moon that was obscured now and then by passing dark clouds. Local legend said the sprawling Victorian house, which overlooked Lake Wallapawakee, was haunted, but the evening of the Fur-ever Friends Pet Rescue gala fund-raiser, the place was spirited in a different way.

"This is so cool," my best friend, Moxie Bloom, said as we passed through tall, iron gates that had concealed most of the property from the road. The gates clanged shut behind us, and I jumped, nearly dropping a big, plastic tub full of pet treats I'd cooked up for the party, which would support my favorite local charity. "Wow," Moxie added. "It's spooky gorgeous."

I had to agree. The curving stone pathway that led to the house was lined with at least fifty glowing jack-o'-lanterns, their flickering faces carved into leering grins, grimaces of agony, and threatening scowls. The twisted branches of the property's many crabapple trees were strung with twinkle lights, while three ornate, black-iron chandeliers—each holding at least twenty candles—were suspended from the sturdier oaks, so the grounds were bathed in a soft, mysterious light. More grim-faced jack-o'-lanterns were propped on the railing that surrounded the house's wraparound porch. It looked like the pumpkins were guarding the mansion, which was dark inside, with the exception of single, lit candles that burned in most of the many tall, narrow windows.

The estate was already movie-set eerie, but the Fur-ever Friends decorating committee—chaired by my perfectionist sister, Piper Templeton—wasn't finished yet. A few people still bustled around the lawn, setting up chairs and lighting even more candles.

Standing just inside the fence with Moxie and my canine sidekick, Socrates, I took a moment to drink in the scene. Then I frowned and turned to Moxie. "Umm . . . Why are we the only people in costumes?"

"I'm not wearing a costume," Moxie said, sounding confused. She looked uncharacteristically demure in a vintage, mint-green, wool suit with a high-collared jacket and a pencil skirt that hit midcalf. A string of pearls circled her neck, and she'd dyed her hair from flame red to a soft blond. "Why would you think *that*?"

"I thought you were Tippi Hedren, from *The Birds*." I resumed watching the volunteers, most of whom wore sweaters and sweatshirts, then I adjusted a tall, pointed hat that kept slipping off my long, unruly, dirty-blond curls. I didn't see one other witch, not to mention any ghosts or ghouls, and I began to get a little sweaty under my polyester cape. "I'm the only person who dressed up!" I glanced down at Socrates, taking some comfort in the fact that he was also in costume—only to discover that he looked like he always did: like a contemplative, sometimes morose basset hound. "Where is your wizard hat?"

"Didn't you see that fly out the window of the van, halfway up the hill?" Moxie asked, answering on behalf of Socrates, who was pretending he hadn't heard me. He stared straight ahead. However, I noticed that the very tip of his tail twitched the way it did when he felt guilty. "I assumed you noticed," Moxie continued, "and just didn't want to turn around, because we were running late."

I'd heard Socrates shuffling around in the backseat of my distinctive 1970s, pink VW bus, which advertised my business, Lucky Paws Pet Sitting, and featured a large, hand-painted dog that was often mistaken for a misshapen pony. I'd thought he was cranky about losing the front seat to Moxie, and I'd ignored him.

"I should've known you'd never really wear the hat," I complained to Socrates, who had started snuffling. The sound was very reminiscent of a snicker. "You were far too agreeable about putting it on. I should've guessed that something was up."

Socrates finally looked up at me and blinked his droopy, brown eyes, as if to say, *Indeed, you should have known that I would never deign to don a costume.*

"Maybe I should go home and change," I said, starting to turn around.

"You're not going anywhere," my sister called, hurrying across the lawn. She took the tub of snacks from me, like she couldn't wait one more minute to get her hands on it. "You're a half hour late! There's no time for you to return to Winding Hill, change clothes, and come back before the gala starts."

Of course, she was right. It would take me at least twenty minutes to drive to Winding Hill Farm, where Piper—a successful veterinarian—let me live rent free in her gorgeous, restored 1860s farmhouse. Well, actually, I was moving into a cottage on the property. The adorable tiny house had recently become available when the former tenant, Winding Hill's caretaker, was arrested for the murder of Piper's ex-boyfriend. I'd solved the crime—not that anyone would give me credit.

"This is Fur-ever Friends' biggest fund-raiser of the year," Piper added. "People and pets will start arriving in less than an hour. You need to set up the snack table for the dogs. . . ." She finally looked me up and down. "No matter how silly you look." Then she turned to Moxie and knitted her brows. "And who are you supposed to be? Tippi Hedren?"

Moxie's cheeks flushed, just slightly. "It's more of an *homage* than a costume," she said, lifting her chin high. "The woman was Hitchcock's muse. An icon!"

She *was* in costume. I'd known it.

"What happened to *you*?" I asked, thinking Piper was being a little judgmental for someone whose blouse was soaking wet.

My sister brushed ineffectually at a dark stain on her sleeve. "Pastor Kishbaugh and I were trying to move the apple-bobbing tub. Water sloshed everywhere."

I located Pastor Pete Kishbaugh, who was across the lawn attaching fake ravens to the branches of a crab-apple. If he was also soggy, his black shirt hid the problem.

"All three of you, come with me now," Piper added, leading the way down the path. Temporary stain aside, she was dressed appropriately in dark slacks and a rust-colored top that hinted at fall, but didn't scream "Halloween," like my getup. Her straight, shiny, brown hair—the polar opposite of the chaos on my head—was smoothed back and held in place with a pretty peach and brown patterned headband. "There's still plenty to do before the guests show up," she informed Moxie and me, over her shoulder. "Let's go."

We all followed Piper, who lugged the plastic bin, while I tried to keep a grip on the billowing fabric of my cape, which kept flapping perilously close to the gauntlet of jack-o'-lanterns. The last thing I needed was to make a bigger spectacle of myself by catching on fire. The tag on the cape had warned that the fabric wasn't flame retardant.

"This is where you'll set up," Piper said, stopping in front of a table with a placard that advertised *Howling Good Dog Treats* in a spooky, drippy script. The tabletop was already decorated with two life-sized ceramic black cats, their backs arched high and their tails sticking straight up. Cute orange and black platters featured similar hissing felines, in a vintage design. The table was also scattered with dog-appropriate bones, all real and available for the munching. Piper set the bin on the grass. "As you can see, I did most of the work, in your absence."

"Why are you so grouchy?" I asked, because Piper, always type A, was even more tense than usual. "This is supposed to be fun."

All at once, my sister's shoulders slumped. "I'm sorry. I'm just worried because Lillian Flynt, who is supposed to be hosting this event, is nowhere to be found. I've somehow ended up in charge of the whole thing. And to make matters worse, the power is out in the house, for some reason. These candles aren't all just for show."

"Miss Flynt isn't here?" Moxie asked, looking around, like she might locate the older woman, who was semi-affectionately known as Sylvan Creek's "professional volunteer."

Gray-haired, never-married heiress Lillian didn't lack for money, so she'd made charity her life's work. The local *Weekly Gazette*'s About Town society column almost always featured at least one photo of Miss Flynt in her signature knit cardigan, doing good things for others. One day, she'd be pictured delivering meals to folks even more elderly than she was, and the next, she'd be accepting an oversized grant check on behalf of the public library or ladling stew at a church soup kitchen. But while Lillian might have appeared kind and grandmotherly, she had a spine of steel. I'd worked with her quite a bit on behalf of Fur-ever Friends, and she always acted like she was my boss, and I was an intern.

As I bent to open the bin, I flashed back to the day she'd approached me about "volunteering" for the gala.

"You are aware of the upcoming Fur-ever Friends party, correct, Daphne?" Miss Flynt had said, stopping me on Sylvan Creek's main street by slamming a cane in my path. She couldn't have been more than sixty-five, and she was probably in better shape than me, so I didn't think she needed the stick for support. I was pretty sure it was a tool to keep others in line.

"Yes, I know about it," I'd told her. Then I'd cut right to the chase. "What do you need?"

"Treats for at least twenty dogs. From your pet bakery."

She always acted like I had a storefront, and I always corrected her. "Um, I just cook for fun, at home. I don't really have a bakery. . . ."

Miss Flynt had answered the way she always did. "Well, get to it, Daphne! What are you waiting for?" Then she'd nodded briskly to Socrates, nearly dislodging her wiry, gray hair from its bun. "Good day to you, wise Socrates!"

A few moments later, Miss Flynt had moved on down the street, and I'd stood there with Socrates, both of us needing a second, as usual, to recover from the very direct, almost curt, exchange. Yet, I admired Miss Flynt. She had a different approach from me, but she was a big supporter of Fur-ever Friends.

"It is odd that she's not here micromanaging," I told Piper, as I removed containers of home-made goodies from the bin. Prying the lid off one tub, I began to place Tricky Treats on a platter. The snacks were "tricky" because they looked and tasted like peanut-butter cups, but I'd substituted dog-friendly carob for the chocolate, which could be lethal to canines. "Where do you think she is?"

"I have no idea," Piper said. "And, as if things aren't bad enough, when Tamara Fox went into the house to get some matches, she accidentally let Lillian's prized Persian cat, Tinkleston, run out the door. Now we can't find him."

Moxie and I shared a look, then we both started snickering.

"What is so funny about a missing cat?" Piper demanded. "Especially since I'm sure I'll get blamed for his disappearance."

"I'm sorry," I said, slipping Socrates a Tricky Treat. He feigned disdain for a few moments, then accepted the sweet from my fingers. "But what kind of name is Tinkleston?"

"It's a horrible name for a horrible cat."

We all turned to realize that we'd been joined by none other than Tamara Fox, who made a mock shudder, so I got the impression that she wasn't upset about the feline's disappearance.

Tamara, whom we'd all known since high school, didn't bother to really greet us. Kind of like she'd snubbed us back in school, too. Tossing her long, dark hair over her shoulder, she gave Moxie and me a skeptical once-over, then didn't ask about the costumes,

either. It was almost like she assumed we'd misread—
or lost—our invitations, as I had done.

In my defense, though, who *wouldn't* assume that a
"gala" held in late October at a haunted mansion
would at least be costume optional?

"Have you seen the cat?" Piper asked Tamara. "I'm
dreading telling Lillian that he's gone."

"I hope I never see that beast again," Tamara said.
She adjusted a large tote that was slung over her shoulder, and her adorable little Maltese, Buttons, poked
out her beribboned head just long enough to blink.
Then the dog disappeared back into the bag, like
something was spooking her. "I swear that cat was stalking Buttons and me the whole time we were inside."

"Most people think cats are aloof, but they actually
like company," I told Tamara. I felt like I had some
authority on the subject since I was a professional pet
care expert. "He was probably just lonely in that big,
dark house and wanted to be friends."

Tamara shot me a look that said she wasn't interested
in my credentials or my opinions. "There's nothing
friendly about that animal. It's evil."

Giving her hair one more dramatic toss with a hand
smothered under heavy rings, Tamara took her leave
of us without another word. We all watched her sashay
off with the same hip-swaying stride she'd had back in
her cheerleading days. Soon after graduation, she'd
surprised all of Sylvan Creek by marrying much, much
older—and very, very wealthy—attorney Larry Fox.
Tamara hadn't worked a day in her life and was considered heiress-apparent to Lillian's informal title of
"professional volunteer." On days Lillian wasn't in the
Gazette, Tamara could usually be found smiling for
the camera.

"What does she have against cats?" asked Moxie, who

had a wide-eyed kitten tattooed on her wrist. "They're adorable!"

"Actually, Tinkleston—née Budgely's Sir Peridot Tinkleston—is a difficult animal, to put it mildly," Piper informed us. "I've had to give him shots, and I have the scars to prove it."

I didn't think it was fair to judge a cat based upon his behavior while getting stuck with a needle, but I didn't mention that to Piper.

"We'll keep an eye out for the runaway and finish setting up the table," I promised, waving my fingers to dismiss my sister. "You go oversee everybody else."

"Okay, thanks," Piper said. "I actually need to track down an old CD player Miss Flynt promised we could use to play spooky music. That thing's missing, too." My sister eyed the table warily as she backed away. "You two do a nice job, okay?"

I didn't dignify that with a response. I just started arranging Batty-for-Pumpkin Cookies on a plate—a task that absorbed me until Moxie tapped my shoulder.

"Hey, look," she said. "Somebody else dressed up, as a priest!"

"That's not a costume," I corrected Moxie. "That's Pastor Pete Kishbaugh, the guy Piper was just talking about. He always wears a black shirt and a clerical collar. Don't you know him?"

"No," she said. "He's completely bald. How would I know him?"

Moxie was the owner of Spa and Paw, Sylvan Creek's unique salon, which catered to people *and* pets. She seldom met anyone who didn't have hair. Or fur.

"He's kind of cute," Moxie noted. "Some guys can pull off the shaved head."

"He's also involved in a scandal right now," I whispered. "You've probably heard the rumors about his church, Lighthouse Fellowship." Moxie might not have recognized Pastor Pete, but she was the motor that turned Sylvan Creek's busy gossip mill, and I knew she'd at least be familiar with the stories surrounding him. "I don't know the details, but I heard something about embezzlement, or misappropriated funds."

"Oh, he's *that* minister?" Moxie mused, just as Pastor Pete—thirty-something, with a gleaming white smile and kind eyes—noticed me and waved. I sometimes watched his golden retriever mix, Blessing, while Pete was on mission trips. He was a very peripatetic man of the cloth. "Yeah, I've heard about that mess," Moxie added. "That's probably going to be fall's big story. I can just tell."

Feeling guilty because the subject of our discussion was still smiling at us, I told Moxie, "You know, Socrates—the logician, not the dog . . ." I often quoted the ancient Greek scholar, who'd been central to my doctoral dissertation, so I was always making that clarification. "Socrates once said, 'Strong minds discuss ideas'—not people. I kind of wish I hadn't even brought up the rumors."

Moxie waved off my concerns with a gloved hand.

Why had I believed for a minute that she wasn't in costume?

"I've seen pictures of that old philosopher," she informed me. "He could've used a haircut. And I bet he would've dished on Plato for hours, if he'd ever sat in my chair."

At my side, the canine Socrates lifted his big head and rolled his baleful eyes, as if he disagreed. At least, it appeared that way. Or maybe he was just sniffing the air, which smelled wonderful. The night was crisp and the breeze off the lake was fresh, but tinged with the bittersweet aroma of falling leaves. And somewhere inside the mansion, a fire burned in a fireplace. The smoke, coiling from the chimney, gave the air a distinctly autumnal tang. Raising my slightly upturned nose, I sniffed, too, and I was pretty sure I could also identify the scents of apple cider, cinnamon, and pumpkin.

"Do you think we could take a little break and wander over to the table with the people food?" I asked Moxie. I glanced at my bin of treats, which was still pretty full, while the platters I needed to fill were mostly empty. "We wouldn't be gone long."

"I could go for something sweet," Moxie agreed. She was already heading across the lawn. Passing under a crabapple tree, she ducked and placed a protective hand on her blond bouffant while warily eyeing one of the ravens Pastor Pete had wired to a branch. Then she called back to me, "I'm pretty sure I see cookies for humans."

What could I do but follow, with Socrates in my wake?

"You know, I'm actually surprised Lillian threw this shindig," I said, when we reached another table that was completely stocked with an array of very clever treats, including meringue ghosts, chocolate cookie "spiders" with licorice legs, and cheese sticks decorated to look like severed fingers, with almond-sliver fingernails and marinara-sauce blood. That was sort of gross, but I took one anyhow, adding, "I know Miss Flynt loves animals, but I can't recall her ever opening up her house for a party."

"She doesn't love all animals!"

Both Moxie and I started at the sound of an indignant, almost angry, voice, coming from right behind us.

"Hey, Ms. Baumgartner," I said, taking a step backward and greeting the head of the local cats-only shelter, Whiskered Away Home. Beatrice Baumgartner was also active with Fur-ever Friends and held a plastic-wrapped plate of snacks to donate. "We didn't see you there."

Now that Bea was upwind, I could *smell* her. She carried the faint odor of a litter box that needed to be emptied. I didn't understand that. I worked in lots of homes with multiple cats, and that smell was avoidable. It kind of put me off my cheese finger, and I had no intention of trying one of the chocolate-chip cookies she was unveiling from under the crinkled sheet of plastic, either.

Moxie's nose was wrinkling, too, but she wasn't dis-suaded from eating the meringue ghost she'd chosen. "Miss Flynt loves stray dogs, and she must love cats, too," she said, pausing to bite off the specter's head. "We were just talking about Tinkleston, who is supposedly on the loose."

For a woman dedicated to saving felines, Bea didn't seem overly concerned about a missing prize Persian.

"Lillian is no friend to cats—except *purebred* show animals," she said, crossing her arms over an ample bosom. She had to be in her late sixties, and while I was definitely the least appropriately dressed person at that party, Bea wasn't exactly up to code, either. She wore stained khaki pants that I was pretty sure came from the men's department and a frayed sweatshirt that fea-tured an appliqué of a black kitten sitting inside a pumpkin. I supposed I could at least give her credit for making an effort to honor the holiday. The expression on her deeply lined face was also suitably scary. "I am positive that Lillian only agreed to host this fund-raiser to get herself noticed by the media. Again."

I wasn't sure I'd call the *Weekly Gazette* "media." It was delivered free, whether anyone wanted it or not, and it only reached about two hundred homes. As I made my pet-sitting rounds, I found a lot of copies on floors in houses where puppies were being potty trained. However, I didn't argue that point with Bea, who was excusing herself, anyway. She nodded at me, Moxie, and Socrates. "Enjoy the party."

"Well, that was awkward," Moxie observed, when Bea was out of earshot. All at once, her eyes gleamed. "And while we're on the subject of uncomfortable situations, what are you going to do if Dylan and Detective Black *both* show up tonight?"

She was referring to one guy I sometimes dated, and another I hadn't seen since I'd solved a murder for him, after numerous clashes.

I really didn't want to discuss either of those men.

I was also suddenly distracted by something I could see inside the mansion, over Moxie's shoulder.

A shadowy figure, who stood at one of the tall windows, observing the party preparations from behind a curtain.

I blinked twice to make sure my eyes weren't playing tricks on me, then I got a funny, nervous feeling in the pit of my stomach.

What was that person doing *there*?

Chapter 2

I wasn't especially eager to enter Flynt Mansion. I'd only been inside the house once, years ago, when Piper had dared Moxie and me to trick-or-treat there.

Kids never used to approach the property, which was said to be haunted by the ghost of a woman who'd been strangled there, decades before. Some people in Sylvan Creek swore that an elegant, dark-haired specter in a red evening gown floated past the windows on moonless nights.

Moxie and I couldn't bear to look like chickens, though, so we'd lumbered up onto the unwelcoming, unlit porch, both of us moving awkwardly, because we'd made a dinosaur costume out of a big cardboard box. I'd been the rear end. Moxie had rung the bell, and as I'd tugged on her green leggings, begging her to run away, the massive door had opened and some-one had waved us inside. I'd tried to pull back, but Moxie had dragged us both into the foyer. I hadn't been able to see a thing except a worn Turkish rug and my sneakers, but the house had smelled musty. A few minutes later, we were back outside, and Moxie'd informed me that we'd received a single, mushy apple for our troubles.

Piper, dressed as Dorothy from *The Wizard of Oz*—right down to ruby-red slippers she'd hand-sequined—had enjoyed a rare fit of genuine laughter at our expense.

I wasn't any more keen on opening the huge, wooden, front door that night, in part because this time, I was pretty sure I knew who lurked inside. And that person was scarier than any unknown, potentially menacing entity.

Still, I turned the knob, pushed open the creaking door, and poked my head into the foyer, which I was pretty sure had the same carpet I'd seen as a kid. Then I called softly, "*Mom?* Are you in here?"

Chapter 3

"You're showing this house *tonight*?" I asked, confused by my mother's presence in Flynt Mansion on a Saturday night. Or any night, for that matter. She wore a conservative, dark suit she called "the Closer" and moved quickly around the house, straightening up, like she always did before presenting a property to potential buyers. I followed after her, still asking questions. "And in the dark? During a party?"

"It's not exactly a *showing*," Mom clarified, lighting a candle she'd dug out of her black canvas tote, which advertised her business, Maeve Templeton Realty. Unlike the tapers in the windows, her candle was scented, and I suspected that, more than to dispel the gloom, she wanted to mask a musty odor that I also recognized from my childhood trick-or-treating escapade. She set the glowing jar, labeled *Autumn Breeze*, on a rolltop desk that probably dated back to the mansion's Victorian days. "The buyer has already toured the house and is returning for one last look before making an offer. But it's really a formality. I can tell that she's very eager to begin negotiating." Mom adjusted a few knickknacks on the desk, then stalked off, talking over her shoulder. "I don't know why you are so surprised by any of this!"

"I didn't even know the house was for sale," I said, following her into a spacious kitchen, which actually had a lot of potential. Classic white cabinets lined the walls, and the countertops were appealingly worn butcher block that had obviously outlived quite a few passing trends. The cherry floors were also scuffed, but could easily be returned to their former gleaming glory. Best of all, a large bank of nearly floor-to-ceiling windows overlooked the lake. The full moon had emerged from behind the clouds and was illuminating the water. The view was stunning, and I could imagine sipping tea while watching the sunrise. Then I turned back to Mom. "To be honest, I'm kind of shocked that Miss Flynt would move. Her family's been here forever."

"I was also surprised," Mom admitted, retrieving yet another candle from her bottomless bag. My mother—like my sister—was always prepared, which was no doubt why Templeton Realty had steamrolled most other competitors in Sylvan Creek. Well, Mom's rather strong personality—to put it kindly—had probably helped her get ahead, too. "But when I told Lillian that I'd been approached by a potential buyer, she agreed that it was time to put this place on the market." Mom lit the second candle and shook her hand, extinguishing the match. "This property *is* far too large for one older person."

"So, if the house is already essentially sold, why are you 'staging' it?" I asked, leaning against a counter and crossing my arms, so my cape swooped. Fortunately, Mom had been too preoccupied with preparing the mansion to lecture me about appropriate party attire. Although she had suggested that I take off my "ridiculous" hat. In retrospect, I wasn't sure why I'd kept it on for so long. "And why did you schedule this meeting on a Saturday night?" I added. "During a big fund-raiser?"

My mother shook her head and sighed, like everything I'd just said exasperated her. "And you expect me to believe that you sold Detective Black a property. Honestly, Daphne! You don't seem to know anything about real estate!"

I *had* convinced Jonathan Black to buy an A-frame log cabin that was perfect for a privacy-loving ex-Navy SEAL. But my mother would never believe me, and Jonathan apparently wasn't corroborating my story, either.

"The interested party is a very busy, high-powered executive in New York City, and she had difficulty working this meeting into her schedule," Mom continued. "We finally settled on this evening, in spite of the event." The countertop was messy, and as she talked, my mother stashed items in cupboards and drawers. "Unfortunately, she couldn't leave the city until at least six p.m., and it's a two-hour drive from Manhattan to the Poconos." She shot me a pointed look. "Businesspeople often work weekends and well into the evening, you know."

I knew. *I* was a businessperson. One who had to take a Yorkshire terrier out to potty at ten o'clock that night, long after most nine-to-fivers were in their jammies.

"Well, I still don't understand why you're making such a fuss about how the place looks—and smells," I said, moving over to the refrigerator, where a single, typewritten sheet of paper was attached to the door by a magnet advertising a local pet boutique called "Fetch!" Scanning the document, I realized it was a schedule, titled *Tinkleston—Supplements—October*. Beneath that was a spreadsheet, arranged by date and listing all of the probiotics, omegas, and fish oils that Miss Flynt's pampered feline apparently consumed on a regular and regulated basis. I kind of wished anything in my life was as organized as the cat's vitamin regimen. Then I returned my attention to Mom. "Again, what's up with the candles, if the offer's essentially in the bag?"

"Candlelight bathes everything in a warm, forgiving glow," Mom said, with a glance at the ceiling. "To be honest, I find the power outage rather serendipitous. The house looks even better than when I initially showed it."

I looked up at the ceiling, too, and saw a jagged crack in the plaster. I probably would have noticed the flaw sooner if the overhead light was working, and for just a moment, I pictured my mother creeping around a fuse box, cutting wires. Then I dismissed the image as absurd. Well, at least unlikely. "So you're trying to trick this person into making a *bigger* offer?"

"It's no different than having dinner by candlelight, with a date," Mom pointed out. "Aging ladies, like this lovely old girl"—she patted the countertop— "can benefit tremendously from a little 'soft focus.'"

I wondered if my mother had used that realtor trick to her personal benefit, too. Not that she had wrinkles or dated much since my father left town, ages ago.

"As for the fund-raiser, that's also beneficial," Mom noted, with a smug half smile.

"How so?" I asked warily. I was starting to worry that my mother was even more crafty than I'd thought.

"The purchaser is an *executive producer* with the Stylish Life television network," Mom informed me, sounding somewhat triumphant. I got the sense that my mother felt she'd personally reeled a big fish into our little pond. "How better to impress her than with a soiree, beautifully and atmospherically decorated by Piper?" Maeve Templeton rarely grinned—grinning caused creases around the mouth—but she couldn't contain her glee at the prospect of a big sale. "I guarantee you, this particular buyer will take one look at the gathering, then another look at the lake, and write a check for the full asking price of *one point five million dollars.*"

My greenish gray eyes nearly bugged out of my head. "Seriously?" I resumed walking around the kitchen, giving the mansion—and my theory about Mom cutting wires—more careful consideration. "That's how much this place is worth?"

"It's an historic lakefront property in a quaint tourist town," Mom reminded me. "I think the price Lillian is asking, based on my expert advice, is very fair." She looked around, too, but with sudden concern. "Speaking of Lillian . . ."

"I think she's out of town," I said, stopping near the sink, because I'd noticed something my mother hadn't yet cleared off the countertop. A note, weighted down by a can of Cleopatra's Choice Cuts cat food. Although I fed a lot of cats, I didn't recognize the brand. "She left instructions for the care of Tinkleston."

"What. . .? But I just met with her. . ." My mother hadn't been bothered by a power outage, but she seemed genuinely alarmed by my news, which had surprised me, too.

Who didn't stick around for her own party?

However, the note made it pretty clear that Miss Flynt was not only away, but out of reach.

I read the message again, thinking Miss Flynt's handwriting was atrocious.

*While I am away, please feed the cat at least once a
day and change the litter when necessary. I have been
advised that cell phone reception is poor where I'm
traveling. Therefore, I will be extremely difficult to
contact during my absence. If you have any trouble,
please call a veterinarian. LF.*

"Give me that," Mom demanded, plucking the
paper from my hand and silently reading by the light
of the moon. She frowned, which almost *never* happened, and I saw two faint lines form between her knitted brows. "Oh, no . . ."

"Where the heck did she go?" I wondered aloud.
"Timbuktu? Where can't you get cell service these
days?"

"I don't know, but this is very inconvenient," Mom
grumbled, handing the paper back to me. "And there's
no indication of when she'll return. What if I receive
an offer tonight, as I expect? What will I tell the buyer
if she *doesn't* agree to the full asking price? That I have
no idea when I'll be able to negotiate?"

I noticed, finally, that my mother kept referring to
the potential purchaser as a "she." So *another* single
woman wanted such a big place? And just how "high
powered" was this producer? What would bring her to
sleepy Sylvan Creek?

"Well, there's nothing I can do," Mom said, tossing
up her hands. "It's too late to cancel everything now."
She surveyed the room, giving it a final once-over, then
sniffed and pointed to something on the floor behind
me. "Daphne, please set that outside."

I turned to see that she was gesturing to Tinkleston's
litter box, which was placed next to a door that led to
the sloping lakeside backyard. "Why me?"

"You are a *pet sitter*," Mom said. "This is the type of task you enjoy, correct?"

Once again, there was no use arguing with Maeve Templeton, so I sighed and went to get the kitty potty. Realizing that I was still holding the note, I started to slip the paper into the pocket of my black, skinny, hopefully witchy pants, with the intention of replacing it under the cat food when I completed my task. Then I paused and read the instructions one more time, thinking there was something odd about them. But I couldn't put my finger on what was wrong.

Well, I could pinpoint one big problem with the message. It should've been addressed to *me*, a professional pet sitter. Miss Flynt knew what I did for a living.

Heck, everybody in Sylvan Creek knew. My van was *really* hard to miss.

"Daphne, hurry, please," Mom said, glancing at her wristwatch. She fidgeted with the candle she'd placed in the kitchen, as if its proper placement would be key to getting that full asking price she craved. "And set the box far away from the house. Someplace it won't be seen."

"Sure," I promised, finally cramming the note into my pocket and picking up the litter pan, which was a mess. Two bowls that should've held food and water were empty, too. Whoever was watching Tinkleston— who was aptly named—wasn't doing a very good job. Then I carefully opened the door, telling Mom, "This litter box really needs a good cleaning—"

That observation was cut short when something ran past my feet, nearly tripping me, which would've been a disaster, given what I was carrying.

My mother had spied the black blur darting across the kitchen, too, and she cried, "Forget the litter box, Daphne! Get that *awful* cat out of here!"

Chapter 4

"Daphne, you must find that nasty creature and corral it safely away," Mom said, shooing me with her hands. "And hurry. I can't have that thing hurling itself off the refrigerator, attacking someone during a tour of the house!"

That scenario was strangely specific. "Did that happen to you? The first time you showed the house?"

My mother's sculpted cheeks turned a rarely seen shade of red. "Just find the cat!"

I turned away before she could catch me laughing at the image of Maeve Templeton under assault from a feline whom I still couldn't blame for misbehaving. My mother brought out the worst in animals. Even Socrates, who barely took notice of most people, had chosen to wait outside and risk having to mingle with other dogs rather than spend time with my mom.

"Just relax, okay?" I urged, picking up the candle Mom had just carefully adjusted on the counter. The scent was *Falling Leaves*. "I'm sure I can find Tinkleston and keep him calm."

"Lillian said he likes to hide upstairs in the closets

when he's not on top of the refrigerator," Mom advised me, as I left the kitchen. "He also lurks under beds."

That was pretty typical cat behavior. Unfortunately, Flynt Mansion probably had about fifty closets, and the place was very dark once I left the kitchen, with its bank of windows. The rest of the first floor had lots of windows, too, but most of them were smothered under heavy velvet drapes. Passing through a formal dining room, I paused in a parlor and held the candle lower, near my waist, trying to let my eyes adjust to the gloom.

The room was filled with furniture that had to be original to the house. The chairs, scattered randomly around the space, were carved of dark wood and covered in either more velvet or needlepoint. Almost every flat surface was shielded with a lace doily, and the floors were smothered under scattered, threadbare Persian carpets. Yet the place had "good bones," as my mother would say. The ceilings soared and each wall was defined by wide, wooden crown molding. It was easy to imagine the space swept clean of lace, freshly painted, and the windows thrown wide open to let in a cleansing breeze.

All at once, the hairs on the back of my neck prickled, like I was being watched, and I turned slowly to discover the source of the eerie feeling: a large portrait that was propped against a wall. The painting, which was partially covered by a tarp, depicted a gorgeous but severe-looking woman in a red evening gown with an angular neckline. Silky gloves covered her arms up past the elbows.

Moxie always wore vintage 1950s fashion, and I felt confident that the portrait dated roughly to that decade.

I studied the woman's face. Clearly, the painter hadn't suggested that she say "cheese" while her image was committed to canvas. Her mouth was drawn down and her eyes radiated disapproval.

"Are you the ghost in the gown?" I asked her quietly. "Because you are a little frightening."

She didn't answer—thankfully—so I raised the flickering candle again and headed toward a wide flight of stairs I'd seen when I'd entered the foyer.

Resting one hand on a wobbly banister, I set a foot on the bottom step, only to hesitate.

The second story was *really* dark.

"Don't be a fraidy cat," I muttered, resuming my ascent.

The stairs squeaked underfoot like dying mice, but I kept going.

What could be scarier than returning to the kitchen and telling my mother I'd failed my mission to find Tinkleston?

Nothing that I could imagine.

However, when I reached a landing, halfway up, I paused again, this time to push aside a curtain and gaze out the window, because I could hear the reassuring sounds of a party outside. And, indeed, guests were starting to arrive.

Not surprisingly, between my involvement in Fur-ever Friends and the fact that Sylvan Creek was very small, I knew most of the people who'd gathered on the lawn. Piper and Moxie were conferring about something, while Pastor Pete and Bea Baumgartner lingered awkwardly alone, on the fringes. Socrates and Pastor Pete's golden retriever, Blessing, were also ignoring each other. Socrates stared at the gate, like he wanted to go home, while Blessing sniffed at the treat table I hadn't finished stocking.

Fortunately, someone was doing that job for me. Martha Whitaker, head of the Sylvan Creek Public

Library, was unpacking the plastic bin. Her delightfully doleful bloodhound, Charlie, whom I sometimes walked, was asleep under the table, obviously not bothered by the fact that Martha and her husband, Asa, were arguing. I could tell by the hurried, heavy-handed way Martha slapped the treats onto the platters that she was upset. She paused now and then to jab a finger at Asa, who worked at the library, too, as an archivist. He was also president of the Sylvan Creek Historical Society and had written a new book about the town's past, according to a recent article in the *Weekly Gazette*.

I raised my free hand to my mouth, suddenly struck by the need to yawn.

Asa, meanwhile, seemed to be crumbling under his wife's anger. He was a slight man to begin with, and his curved spine, probably earned by poring over old texts, bent more deeply into a question mark each time Martha pointed that finger at him. Her auburn, sharply cut bob swung in time to her gestures, while Asa repeatedly flinched and stroked a tribute-to-Freud gray goatee.

I'd had a few run-ins with Martha myself, and I felt sorry for her husband. She usually wore outfits that appeared cheerful—like her sweatshirt that night, which featured an embroidered owl sitting on a pile of books, under a thought bubble that said, *Reading is a hoot!* But Martha Whitaker was deadly serious about libraries. Woe to the person who had an overdue book. Or twenty . . .

"Daphne? Did you find the cat yet?"

My mother's distant, muffled call compelled me to drop the curtain—but not before I saw someone I *didn't* know. A slight, young woman who stood alone under one of the oak trees. She was pale and wore a flowing, gauzy, white tunic over black pants, so she appeared almost spectral. There was a haunted aspect to her face, too. Her eyes were sunken, and the shadows cast by a chandelier above her head created the illusion that her sockets were empty.

Who was she?

And did she just turn to look at me, as if she'd felt me watching her . . . ?

"Daphne!" My mother spoke more sharply. I could hear her moving around the first floor, no doubt stuffing clutter into her tote bag. The final step in her staging ritual was always to make a clean sweep of the property, and she sometimes walked away with the things she'd picked up. We'd never lacked for pens, catalogs, and umbrellas when I was growing up. "The cat!"

"I'm getting him," I called back. "It's under control."

Mom didn't reply, but I could imagine her muttering under her breath, so I grabbed the banister and resumed my upward trek.

When I reached the last step, I knocked into the decorative top of the newel post, and the heavy chunk of wood tumbled to the floor.

"What is this?" I mumbled, bending to pick up the finial and balance it back in place. *"It's a Wonderful Life— The Haunting?"*

Then I peered in both directions down a long hallway that was lined with doors, most of which were closed. But, to my surprise, the corridor wasn't quite as dark as I'd expected. Faint light glowed from behind a door that was slightly ajar at the far end of the hall, to my right.

All at once, I recalled the smoke I'd seen spiraling from one of the mansion's several chimneys.

I was surprised that Miss Flynt would leave a fire burning while she was out of town, and confused about why the flames hadn't sputtered out by then. Surely, Lillian had been gone at least several hours, if not longer. Piper had mentioned trying to contact her.

Then again, maybe whoever was caring for Tinkleston had lit a fire for the cat. If Miss Flynt really spoiled her furry housemate, as the supplements chart indicated, she might want him to have a warm hearth to curl up near, in her absence.

"Here, Tinkleston," I called softly, making my way down the corridor. "Here, kitty, kitty."

I didn't really expect a response, and I was pleased when I heard a soft "meow," coming from behind the door.

Pushing it open, I looked around the room, which was lined with busy floral wallpaper. Lace curtains fluttered when the breeze blew through a window that had been left open, perhaps so the room wouldn't get too warm as a stack of wood—and papers—burned in the fireplace. Whoever had built the fire had tossed what appeared to be a manuscript in with the logs. The edges of the document were singed and curling, and as I watched, part of a flaming sheet drifted upward into the chimney.

"That's odd," I noted softly.

Then I resumed my search, first bending down and lifting the bed skirt.

Sure enough, Tinkleston was there. The pure black Persian, who had tucked himself into a slipper, was perhaps the cutest cat I'd ever seen. He was small, but as fluffy as a duster, with paws like tiny, ebony pom-poms and the widest, most intensely orange eyes I'd ever seen. His smushed-in face reminded me of a toddler's pout, and I couldn't resist reaching for him.

"It's okay, Tinkleston," I promised, *certain* that he was misunderstood. "Come here, sweetie . . ." I really wanted to comfort that poor, lonely little guy, who'd probably been terrified when he'd wandered outside amid all the commotion at his house, and I reached farther under the bed. "Can I pick you up?"

Wearing a witch outfit to a non-costume party was a pretty big gaffe on my part.

But trying to cuddle Budgely's Sir Peridot Tinkleston . . .

That was my *worst* mistake of the evening.

Chapter 5

"Tinkleston, wait!" I called, hurrying after the
Persian and shaking out my hand, which he'd slashed
with a set of tiny but sharp claws before darting out
from under the bed and through the bedroom door.
"Come back here!"

Being a cat, he didn't listen to me, and I followed
him down the corridor, hoping that he wouldn't run
down the steps. My mother would never forgive me if
he ruined her meeting.

Fortunately, Tinkleston stopped in the middle of the
hallway. I'd forgotten my candle, but I'd left the bedroom door wide open, and I could see his orange eyes
glowing, reflecting the light from the fireplace. Then
he spun around and slipped through a door I hadn't
realized was also open, just a crack.

"Tinkleston!" I said, following him and closing the
door behind us both, to trap him inside. "Easy, little guy!"

I didn't hear a sound, and I stood quietly, too, trying
to figure out what kind of room I'd entered.

Then my ears picked up a faint dripping noise, and

my eyes grew accustomed to the dim glow of moonlight through a window.

A bathroom. We were in a bathroom.

I blinked and found Tinkleston, who was perched on the edge of a claw-foot tub. His back was arched and his tail stood straight up, so he looked like a much fatter version of the ceramic cats on the table outside.

"Easy, there, Tinks," I said, moving closer. Water dripped from the faucet into the tub. "There's nothing to be scared of. . . ."

Even as I made that promise, I realized I was lying. There was plenty to be frightened of in that room.

Leaning over the tub to twist the old porcelain knobs and stop the drip, I saw someone staring back at me, with wide, wide, lifeless eyes.

Lillian Flynt, in a sopping wet bathrobe.

And there was something big, black, and boxy at her feet.

I rested my hand against my stomach, feeling queasy.

I was pretty sure I'd just found the CD player Piper was looking for—and the reason the power was out.

Chapter 6

"I can't believe you found *another* body," my mother said, in a somewhat accusing tone. She paced back and forth in the mansion's kitchen, where Piper, Moxie, Socrates, and I waited while coroner Vonda Shakes, some EMTs, and a few uniformed police officers tromped around upstairs. Needless to say, the fund-raiser had come to an abrupt end when the ambulance had arrived. "And you had to do it when I'm trying to sell a house," Mom added. "Really, Daphne!"

"I *helped* you by catching Tinkleston," I reminded her, raising my hands, which an EMT had been nice enough to wrap in bandages. I looked like a boxer—which was appropriate. The cat had really put up a fight when I'd tried to capture him so he wouldn't get lost in what I'd known would be inevitable excitement. I'd barely managed to carry him a few feet down the hall and secure him in the bedroom with the fireplace. "And don't you think it's best that I found Miss Flynt before your big-city socialite buyer arrived? What if she'd asked to see the bathroom again? I don't think finding a body on a house tour bodes well for getting that 'full asking price'!"

"Daphne's probably right," Moxie said. "I wouldn't be able to even *think* about the wallpaper if there was a dead person in the tub."

My mother gave Moxie one of her signature funny looks.

Then the reality of Miss Flynt's death began to sink in for me, and I suddenly felt sad.

"Could we all stop talking about Miss Flynt like she's an object? Or an *inconvenience*?" I requested. "She wasn't the easiest person to deal with, but she did a lot for Sylvan Creek and animals."

"Daphne's right," Piper agreed. "I think, in our shock, we're acting a little callous." She rubbed her arms like she was cold, although her silk shirt had finally dried, leaving behind a water stain. "And where is this 'buyer,' anyhow, Mom?" she asked, taking a seat on an upholstered bench that ran the length of the bank of windows. It really would be a lovely spot for morning tea. Then my sister checked the wristwatch she always wore, in case her phone ever died. Which never happened. "It's getting late."

"I don't know where she is," Mom said. "I've been trying to text her, to postpone, but she's not responding. I suppose she's still en route. Traffic between Manhattan and the Poconos can be dreadful, even on a Saturday evening."

That was true. A lot of city folks had weekend homes in the mountains, and the commuter route was perpetually backed up, even at odd hours.

"I'm stepping outside for a moment," Mom told us, tapping at her cell phone. "Reception is sometimes bad in these old houses. Maybe she's not even receiving my messages."

Piper, always restless, rose again as the back door

shut behind our mother. "I'm going outside, too, to clean up."

Either Moxie or I—or both of us—probably should have offered to help gather up the jack-o'-lanterns and take down the chandeliers, but neither of us volunteered.

Moxie began fidgeting with her nails, pretending she hadn't heard Piper, no doubt so she wouldn't miss any gossip-worthy news from the coroner or police.

Socrates, sitting quietly at my feet, also averted his gaze.

"Come on, Moxie," Piper finally prompted. "I'm sure you won't miss anything if you're on the lawn."

Moxie stuck out her lower lip, like she doubted that. Then her shoulders slumped. "Oh, fine. I'll help."

Piper turned to me, her eyebrows raised over her wire rims. "Daphne?"

Before I could answer, the doorbell rang. "I need to get that," I said, grabbing the *Falling Leaves* candle off the counter again. Resourceful and brave Piper had located a fuse box in the basement, but she hadn't been able to restore the power. "It's probably Mom's big commission."

"Oh, fine," Piper grumbled, taking Moxie by the arm. "We'll see you in a few minutes, though, right?"

I didn't make any promises. I just hurried toward the foyer, with Socrates lumbering along behind me, and opened the front door. "Welcome to Flynt Mansion . . ."

I started to greet the visitor in a way I assumed my mother would. Then I realized who was actually standing on the porch, and the words died on my lips.

The person waiting to come inside wasn't speechless, though.

"So, you're mixed up in another possible murder," Detective Jonathan Black said, shaking his head and marching right past me into the house. Then he looked me up and down, frowning. "And are you dressed as a *boxing witch?*"

Chapter 7

"Why didn't you just come in?" I asked, as Jonathan walked around the first floor of Flynt Mansion, studying everything by the feeble light of my candle. Socrates remained in the foyer, sitting on his haunches and observing my reunion with a detective who frequently infuriated and, I had to admit, always intrigued me. "Since when do homicide detectives knock on the door at a crime scene?"

All at once, I realized that Jonathan's arrival meant that, at the very least, Vonda Shakes suspected foul play. Up until that moment, I'd assumed that Lillian's death had been accidental.

"The door was locked," Jonathan informed me. He studied the portrait of the dour lady, and I wasn't sure who looked more stern. "What else could I do? Climb in through a window?"

"That's weird," I said. "I thought I left the door open."

Jonathan faced me. He definitely looked more grim than the lady in the painting. "Please—*please*—don't start speculating about this *potential* homicide," he requested. "Old houses can be quirky. The lock probably malfunctioned."

"Okay, fine," I agreed, backing up a step and raising my bandaged hand in a gesture of surrender. "I just thought it was odd!"

I fully intended to check that lock later, though.

I also had about a million questions for Jonathan, whom I hadn't seen since August, when I'd helped him solve a murder *and* compelled him to take custody of two dogs.

The first, a chocolate Labrador retriever named Axis, had been left homeless by the homicide. I'd known that Axis, a prize-winning agility dog, would be a great match for Jonathan, who'd had a canine partner when he was a SEAL. I'd also believed Jonathan would come to love the other rescue I'd convinced him to take home. Artie—a one-eared Chihuahua with a severe overbite—was as lawless and exuberant as Jonathan was regimented and reserved. But the little dog had a way of winning people over, and I believed that, under his tough exterior, Jonathan was a big softie who would eventually cave to Artie's unique charms.

"How are Artie and Axis?" I asked, as Jonathan handed back the candle and headed for the staircase. I knew he didn't have time to talk, but I kept pestering him anyhow. "How's the house working out?"

"The house is fine, thanks," he replied, ignoring my question about the dogs. That worried me. Maybe he wasn't the softie I'd hoped. He paused at the foot of the stairs, and I followed him, holding up the candle so I could see his face better. He was even more handsome than I remembered. He wore a suit, as he always did when on duty, but his black hair was a little longer than usual, like he hadn't been to see Moxie in a while. His incredibly dark blue eyes hadn't changed, though.

They were still difficult to read. I'd spent a decent amount of time with Jonathan during our joint murder investigation—not that he'd wanted me as a partner—and he'd only really let his guard down with me three or four times.

Jonathan was studying me, too, and I suspected that I was failing to pass muster, as usual. I'd once appalled him by sniffing a boot covered with guacamole, and on another occasion, he'd had to pluck cheese from my hair. I doubted that my cape impressed him.

Then all at once his expressions softened, and he nodded to my bandaged hand. "Are you okay? Do you need me to send down one of the paramedics?"

"They already fixed me up," I said, raising my hand again, so he could inspect the mummylike wrap. "This is their professional handiwork."

"I suppose I'll have to ask what happened, later," he noted.

I wasn't sure what he was talking about, and I cocked my head. "Later?"

"Yes. If I question you. And whoever else had access to this house recently." He must've seen the gleam of interest in my eyes, because he raised one cautionary finger. "Assuming that Miss Flynt's death is determined to be a homicide. Vonda Shakes isn't certain yet. I'm only here based upon her early suspicions."

My interest had been piqued, but all at once I got a cold knot in the pit of my stomach.

Piper had probably been in and out of the mansion all day while setting up for the party. If Lillian Flynt had been murdered, would my sister be a suspect *again*?

Then I realized that my mother also had access—and probably *keys*—to the mansion, not to mention a killer instinct.

"Oh, no," I muttered. "Here we go again."

Jonathan leaned closer. "What was that? Do you have something to say, Daphne?"

Jeez, it almost seemed like he considered *me* a potential suspect. Which probably made sense, since I'd found the body.

"Nothing," I said, for once holding my tongue. "I've got nothing to say."

"Why don't I believe that?" Jonathan asked, with the slightest glimmer of amusement in his eyes. Then he glanced over his shoulder, up the staircase. The whole time we'd been talking, the second floor had been creaking under the weight of the EMTs and police officers, and the corridor had been splashed with light from the moving beams of flashlights. "I need to get upstairs. But don't go anywhere. And tell your sister, whom I saw out front, to stick around, too."

"You should probably know that my mom is also here somewhere," I said, thinking there was no sense in hiding that fact. "And Moxie."

Jonathan was halfway up the stairs, but even by the dim light, I saw his back stiffen. Then he sighed and turned to face me again. "How about Taggart? Is the entire gang here? Is this a reunion of people involved in the *last* murder?"

He was referring to Dylan Taggart, a vet tech with my sister's practice whom I sometimes dated.

"Dylan was supposed to come to the fund-raiser," I said. "But you know that he tends to run late. He'll probably show up around midnight."

Jonathan didn't reply. Like Piper, he probably didn't know what to make of Dylan's refusal to live by the dictates of a clock. My sister sometimes threatened to fire Dylan—a California-transplanted surfer—for wearing board shorts to work and showing up pretty much whenever he pleased.

"Just tell everyone to stay here," Jonathan urged. "Moxie, your mother . . . everyone."

Before I could respond, the doorbell rang again and he resumed climbing the stairs.

"That's probably Detective Doebler," he added, addressing me over his shoulder. "Please send him upstairs."

"Sure," I agreed, glad for a chance to be genuinely helpful, if only in the smallest way.

Then I turned around and opened the door, prepared to greet Jonathan's older partner, who acted more like a subordinate than an equal.

I couldn't blame Detective Doebler. Who wouldn't be cowed by Jonathan?

Yet, I was again surprised by the person waiting on the porch.

Far from being a frumpy, middle-aged man in an ill-fitting suit, the visitor was female, gorgeous, blond, and accompanied by two regal greyhounds, who sat completely still on either side of her, like those dog statues that sometimes flank driveways.

Although I'd never met her before, the woman was also familiar. I'd seen her in several photographs when I'd been snooping around online. In one picture, she'd been kissing Jonathan at a fancy party. And in another she'd stood at his side, wearing a wedding dress.

I froze like I was carved out of stone, too, and stared stupidly, until she took the initiative to greet me, holding out her hand, smiling broadly, and saying, "Hi. I'm Elyse Hunter-Black."

Chapter 8

"I can't believe Jonathan's ex-wife still uses his name," Moxie noted, rolling cream-colored paint onto the walls of my new cottage's living room. She wore a vintage men's blue work shirt, the sleeves rolled up, and she'd secured her hair with a red and white polka dot scarf, so she looked very much like Rosie the Riveter. Apparently, she was going through an "homage" phase. "And Elyse honestly wanted to look at the house again? With a dead person in it?"

"I only spoke with her for a minute or two, but I got the sense that Elyse Hunter-Black doesn't let much—including the occasional body—stand in the way of getting what she wants," I said, pouring more paint into my roller pan.

Straightening, I took a moment to appreciate how the tiny house was evolving. It had been adorable when Winding Hill's former caretaker, Mr. Peachy, had occupied it, but now that he was headed for something even smaller—a jail cell—I was brightening the place up a bit. I'd taken down dusty drapes that had all but enveloped the living room, allowing soft light to stream through arched, leaded glass windows. I'd also removed a bunch of worn rugs and polished the wooden floors until they gleamed. Old beams crossed the ceiling, making the house feel sturdy and secure, and a cheerful fire burned in the stone fireplace, dispelling the chill on that gray, gloomy day. I already felt very much at home in the fairy-tale space, and Socrates clearly agreed. He dozed on the single antique Turkish rug I'd placed near the hearth, his big, dappled paws twitching now and then when he dreamed.

"What do you think she wants?" Moxie asked.

"What?" I'd lost track of the conversation and had no idea what she was talking about.

"Elyse Hunter-Black." Moxie dropped her roller and wiped her sleeve across her face, like she was ready for a break. "What do you think she wants?"

I put down my roller, too, and led the way to the itty-bitty kitchen, which I didn't intend to change at all. I loved the soft blue-green color on the cabinets, and the farmhouse sink was perfect for the room. I was even maintaining Mr. Peachy's windowsill herb garden. It wasn't the plants' fault that he'd tried to kill me with a hammer.

"Elyse definitely wants Flynt Mansion," I said, putting a pot of water on the stove. Moxie, always able to identify vintage goods, dated the cute, two-burner oven to the mid-twentieth century. But it was in perfect condition. I turned a knob, and gas flames jumped to life with a small *whoosh*. Then I cut a few pieces of still-warm pumpkin bread from a loaf I'd baked that morning and set them on two small, olive-green plates shaped like oak leaves. "Although Elyse couldn't really tour the house again last night, except to poke around the first floor a little, Mom's still confident she'll make an offer."

"I think Elyse wants more than the house," Moxie

said, taking a seat at a spindle-legged, two-person table I was also keeping. Accepting one of the plates from me, she immediately tore a piece off her share of the pumpkin loaf, which smelled deliciously of cloves and nutmeg. "I think she wants *Jonathan* back."

"You haven't even met her," I reminded Moxie. Deciding to make chai tea, I dropped some crushed ginger into the water. I'd learned the technique in India. "Elyse left while you were still trying to pry fake ravens out of trees."

"I think Piper assigned me that job on purpose," Moxie complained. She lightly touched a few strands of her still-blond hair, which peeked out from under the kerchief. "Those birds were freaking me out."

The water came to a boil, and I added sugar and loose Indian tea, too. A moment later, I streamed in some milk. "Getting back to Elyse . . . Mom says she wants a place away from the city."

Moxie rolled her eyes. "And she just had to pick Sylvan Creek? Out of all the little towns in America? She just had to choose the one where her handsome ex-husband lives?"

"Apparently, she's also considering shooting a TV show here," I informed Moxie. Grabbing the pot off the stove, I strained the tea into two earthenware mugs I'd picked up in New Delhi. The tea's warm, spicy aroma was the perfect antidote to the dreary day. "I told you she's a high-powered producer with Stylish Life Network, right?"

"No, you didn't mention that." Moxie accepted her mug, lifted it to her lips, and blew gently across the steaming surface. "That's a pretty big deal."

Yeah, it was a big deal. I didn't aspire to be a New York City power broker or live in a mansion on a hill. I was quite content in a cottage, enjoying a snack with my best friend and a still-sleepy basset hound, who yawned as he entered the kitchen, looking for something to eat. But I had to admit that I'd been a little intimidated by Elyse Hunter-Black, with her hyphenated name, her dark suit and low-cut silk blouse that exuded authority but managed to be feminine, too, and her matched duo of sleek, silver-gray greyhounds, who reminded me more of accessories than companions. Socrates was quiet, but Elyse's dogs had seemed to float on air, like ghosts. Their toenails hadn't even clicked on the hardwood when they'd followed Mom and Elyse around the mansion's first floor, Elyse nodding approval at most features and quickly assessing how to fix those that didn't meet her standards.

And then Jonathan had come downstairs to discover the woman he'd married at one point. . . .

"Daph?" Moxie's voice brought me back to the present. She snapped her fingers. "You're daydreaming. I asked what the show's about."

"Something about America's most pet-friendly small towns," I said, opening the refrigerator, which was a square little cabinet that Moxie said was more accurately called an icebox. Digging around, I found a container of Liverin' It Up dog treats I'd made from pureed chicken livers, chicken broth, wheat germ, and eggs. "Apparently, Spa and Paw is one of the businesses that caught her attention," I added, putting two treats on a plate for Socrates, whose tail quivered in a restrained wag. He *really* loved liver. "You might help put Sylvan Creek on the map."

"I don't know if I want to be 'on the map,'" Moxie noted. "I like things the way they are. We have just enough tourists, right now."

I kind of agreed.

"I still think Elyse mainly wants to be near Jonathan," Moxie added, sipping her tea. "It's pretty transparent."

I sort of agreed with that, too. But I wasn't going to speculate with Moxie, who would start spreading rumors all over town. And fortunately, she'd already moved on to a new topic.

"Do you really think Detective Black might consider Piper, or you—or *me*—suspects in Miss Flynt's murder?" she asked. "He hinted at that last night. And he didn't seem pleased by the fact that your Mom had keys to the place, either."

My heart sank every time I thought about being forced to solve another murder before Jonathan could pin it on a Templeton or my best friend. But Moxie's eyes gleamed, as if she was pleased by the prospect of getting interrogated by Jonathan.

"As far as I know, Miss Flynt's death still hasn't officially been declared a homicide," I reminded Moxie—and myself. "Jonathan said the coroner's inquest could take a day. But yes, I assume that if Miss Flynt was murdered, we will all be questioned again. Detective Doebler hardly asked me anything last night."

And Jonathan hadn't questioned me at all, like he'd said he would. I'd been disappointed, because I'd had a few things to tell him, and a lot of questions of my own. Which was probably why Jonathan had assigned his subordinate to debrief me.

"Well, in the meantime, what do you think about adding a mural to the living room?" Moxie asked, abruptly changing the subject yet again. She turned and swept her arm in the air, as if painting across the wall near the fireplace. "I was thinking that a single, stark, twisty branch, echoing the plum tree outside, might be a cool way to incorporate nature into the space."

Moxie was an incredibly talented artist, but her other

attempt at large-scale painting, on my van, had gone pretty awry. "Thanks, but I'm going to stick with plain walls for now," I said. She looked crestfallen, so I added, "I think you might've just christened the house, though. How about *Plum Cottage*?"

She immediately brightened, and I looked down to see that Socrates had stopped eating for a moment. He also seemed to approve.

"I like it," Moxie said. "It's better than *that place where Daphne almost got hammered to death,* which is what I usually call it, in my head."

"It's *definitely* settled." I raised my mug. "To Plum Cottage."

We tapped earthenware, then Moxie suggested, with clear reluctance, "I guess we should get back to work."

"I suppose so."

I stood up and carried our empty mugs to the sink, while Moxie disposed of the last few crumbs of pumpkin bread by cramming them into her mouth.

As I entered the living room, I noticed that the fire was dying down, and the big brass tub that usually held kindling was empty.

"Oh, no," I muttered, thinking Socrates, especially, would be disappointed when the fire guttered out entirely. He was already curling up on the rug for a post-snack nap. "We're out of logs."

Moxie followed me into the room and looked around, searching for something to burn. Then she pointed to a tall bookcase, still filled with Mr. Peachy's collection of reading material. There was no cable or Wi-Fi in the cottage, so he'd apparently read quite a bit—usually about hardware.

"Maybe you could burn one of these instruction booklets," Moxie suggested, taking a volume down from a low shelf. "I really doubt you'll ever read the

John Deere operations and maintenance manual for a compact utility tractor."

I wasn't so sure about that. Winter in the Poconos could be isolating, especially at the top of Winding Hill. Snow and ice sometimes made the road impassable, at least for a 1970s van with balding tires. I might get desperate enough to read about fluid-check dipsticks and fuel filters. Or I might need to ride a compact utility tractor to the grocery store.

Then again, maybe not.

I accepted the manual from Moxie, prepared to toss it on the fire.

But as I pictured the booklet going up in flames, I suddenly remembered something from the previous night.

Two things, actually.

"I think we're done painting for the day," I told Moxie. "I have somewhere to go."

Moxie lowered one skeptical eyebrow. "Where?"

"Flynt Mansion," I informed her. "I need to see a fireplace and find a cranky cat—hopefully with the help of the one person who *might* be able to tame a wild Tinkleston!"

Chapter 9

Not surprisingly, Dylan Taggart was late for our meeting at Flynt Mansion, so I let Socrates and myself into the house by jiggling the knob on the front door.

I'd checked the lock the previous night, after Jonathan had gone upstairs, and discovered that he'd been right about the old mechanism being temperamental. It had only taken me a few minutes to figure out how to consistently lock and unlock the door without a key.

"Don't look at me like that," I said, with a glance down at Socrates, who clearly disapproved of my plan to capture Tinkleston at the site of a possible homicide. "The house isn't technically a crime scene yet," I reminded him, bending down to pick up a bulky cat carrier. "There's no yellow tape!"

Socrates made a skeptical rumbling sound, deep in his broad chest.

Ignoring him, I lugged the carrier over the threshold, bumping it against the door frame and leaving a mark in the wood. Elyse Hunter-Black would want to fix that, if she really bought the place.

"Should I catch Tinkleston myself?" I asked Socrates, who stood at my side in the foyer.

Socrates snuffled, then shook his head so his long ears swung.

I took that for a no and decided to wait for Dylan to tackle—perhaps literally—the cat.

"I guess I should at least check upstairs, in case Tinks is still stuck in the bedroom," I added, leading the way to the staircase. "I told the police officers to let him out before they left last night, but they probably forgot. Tinkleston wasn't their top priority. And, in spite of that note in the kitchen, I'm not sure anyone is really checking on him."

All at once, I realized that, in the previous evening's excitement, I'd forgotten to slip the instructions for Tinkleston's care back under the can of Cleopatra's Choice Cuts. The note was still in the pocket of the black pants I'd worn with my witch cape.

Then I looked up the stairs, more concerned about the cat than my involuntary theft of a small piece of paper.

If the little Persian was still locked away, as I feared, the mansion's next owner would need to clean up some Tinkleston tinkle stains, too.

"Come on, Socrates," I said, hauling the carrier up the steps.

I didn't hear anyone behind me, and I looked over my shoulder to see that Socrates was sitting at the foot of the staircase. I was familiar with the expression on his face. He wasn't going any farther.

"Fine," I said. "You wait there."

Then I resumed climbing the stairs, the carrier nicking the banister, too. Reaching the top, I was careful not to bump the loose finial and to avoid a cat toy that someone had left right on the edge of the last stair. Anyone who stepped on the little pink ball would probably tumble backward.

Maybe someone really was checking in on Tinkleston and had been playing with him.

There was also a chance one of the police officers or EMTs who'd been tramping around had kicked the ball, not even realizing that it had landed in a dangerous spot.

Or maybe Tinkleston was booby-trapping the place.

Or a ghost in a red dress . . .

Any of those options seemed possible, and the hairs on the back of my neck prickled as I nudged the ball with my foot, sending it to a safer spot. Then I tiptoed down the corridor toward the bedroom door, pausing for a moment in front of the bathroom where I'd found Lillian's body. The tub was empty, of course, and the CD player was gone, probably taken as potential evidence. But I could picture, too vividly, Miss Flynt's wide-open, blank eyes. . . .

Shaking off the image, I continued on to the very end of the hall, where I slowly pushed open the bedroom door.

The hinges creaked, the sound echoing loudly in the otherwise empty house.

Hesitating, I inspected the raised, red scratches on my hand. Then I dared to poke my head inside the room, first spying the now cold, dark fireplace that I really wanted to examine.

I next found Tinkleston, who sat on the bed, between me and that goal.

His pitch-black body was unnaturally still, his scowl seemed deeper than ever, and he blinked directly at me with angry, orange eyes.

It was almost like he'd been waiting for me.

Chapter 10

"You are in big trouble, mister," I advised Tinkleston, who glared at me from behind the bars of the cat carrier. I wasn't sure how I'd managed to get him inside the crate. Maybe I'd be able to reconstruct the struggle later by examining the pattern of scratches on my arms. "I feel very sorry for you, losing Miss Flynt, but that is no excuse to lash out," I added, leaning down to meet his eyes. "There are better ways to channel grief."

In response, Tinkleston darted out a little paw, his claws extended.

No wonder Socrates, who was very prescient, had refused to come upstairs.

Why hadn't I taken his advice and waited for Dylan, like I'd planned?

Pulling back, I muttered under my breath, "What am I going to do with you, Tinks?"

As a pet care professional, I didn't feel like I could leave Tinkleston alone in the mansion if I wasn't *positive* that someone was caring for him. And if Vonda Shakes declared Miss Flynt's death a homicide, Jonathan and his crew of investigators would tramp in and out of the place, maybe for days. Finally, if the house *wasn't* eventually sealed off as a crime scene, my mother and Elyse would almost certainly go through the property at least one more time.

What if Tinkleston ran outside again, and no one even noticed?

"I'll find someplace safe for you until things calm down," I promised the cat. "Just try to be nice, okay?"

In response, he hissed.

"Oh, fine," I grumbled, rising and leaving him alone in his snit. "I have things to do while you calm down."

I heard another hiss behind me as I crossed the room to the fireplace, where I'd seen that pile of papers burning the night before.

Kneeling down, I began to sift through the ashes.

At first, it appeared that every scrap of the document had been consumed by the flames. If I hadn't seen the manuscript while it had still been partially intact, I never would've known anything but logs had burned there the previous evening.

Then I glimpsed something at the very edge of the ashes. A scrap of paper that was only half burned.

Lifting the singed piece, I dusted off some cinders. And while I couldn't read much of the scorched paper, the words—and partial words—that I could make out were intriguing.

Benedict Flyn . . . 195 . . . congregation . . . scandalo . . .

Setting that fragment carefully aside on the brick hearth, I edged farther into the fireplace and brushed my fingers around until I found more sheets, including two pages that had survived the fire almost intact.

Unfortunately, those were less compelling. In fact, the text was dull, both in terms of writing style and content. Yet I quickly skimmed, looking for clues to the author.

In 1852, a second mill was constructed. . . . Railroad service was expanded. . . . Four new roads were built to link Sylvan Creek with surrounding communities. . . .

Raising my hand to my mouth, I fought back a yawn. The yawn won.

The last time I'd stifled a boredom-induced reaction like that, I'd been looking out a window at Asa Whitaker, archivist at the public library and author of a soon-to-be-published history of Sylvan Creek.

"Is this Asa's manuscript?" I mused aloud. "But why . . . ?"

In the distance, I heard the front door open and close, then footsteps coming up the stairs.

I assumed Dylan had arrived, and I told Tinkleston over my shoulder, "You'll meet your match now, Tinks. Dylan will have you achieving Zen in no time."

Then I heard voices—two of them—and I realized that I was wrong. Dylan wasn't in the house.

As I turned slowly around, still crouching down, the bedroom door creaked open even wider and someone demanded loudly, "Daphne Templeton, what in the world are you *doing*? And what is *on your face*?"

Chapter 11

I reached up and wiped the back of my hand across my cheek, then looked at my knuckles, which were smeared with gray.

"Oh, that's just soot," I said, crawling backward away from the fireplace and standing up. "I was digging around in the ashes, and I must've touched my face. . . ."

I let my voice trail off, because my mother and Elyse Hunter-Black, who'd entered the room, were both giving me funny looks. The greyhounds that again flanked Elyse had their heads cocked, too.

"Why in the world were you hunting through ashes?" my mother inquired. "What could *compel* you?"

I suddenly realized that my behavior did seem somewhat erratic. And, intriguing snippet aside, the papers I'd found were most likely meaningless. Miss Flynt had probably just used a boring book as kindling, like I'd nearly burned the tractor manual.

"I, umm, thought I saw something that shouldn't have been burning, last night," I explained, weakly. I brushed my hands against my jeans, which was also a bad idea. Smears of soot covered my legs. "It was nothing though." It finally struck me that I wasn't the only one behaving oddly. "What are you doing here?" I asked Mom, shooting Elyse a confused glance, too. Then I turned back to my mother. "You can't be showing the house after what happened last night, can you?"

"On the contrary, this is the most opportune time," Mom noted. "If the mansion is declared a crime scene, we may not be able to get in for weeks. This may be our window of opportunity."

"Not to seem callous, but your mother is right," Elyse agreed, reinforcing my initial impression that a few dead bodies wouldn't stand in the way of her getting what she wanted. "I spoke with Jonathan this morning, and he mentioned that he still wasn't sure Miss Flynt's death was a homicide. I know how these things work, and I quickly called your mother. . . ." All at once, Elyse grew distracted by something right at my side. I wasn't sure what she was looking at, until she frowned and gestured to the fresh scratches on my arms. "At the risk of being rude, what in the world *happened to you?*"

"Miss Flynt's angry cat, Tinkleston, happened," I said, pointing at the carrier. "I'm afraid no one is caring for him, so I'm taking him with me."

Hearing his name, or my plan, Tinkleston yowled, and the greyhounds again showed hints of emotion. Both of them flattened their ears against their already narrow heads.

"Oh, that's nice of you," Elyse said, smiling. She bent to look into the carrier. "Poor thing!"

Mom finally rejoined the conversation. "I hope you don't plan to keep that beast at your cottage, Daphne. I will refuse to visit."

I had hoped Dylan would take Tinks for a while, since Socrates wasn't fond of even friendly felines, but

I suddenly started to give serious consideration to keeping him myself.

"I'm going to find a powder room downstairs, clean up, and get going," I said. Of course, there was a bathroom right down the hall, but I didn't think I should use it. Nor did I want to enter that room. "You two continue with your showing. Don't let me get in your way."

"Don't forget to take your dog when you leave, Daphne," Mom reminded me. "He's in the parlor staring fixedly at a hideous portrait. It's rather off-putting behavior."

First of all, I would never "forget" my closest companion. And I wasn't surprised to learn that Socrates was contemplating the picture that had given me the willies the night before. Socrates was very interested in art of all periods and levels of quality. I really wished he could get into the MOMA, but they had a shortsighted policy about animal visitors. Socrates and I had learned that the hard way.

"We'll all be out of your way in a minute," I promised Mom.

"Actually, I think we're almost done here," Elyse said. She turned to my mother. "I don't need to see the whole house again. I'm ready to make an offer—and I am going to surprise you by asking for the inclusion of the portrait downstairs." She tilted her head, seeming thoughtful. "I believe it just *belongs* with the property."

I was bending to pick up Tinks, but I jerked upright. "You're seriously buying the house? And you *want* that ugly painting?"

I shouldn't have said any of that, and my mother shot me a warning look, trying to stop me before I could ruin her sale. "Daphne . . . Weren't you going to wash your face?"

I took a step backward. "Oh, yes . . . I was."

But Elyse smiled again. "I can understand your surprise, Daphne. This old place does look like quite a project." She surveyed the bedroom, and I followed her gaze, noting some water damage on the ceiling above one of the two windows. Then she returned her attention to me. "I have a fondness for classic architecture, though. I think that, in the right hands, this house could be a gem."

She obviously judged *her* hands to be the right ones, and she was probably correct. Jonathan's ex-wife had impeccable taste. She wore a pair of dark-washed skinny jeans and a simple but expensive-looking silver-gray silk top that mirrored her unusual blue-gray eyes. The blouse also echoed her dogs' coats, making them again seem like accessories. Her blond hair was slicked back into an artfully spiky bun, and her burgundy suede ballet flats probably cost more than my van. I could just tell.

I glanced down at my outfit. I'd left the cottage feeling pretty good about my intricately patterned, gauzy blouse, which I'd bought at a street market in Mexico. I wore my favorite pair of jeans, too. But all at once I felt more shabby than chic. I swiped my hand across my cheek again, removing, or maybe depositing, more soot.

"Daphne?"

I raised my face to realize that Elyse was addressing me.

"What? Did you say something?"

"I was asking you about Paris and Milan."

For a second, I thought she was interested in hearing old travel tales about two of my favorite European cities. Then, when she rested her hands on her dogs' heads, I realized she was talking about her greyhounds. Of course, her pets would have classy names.

"There will be times during the remodel when the house isn't safe for them, and I'll need someone to watch them," Elyse added, so I finally figured out she'd been asking about my pet-sitting services. "I already know for certain that the entire place needs to be rewired and the fuse box updated." She grew solemn. "If there'd been safety outlets in the bathroom, Lillian Flynt might still be alive."

I didn't mean to sound morbid, but I had to ask. "So . . . she was definitely electrocuted?"

Elyse fidgeted with a silver circlet that hung from a chain around her long, graceful neck. "Oh, goodness. I've probably said too much. Jonathan mentioned some things in confidence."

"It's okay," I said, feeling strangely crestfallen, because Jonathan had never shared confidential details about an investigation with me. At least, not voluntarily.

Then again, I'd never been married to him, and I did have a habit of blurting things out, like I was about to do right then.

"I can't believe two people have died violently here," I noted, recalling the legend about the woman who'd been strangled. "That's kind of eerie—assuming the old tale is true."

"I believe Elyse was asking about your *professional services*, Daphne," Mom said sharply. "Don't you want to build *your own* business?"

My mother was staring daggers at me, and I realized that Elyse might not be familiar with the story about the first murder. At least I hadn't brought up the haunting—although I'd almost mentioned that, too.

Regardless, Elyse didn't seem bothered by anything I'd said.

"Would you add me as a Lucky Paws client?" she inquired. "Is it possible you could sometimes squeeze

Paris and Milan into your schedule, which I'm sure is busy?"

My mother coughed into her hand, like she was choking on Elyse's comment.

"Yes, I'd be happy to watch the dogs whenever you need me," I said. In fact, my schedule had a big gap, now that three rottweilers I used to walk had been adopted by a loving family with a huge yard and three kids who did agility work with them. Macduff, Iago, and Hamlet got plenty of exercise without me. I glanced at the greyhounds. "I'd love to take care of these two. They're beautiful. And so well behaved."

"Yes, they are well mannered," my mother agreed, although I knew she wished the dogs weren't even there. "They are lovely animals."

I resisted the urge to roll my eyes, while Elyse beamed proudly and stroked Paris's—or maybe Milan's—head.

I would have to learn to tell the dogs apart. They were nearly identical in color, shared the same placid expressions, and even wore matching three-inch-wide, chokerlike, jeweled collars.

"Thank you for the compliments," Elyse said. "But I have to confess that Jonathan trained them, back when we were . . ." Her eyes clouded over, and she didn't finish her sentence, even though it was pretty obvious she'd been about to say "married." Then she forced a smile and extended her hand to me. "Do you have a business card, Daphne?"

"I do have cards," I said, with a quick glance at my mother, so I could see her look of disapproval when I admitted, "But I have no idea where they are."

"No problem." Elyse reached into a handbag with a familiar designer pattern. I'd seen it on bags sold on Manhattan street corners. I doubted Ms. Hunter-Black was toting around a knockoff, though. She pulled out a phone. "I can just add you to my contacts."

"Um, my cell phone isn't working very well lately," I said. My mother, who knew that, groaned softly, and I tried to explain to both of them, "I'm kind of in the middle of moving. Things are a little chaotic."

"You're moving, too?" Elyse smiled more broadly. "We have that in common."

That was probably the only thing we shared. And we didn't even have that yet, as my mother reminded Elyse.

"We need to write up that offer first," she said. "And determine who is in charge of the estate." A shadow of concern darkened my mother's eyes as she finally grasped that her sale might be jeopardized. She'd apparently been so blinded by dollar signs, and the potential to score a local real estate coup by selling Sylvan Creek's most fabled lakeside property, that for once she'd overlooked an important detail. "I haven't heard anything about the mansion being taken off the market," she added. "But I suppose that's possible, depending on Lillian's provisions for the house in her will."

"I've considered that possibility," Elyse said. "But I refuse to believe that this lovely home isn't destined to be mine. I'm very eager to take possession of it."

Yup, she was definitely used to getting what she wanted.

"Are you really going to shoot a television show in Sylvan Creek?" I asked. "I heard something about a series on America's most pet friendly towns."

My mother, who had spread that rumor, cleared her throat and fidgeted with some oversized rocks on a chunky necklace that covered half her chest. "Daphne, where would you hear something like that?"

Mom clearly feared that she'd broken "realtor-client privilege"—a thing I was pretty sure she'd made up—but Elyse just laughed and assured my mother, "It's okay. It's no secret." She addressed me. "Yes, Daphne. I am producing a show about pet friendly communities for my network, Stylish Life. And I really think Sylvan Creek would be perfect for the series. It seems as though animals are very central to life here."

"That's true," Mom muttered, without much enthusiasm.

I still wasn't excited about the prospect of national exposure for Sylvan Creek, but I said, "Well, good luck with the show!"

"Thanks." Elyse turned to my mother. "So, what do we do next, about the house?"

"I'll contact Larry Fox," Mom said. "He's a local attorney. I'm fairly sure he's in charge of the estate."

They were starting to talk serious shop, so I took that as my cue to leave. I picked up the carrier, being careful to avoid paws that were reaching through the bars, swiping at my legs. "There's some paper in the kitchen," I said, backing away. "I'll leave my landline number and some other contact information on the counter, Elyse." Piper probably wouldn't mind me handing out her cell number until I fixed the situation with my phone. "Let me know whenever you need help with Paris and Milan. And good luck with the house, too."

My Mom and Elyse were already deep in conversation and barely acknowledged my departure, so I headed downstairs, where I found Socrates in the parlor. He still sat in front of the painting, and I glanced at the gorgeous, imperious woman, too.

Why did she give me such a bad case of the heebie-jeebies?

"Let's go," I said, because Socrates wasn't moving.

He sat with his back to me, but he turned his head, so he could give me—and the carrier—a dubious look.

Tinkleston seemed to understand that he'd been nonverbally insulted. He made a low growling sound. I'd never heard a cat do that.

"That's enough, you two," I said. "Let's all try to get along."

Socrates reluctantly rose and joined me and Budgely's Sir Peridot. But he gave the carrier a wide berth.

I couldn't blame him. A little paw kept poking out of the side air holes, patting at my jeans. Every few swipes, Tinks's tiny claws pierced the fabric.

"Ouch," I complained, setting the crate on the kitchen floor. Then I began to search for a pen and paper, so I could leave the promised contact information for Elyse.

That was when I noticed the can of cat food on the counter—and the chart that listed all of the supplements Tinks was supposed to take, hanging on the fridge.

Hesitating, I pulled the paper from under the magnet, thinking that I should at least try to make sure Tinks got his vitamins, although the regimen looked pretty expensive.

"Hopefully, Piper will tell me most of this stuff isn't necessary," I told Socrates. "Don't you think a natural diet is usually sufficient?"

Socrates snuffled agreement. Still, I folded the paper and tucked it into my back pocket. Then I grabbed the can of Tinks's special food, too, before bending to pick up the carrier and leading the way to the foyer.

Just as I opened the front door, I heard the sound of vehicles pulling up outside and car doors opening and closing, loudly and decisively.

I couldn't ever recall Dylan Taggart slamming a door, and I stepped out onto the porch to discover that a black and white squad car and a plain, dark sedan were parked behind my van, my mother's SUV, and a sleek pewter BMW that obviously belonged to Elyse.

Opening my mouth, I started to greet Jonathan Black, who strode toward the mansion, with Detective Doebler and some uniformed officers trailing in his wake.

But before I could even say hi, Jonathan asked, with ill-concealed frustration, "What in the world compelled so many people to visit the scene of a homicide?"

Chapter 12

"Sorry you had to catch this little guy alone," Dylan said, accepting the cat carrier from me. Inside, Tinkleston hissed and thrashed, so the portable kennel swung wildly. Dylan didn't seem to notice, nor did he explain why he was so late. His ancient, rusted-out Subaru had pulled up to the mansion just as my mother's SUV and Elyse's BMW were driving away. My mother had been in a huff about Jonathan's apparently curt dismissal, while Elyse had paused at the gate to consider whether she'd tear out the crabapple trees once she took possession of the property. I'd urged her to leave the trees alone. "He really did a number on you, huh?" Dylan noted, setting the carrier on the curb, so he could take one of my arms in his hand and examine it. "You look like you hit a reef without a rash guard."

Dylan Taggart often talked in surfing parlance. And he was, as usual, dressed for the beach that day. In spite of the late-October chill, he wore a pair of blue and red striped board shorts and a T-shirt that advertised a surfing competition he'd participated in two years ago in Maui. The white shirt made his ever present tan appear even deeper and framed his biceps pretty well, too. His sun-streaked hair was pulled back into a ponytail. All in all, he looked like he was ready to jump into the ocean.

"Can you keep Tinks for a while?" I asked, withdrawing my arm and glancing at the mansion.

Would Jonathan and his crew check the fireplace?

Should I go back inside and suggest that they do that . . . ?

"Sorry, Daph." Dylan interrupted my speculation. "I'm in a new place for a while. The landlord says no pets."

I was so stunned by that news that I forgot all about murder. "You *moved*?"

Dylan grinned, so the corners of his eyes crinkled. "Only a block. It was no big deal. My old lease was up, and I didn't want to sign on for another year."

One block wasn't too far. But the fact that he'd picked up his few duffel bags' worth of stuff and switched apartments without even telling me was more proof that people like Dylan and I weren't cut out for commitments. I hadn't exactly sent him a change of address card since I'd shifted residences, either.

"Where should I take the cat?" he asked, more seriously. "Your place?"

"I don't think so." I eyed the carrier warily, worried that Tinkleston might somehow escape. And sure enough, a black puffball of a paw was fiddling with the latch. Then I looked down at Socrates, who stared up at me with disbelief, like he couldn't fathom why Dylan had made the suggestion. "I disrupt Socrates with a lot of fosters, but I've never foisted an aggressive cat on him," I told Dylan. "I don't know if that would be fair."

"I'll take Tinks over to Whiskered Away Home," Dylan said, picking up the carrier. The cat whose fate was in question hurled himself around again, causing the crate to bang against Dylan's bare leg. He still didn't seem to notice. That was why Piper didn't fire him from Templeton Animal Hospital. He always remained calm, which eventually helped frightened patients to do the same. "Bea Baumgartner'll know how to handle a fractious cat," Dylan added. "She's seen everything at the shelter."

I wasn't sure she'd seen the likes of Tinkleston. And I didn't really like that plan, either. But I didn't seem to have a choice.

"Okay," I agreed. I suddenly recalled how Bea had been so dismissive of purebred, pedigreed cats. "But please tell her it's only temporary. I'll find a home for him soon. Or maybe there's some provision in Miss Flynt's will."

I felt a small shiver go down my spine as I again pictured Miss Flynt's body in the tub. For some reason, knowing that she'd definitely been murdered made the image even more haunting.

Dylan's mind must've turned to the homicide, too.

"I wonder what poor Tinkleston saw the night Miss Flynt got killed," he mused, shaking his head sadly. He opened his car's hatch and placed the crate inside. "If only cats could talk, huh?"

"Yes," I agreed. "I guess the mystery would be solved."

Stepping behind the car, I bent down and peered at Tinkleston's face, which was pressed against the bars. His naturally downturned mouth was even more severely inverted than usual, and I swore I saw sadness and accusation in his eyes.

My heart tugged, and I straightened, then took a step backward so Dylan could shut the hatch.

"Hey, sorry I was late," he finally apologized, wiping his hands on his shorts to clean them of dirt from his car. There was probably some California sand on the bumper of that wreck, which was even worse than my van. The body was riddled with corrosion, the plastic on one of the headlights was cracked, and the window on the rear passenger side had a bad habit of sliding down into the door if Dylan drove more than a mile, as he'd done that day. I hoped Tinks didn't get too cold on his ride to Whiskered Away. "I'd like to make it up to you," Dylan added. "Especially since you got so scratched up."

I waved off the suggestion. "Don't worry about it. I'm fine."

"No, really," he said. "How about meeting me for dinner at the Wolf Hollow Mill? Tomorrow night?" Dylan and I usually split the check when we went out, and he must've seen me mentally calculating the cost of a meal and drinks at Sylvan Creek's most expensive restaurant, because he assured me, "It's my apology, so my treat."

I didn't know how Dylan could afford dinner at the Mill. And I wasn't sure that I wanted to meet up at a place known for its romantic, classy atmosphere. Usually, Dylan and I went to the Lakeside, a seafood shack that teetered on a pier above Lake Wallapawakee. A vegan, he ate lettuce and tomatoes normally used as burger garnishes, because there wasn't even a salad on the menu, and I ate whatever cheese was available that night, usually in the form of gooey, melted mozzarella sticks or nacho topping.

Were we really going to eat thirty-dollar entrées in a gorgeous stone house dating back to the 1700s?

My continued reluctance must've been written all over my face. "They have a really cool bar, if you don't want to eat in the fancy dining room," he said. "You'll recognize lots of people from the Lakeside."

I still didn't understand how he planned to pay. Even

pub food would be expensive at Wolf Hollow. But what he was suggesting did sound fun. And he did owe me.

"Okay," I agreed, with one last glance at the mansion. I couldn't help wondering what was going on in there. But I knew that Jonathan wouldn't want me to so much as peek in the windows, and I faced Dylan again. "I'll meet you there."

Dylan grinned and opened his mouth to respond. Then something to my right caught his attention, and for the first time I could recall, his eyes widened with alarm.

Needless to say, I spun around, and a moment later cried out, "Tinkleston! No!"

Chapter 13

"You're going to be just fine," Piper promised Socrates, dabbing antiseptic onto his nose, which Tinkleston had scratched after escaping from his carrier and jumping out of the Subaru's perpetually open window. Fortunately, Dylan had quickly scooped up and crated the fearsome little Persian, suffering a few minor injuries in the process. However, Dylan hadn't bled like poor Socrates, who was, of course, acting stoic. I knew that he was mainly pained to be the center of attention—and he hated visiting Piper's office, too. But he sat quietly, enduring my sister's ministrations until she backed away from the silver exam table, stepped on a pedal at the base of a shiny trash can, and disposed of a few soiled cotton balls. "Honestly, it's just a deep scratch," she assured me, moving to the sink to wash her hands. "Dogs' noses and ears tend to bleed a lot, if nicked."

"Well, thanks for taking care of him," I said, pressing a different foot pedal. One that lowered the table so Socrates could jump off without assistance. Nothing would have mortified him more than to be *lifted*. Even the slow ride toward the floor clearly embarrassed him. But he kept his muzzle high as he descended at a snail's pace. I pretended I didn't even notice. "I got worried when he was still bleeding now and then, after hours had passed." Socrates stepped off the table with as much dignity as possible and walked directly to the door, signaling that he was ready to leave. Then I gave my sister a quizzical look as I removed my foot from the pedal. "And speaking of time," I added. "What are you doing here so late on a Sunday evening? You can't have that much paperwork, can you?"

"There's *always* paperwork when you run a business with high liability and several employees," Piper said, drying her hands with a paper towel. She tossed that into the trash can, too. The lid clanged shut. "And since I was summoned to town anyway, to speak with detectives Black and Doebler, I stopped in here to get some things done."

I drew back. "You were already questioned?"

Piper nodded. "Yes. Briefly."

"So, what did they ask you about?" I inquired, feeling strangely slighted. Not that I wanted to be interrogated under a spotlight, but I *had* been at the scene of the crime. I was also concerned for my sister. "Are you a suspect?"

"I don't think so." Piper leaned against the exam room's counter and crossed her arms over the lab coat she'd donned when I'd brought in the day's only patient. "They were both curious about my wet shirt, since Miss Flynt struggled with whoever pushed her into the bathtub, but Pastor Pete apparently corroborated my—true—story about moving the tub full of apples." She shrugged. "Plus, I had no motive to kill Miss Flynt."

"Yes, I guess motive is always the key," I noted softly. Then I grew preoccupied, trying to picture everyone I'd seen the previous night.

Tamara Fox, who was tired of playing second fiddle as a philanthropist.

Bea Baumgartner, who'd complained bitterly about Miss Flynt's preference for purebred cats.

Archivist Asa Whitaker and his wife, librarian Martha.

That spectral young woman in the shadows . . .

"Daphne, you're getting a funny gleam in your eyes," Piper said, snapping me back to reality. "And I bet you did more than retrieve Tinkleston from Flynt Mansion. You snooped, didn't you?"

Socrates, still waiting by the door, made a grunting sound to let Piper know that she'd guessed correctly.

"Hey!" I cried, glancing down at him. Then I turned back to Piper. "I just looked around a little."

"Daphne . . ." There was admonition in my sister's tone. "There's no reason for you to investigate this murder!"

All at once, I pictured one more person who'd been inside Flynt Mansion the previous night.

"What about Mom?" I noted.

My restless, perfectionist sister had begun straightening up the already tidy counter, but she turned to shoot me a quizzical look. "What about her?"

"Mom was in the house with Miss Flynt, *preparing to seal a million dollar real estate deal,*" I pointed out. Not that I believed my mother was capable of murder, but a plausible scenario quickly came to mind. "What if Miss Flynt had changed her mind about selling her ancestral home? What if she was about to cost Mom a big commission *and* ruin our mother's chance to brag about being the realtor who sold Flynt Mansion?"

Even as I speculated, I realized that my scenario was almost *too* plausible. And Piper's cheeks got pale. "Daphne," she cautioned me again, more gravely. "Don't ever say anything like that to Detective Black. He'll no doubt look at money as a possible motive, but don't give him any ideas."

"I won't," I promised, raising my right hand. "I will keep my big mouth shut. I swear."

Piper, Socrates, and I got quiet for a moment, and I knew that we were all guiltily wondering just how ambitious Maeve Templeton really was.

Then I shook off the image of my mother arguing with Miss Flynt and reached into my back pocket.

"If I promise you it has nothing to do with investigating, and everything to do with proper cat care, would you take a look at something I found at the mansion?" I requested, unfolding the list of Tinkleston's supplements. I offered Piper the chart. "It's Miss Flynt's attempt to keep track of all the extra vitamins and minerals she gave Tinkleston."

Piper was clearly skeptical, but she accepted the paper. Then she frowned as she read aloud. "Probiotic . . . salmon oil . . . immune booster . . ."

"Does he really need all that stuff?" I asked. All at once, I started to worry that maybe something was wrong with Tinkleston, in which case he probably shouldn't be in a cat shelter, even temporarily. "Is he sick, that you know of?"

Piper shook her head and handed the paper back to me. "No. He's a very healthy cat. I just saw him a few weeks ago. These supplements probably aren't harmful, but they are overkill. A young cat like Tinkleston should be able to have his nutritional needs met with food. Especially the kind of high quality stuff I'm *sure* Lillian buys."

"She feeds him something called Cleopatra's Choice Cuts," I said, wishing yet again that I'd remembered to give Dylan the can of food I'd taken from the mansion. In the excitement over Tinkleston's near escape, I'd accidentally walked away with it. "I've never heard of the brand," I added. "Have you?"

"No, I haven't." Piper moved to the door, opening it for Socrates, who trotted into the hallway. "Which probably means it's ridiculously expensive." Piper must've seen that I was still concerned about how Tinks would fare at Whiskered Away. "But, trust me, he'll be fine with cheaper food for a while."

My sister obviously wanted to return to work, so I followed her and Socrates out to the waiting room, where she unlocked the front door. Socrates couldn't get outside fast enough, although the street was unwelcomingly dark by then, and the air was pretty chilly.

"Well, thanks again for taking care of Socrates," I said, stepping out onto the sidewalk, too. "You'll send me a bill, right . . . ?"

"Good night, Daphne." Piper moved to close the door without answering my question, but she told Socrates, "And don't bother your nose. It could start bleeding again, and I know you want to be spared the indignity of a bandage."

The door clicked shut before either of us could reply, leaving me and Socrates alone on Market Street. The town was closed down for the night, but most of the businesses' windows glowed with holiday-themed lights, and I took a moment to look around at the displays.

Tessie Flinchbaugh's pet emporium, Fetch!, was perhaps the most elaborately decorated shop, and I found myself walking across the street to get a closer look. "Come on, Socrates," I said, smiling. "Let's go check out Tessie's handiwork."

Socrates didn't appear too intrigued, but he followed along, his toenails clicking on the quiet street.

When we reached Fetch!, we both stopped in front of two large windows, which were even more impressive up close.

On one side, Tessie had dressed the store's mascot, a life-sized, plush Irish wolfhound, as a *were*-wolfhound. The big stuffed dog wore a shredded men's shirt, so it looked like he'd ripped his clothes while transforming, and Tessie had put a set of menacing teeth in his open mouth. The other window had a feline theme. Tessie had painted and carved about ten pumpkins to look like black cats, and she'd placed lights inside each one, causing their eyes to glitter orange from within.

I couldn't help but think of Tinkleston and, feeling guilty, I glanced down at Socrates. "I hope Tinks really is okay at the shelter."

Socrates pretended he didn't hear the comment, so I returned my attention to the display, which wasn't just for aesthetic purposes. Tessie was also trying to sell premium cat food. Expensive cans of organic Natural-Path Salmon Filet Dinner were stacked in pyramids, with the promise of a discount for anyone who bought ten at a time.

I tried to look past the display into the store, wondering if Tessie sold Cleopatra's Choice Cuts. But I couldn't see anything, and Socrates was growing restless. He moved to the street, so I followed him back toward the van, which was parked between Piper's practice and one of Sylvan Creek's few *empty* storefronts.

I still missed Giulia Alberti's Italian coffee shop, Espresso Pronto, which she'd abandoned while fleeing an abusive relationship with local banker Christian Clarke. I couldn't blame Giulia—she'd done the right thing—but I'd loved her biscotti and the atmosphere in the café, which was decorated in a Tuscan style, with warm, terracotta-colored walls and a rustic stone floor.

Although Socrates was waiting impatiently by the VW, I took a moment to cup my hands around my eyes and peek into the shop, standing on tiptoes so I could see over a Templeton Realty FOR RENT sign—and a poster someone had tacked up, advertising a haunted hayride to benefit Pastor Pete Kishbaugh's Lighthouse Fellowship Church. I drew back for a second and studied that ad more closely. The flyer featured scary pictures of maniacal clowns and zombies, and the challenge, *Ride . . . If You Dare!* Followed by, *All proceeds benefit Lighthouse Fellowship community service projects. For more information, or to be a volunteer ghoul, contact Tamara Fox at tfox@lighthouse.com.*

Wasn't a macabre hayride a strange fund-raiser for a *church?*

When Lillian Flynt was in charge of Lighthouse Fellowship's treasury, she used to set up a bake sale table at Sylvan Creek's annual Howl-o-Ween Pets 'n People Costume Parade to raise money for the church's soup kitchen and Pastor Pete's missionary trips.

"Oh, well," I said softly, trying to look inside the bistro again. By the light of a street lamp behind me, I could see that Espresso Pronto's dark, wooden tables were still scattered around the small dining area, and the glass case that used to be filled with delicious Italian pastries remained in place.

"This is such a cute space," I mused aloud, causing steam to form on the glass. I wiped away the cloud with my sleeve. "It could be a bakery again, for people— or pets. . . ."

All at once, Lillian Flynt's words echoed in my mind. *"Well, get to it, Daphne!"*

Then my thoughts were interrupted by a low "woof," coming from behind me.

Pulling back from the window, I turned to see that Socrates, who almost never barked, was standing at attention. His body was stiff, and his tail pointed straight up. His hackles were raised, too.

I'd only seen Socrates look like that once before, on the day old Mr. Peachy had tried to bludgeon me.

The hairs on the back of *my* neck stood up, and I tried to find whatever was bothering my normally unflappable canine friend.

For a moment, I didn't see anything moving except swirling leaves, because the wind was picking up.

Then I noted that Socrates's nose pointed like the needle of a compass down the street, toward Pettigrew Park's entrance, which was lined with *bodies* impaled on sticks.

"They're just scarecrows," I told Socrates, nearly laughing with relief to realize that he was spooked by a display erected every autumn by the Sylvan Creek Garden Club—Lillian Flynt, former president. "They're not really people."

Socrates didn't seem reassured. He continued to stare in the direction of the park, and the ridge of fur that ran along his long spine remained raised.

I was about to laugh at him again when I looked at the park one more time—and one of those scarecrows *slipped into the shadows.*

Chapter 14

The wind continued to rise in advance of a storm as Socrates and I walked down a heavily wooded driveway, shortly after watching a scarecrow seemingly come to life, and I couldn't help jumping every time the branches overhead creaked and the fallen leaves rustled, as if disturbed by unseen feet.

"I know I'm edgy," I told Socrates, who had resumed his normal, placid demeanor. In fact, he seemed somewhat amused by my fears, and I reminded him, "You were nervous, too, back at Pettigrew Park. Not to mention a wreck at Piper's office!"

Socrates swung around to look up at me, his doggy eyebrows raised, as if he disputed those statements.

I knew that he was also skeptical about my decision *not* to go straight home to Plum Cottage. At the last moment, I'd skipped a crucial turn in the road and gone straight, headed deeper into the Pocono Mountains, driving about twenty minutes until we'd arrived at our current destination.

The wind gusted again, and I was glad to see lights glowing in an A-frame cabin just a few yards ahead of us.

Still, I looked over my shoulder, half expecting to discover a somewhat familiar person following us.

I hadn't gotten a good look at the individual who'd lurked amid the scarecrows, but I was pretty sure Socrates and I had been observed by the young woman I'd seen at Flynt Mansion, right before I'd discovered Miss Flynt's body.

The ghostly girl in the flowing tunic had stood alone then, too.

Who was she?

And what was she doing in a lonely park, after dark?

Last but not least . . .

Socrates and I had arrived at the house, and I raised my hand to knock on the door, which swung open, as if our visit had been anticipated.

I probably should've greeted Jonathan Black, who stood in the doorway, leaning against the frame with his arms crossed, but instead, I blurted the final question that kept nagging at me.

"Why in the world haven't you asked *me* anything about the murder?"

Chapter 15

"Detective Doebler tried to contact you several times," Jonathan informed me, still leaning against the door frame. The entrance was also blocked by Jonathan's chocolate Lab, Axis, who sat quietly by his person's side after trying to greet Socrates with a sniff. Socrates had politely declined, although he liked Axis well enough. "But apparently, you don't answer your cell phone or respond to voicemail," Jonathan continued. "And, from what I understand, you don't have an answering machine connected to your landline, either."

I suddenly pictured my unreliable cell phone, which was sitting on my kitchen counter, where I'd left it charging all day while I'd been out and about. And I wasn't sure how I'd hook up an answering machine to the old rotary dial phone that Mr. Peachy had left behind at Plum Cottage.

"But still . . ."

"Moreover, our first priority was to interview all of the people who were roaming around Lillian Flynt's property in the hours before her death," Jonathan added, talking right over me. "By all accounts, you arrived pretty late on the scene, compared to quite a few other people."

I was about to argue that I had nevertheless observed a lot that night, when I was distracted by a soft yipping sound, coming from deep inside the house.

I looked down at Socrates, whose ears were keener than mine, and saw his tail twitch slightly as the noise grew closer, accompanied by the click of toenails on hardwood, right before a one-eared Chihuahua with a severe overbite darted out from behind Jonathan and launched himself at Socrates.

"Artie!" I cried, bending down and scooping up the exuberant little dog, to prevent him from crashing into a much more subdued basset hound. Artie didn't skip a beat and immediately transferred his affection to me. Within seconds, my face was covered with the tiny canine's trademark drool. "It's good to see you, too," I promised him, wiping at my cheeks with my sleeve. Grinning, I again looked at Socrates, who appeared pleased to see his only true nonhuman friend. I hugged Artie, who squirmed with glee. "We've *both* missed you!"

Artie wiggled harder, and I set him down so he and Socrates could finally have a more restrained reunion. The two dogs bumped muzzles, Artie shivering with happiness, while Socrates's tail took a few uncharacteristically wide swings. Then Artie gazed up at Jonathan with wide, hopeful eyes.

I had been worried about whether a reserved detective and a hyper Chihuahua would find a way to communicate, but apparently Jonathan and Artie had connected on some level.

As the high-spirited pup continued to stare up at him, Jonathan rolled his eyes, sighed, and said, "Fine."

Then he stepped aside and extended the invitation I'd been waiting for, the whole time I'd been standing on the porch, trying to see past him into the house I'd first shown him months before. "Won't you all please come inside?"

Chapter 16

The dogs chose to play outside, to the extent that Socrates would play. But I accepted Jonathan's invitation and stepped past him into the house, where I had to stifle a gasp of surprise, to see how he'd transformed the A-frame cabin, which had previously been owned by womanizing dog trainer Steve Beamus.

When Steve had occupied the property, the furniture had been made of deer antlers, the only artwork had been an oversized painting of an elk, and worst of all, Steve had used a taxidermied grizzly bear as a coatrack.

But as I walked into the home's expansive, open living space, I realized that all of the man cave decor was thankfully gone.

"This is incredible," I told Jonathan, who closed the door behind us.

The log structure was still masculine, but the furnishings were modern and sleek. Industrial-looking wood and metal stools flanked the breakfast bar, which had an updated concrete countertop. A deep gray, clean-lined sectional defined the living room, which was anchored and softened by an oversized, artfully worn antique rug in muted shades of red and pale blue. I also noted that two matching dog beds—one large and one small—were placed right next to the couch, within reach of anyone who might absently pat a retriever, or a Chihuahua, while watching TV.

Then I noticed that the huge flat screen that used to dominate the room was also missing. In fact, there was no television at all. The new focal point was the stone fireplace, in which a large stack of logs burned, warming the house.

But the biggest change, aside from the absence of the grizzly bear, was the addition of a floor-to-ceiling bookshelf that took up most of one wall. The shelf was so tall that Jonathan had installed a ladder on wheels, so he'd be able to reach the volumes at the top.

I was very interested to know what Jonathan Black read in his spare time and hoped I'd get the opportunity to explore.

In the meantime, I told him, "This place looks amazing. You have a real talent for decorating."

He smiled. "Thanks, but this is all Elyse's handiwork. She insisted on helping me—for which I'm grateful. I'd probably still have the bear in here if it weren't for her."

I should've known that the stylish woman who produced shows for a network that was all about decorating and living well had planned the space.

"Is that how she found Flynt Mansion?" I inquired, trailing Jonathan toward the kitchen. "While she was redecorating your place?"

Jonathan nodded. "Yes. Elyse saw the property and

decided that it had to be her next project." He gestured for me to take a seat on one of the tall stools at the breakfast bar. "Along with creating a show about pet friendly towns. But I think she's most excited about tackling the mansion's renovation."

"My mother is actually worried about whether she'll be able to sell the house now," I noted, thinking that, if Moxie'd been there, she would've informed Jonathan that Elyse also wanted proximity to him. I didn't mention that, though, and added, "I guess a lot depends on how Miss Flynt disposed of the property in her will."

"I have a feeling Elyse will end up with the house," Jonathan said. Opening a cupboard, he took down two mugs and filled them with coffee from a shiny, black and silver machine. Then he set one of the drinks in front of me. "Now, why don't you tell me why you were snooping around the day after you found *yet another* body?"

"First of all, it's my mother's fault that I found Miss Flynt," I said, wrapping my hands around the mug and inhaling the slightly bitter, almost chocolatey scent of the coffee. "She sent me upstairs to find Tinkleston—"

"What is a Tinkleston?" Jonathan interrupted me.

"That's the cat's name," I said, holding out my arm to show him the old and new red tracks. "The one that scratched me."

"Really? 'Tinkleston'?" He arched an eyebrow. "No wonder he lashes out."

"Yes, everyone seems to agree that Tinkleston's name contributes to his foul temper."

Jonathan moved to the refrigerator to get some cream, and he spoke over his shoulder. "And you returned to the house . . . ?"

"Because I was worried about Tinks," I explained. "I went back to make sure he wasn't still locked away in Miss Flynt's bedroom."

Jonathan closed the refrigerator door. When he turned around, I saw that he was frowning. "But you did more than check on the cat."

I felt my cheeks flush. "How did you know . . . ?"

"I didn't." Jonathan set a container of cream in front of me. "I just assumed. Plus, your face and jeans were smeared with dirt, for some reason." He studied my cheeks, perhaps trying to recall how I'd looked the previous day, then guessed, "Maybe you crawled around the attic? Or basement?"

"Actually, I checked the fireplace in the bedroom," I confessed, pouring a big glug of cream into my mug. The coffee was very dark. "I sifted through the ashes." Jonathan's frown deepened, and I quickly defended myself. "Before I knew for sure that Miss Flynt was murdered!"

Jonathan took a sip of black coffee and made a face, but not because the brew was bitter. I'd confused him. "Murder or no murder . . . why would you dig through cinders?"

"I was curious about something I'd seen burning in the fireplace, the night Miss Flynt died," I said. "A manuscript. I thought I might find remnants that didn't burn."

Jonathan was still unhappy with me, but he was also intrigued. I saw a spark of interest in his blue eyes. "And . . . ?"

"Parts of the document *didn't* burn," I said. "Although, what little I could read was incredibly boring historical stuff about Sylvan Creek. Like when we got a second mill, two hundred years ago."

Jonathan observed me over the rim of his mug. "I get the sense that you found something of interest, though."

"Yes," I said. "One piece of paper had fragments of a sentence on it. Something about a man named Benedict, whose last name started with the letters *f-l-y-n*. And the word 'scandalous.' Or, at least, most of the word."

Jonathan took a moment to consider what I'd just told him. "I'm not sure if that small fragment is important," he finally said. "But the burning manuscript, overall, could be significant."

I was somewhat pleased to think I might have found a clue.

"I'm pretty sure it was a copy of Asa Whitaker's soon-to-be-published history of Sylvan Creek," I added, cradling the warm mug again. "You know him, right? The archivist from the public library?"

Leaning against the counter, Jonathan nodded. "Yes, I questioned him the other night."

He didn't say more, but I could tell that he'd already judged slight, meek Asa an unlikely killer. And I had to agree. Still, I ventured, "What if Asa unearthed some scandal involving the Flynt family? He and Miss Flynt might've argued about him printing the story for the whole world to read."

Jonathan set down his mug and crossed his arms over his chest, covering a nearly worn-off Navy logo on an equally worn sweatshirt. "First of all, I doubt the 'whole world' will read a history of Sylvan Creek—intriguing as the community is." He was being sarcastic, and I started to argue that his ex-wife considered the town interesting enough to feature it on TV, but he spoke over me. "And, second, I don't know if some old scandal is worth killing over."

I cocked my head and dared to ask a personal question. "Where are you from?"

He didn't answer right away, and I rolled my eyes. "Oh, come on. Your past isn't *that* secret!"

Jonathan didn't dispute that he kept a pretty tight lid on his personal history. But he did respond, in his clipped, reluctant way. "My father was in the military. We moved around a lot. Everywhere from Berlin to Norfolk."

Given my own love of travel, I found that snippet of information very interesting. But it wasn't the right time to share stories about places we'd visited.

"So you don't know what it's like to be rooted in a small town, like Miss Flynt?" I asked.

Jonathan watched me warily, like I was trying to trick him. "No . . ."

"Her family lived in that house for generations," I reminded him. "The Flynts are . . . were . . . like royalty here. Lillian's whole *life* was Sylvan Creek, and I guarantee you that her family's reputation was a very big deal to her."

"You have a point," Jonathan conceded. I noted that he didn't say I'd made a good point, but he did promise, "I'll check the fireplace. And talk to Asa Whitaker again, if I think it's necessary."

I sipped my coffee, my thoughts drifting back to the dark bathroom where I'd discovered Miss Flynt's body after chasing Tinkleston down the hallway.

"How do you know Miss Flynt was murdered?" I asked. "How can you be sure that she didn't just fall in the tub with the CD player?"

Which Piper had been looking for, that evening. I wondered if Jonathan knew about that.

"There was a struggle," he told me. He'd already finished his coffee and shifted to rinse his mug in a spotless, stainless steel sink. Shutting the tap, he faced me again. "And . . ."

He hesitated, as if he thought he'd already said too much.

"Oh, just tell me," I urged. "I'm watching Vonda Shakes's dog next week. If you don't explain what happened, she probably will. Or I'll have Moxie drag the story out of her, the next time Vonda gets her hair cut."

"Ah, yes. Moxie Bloom." Jonathan grinned and rubbed his jaw, where he had that intriguing scar. "Provider of great shaves and collector of Sylvan Creek's secrets."

"She'll know everything soon—and call me," I warned him. "So you might as well give me the *correct* story. Because sometimes facts get blurry when filtered through Spa and Paw."

Jonathan paused again, then said, "If you must know, and I guess you must, Miss Flynt had a head injury inconsistent with a fall. And the way the water was splashed around the bathroom . . . There was clearly a struggle."

"But the bathtub was almost empty when I found her," I pointed out.

"The drain plug on the old tub didn't fit properly," he explained, picking up my mug, which was also empty. The dark brew, made richer by the heavy cream, had really grown on me. He set the mug in the sink. "The water probably leaked out between the time she was killed and the time you found her."

I wanted to make sure I had the scenario right. "So somebody first conked Miss Flynt on the head, then shoved her in the tub and tossed in the CD player, zapping her."

Jonathan nodded, and in spite of the grim topic, I saw a twinkle of amusement in his eyes. "That's not how I'd put it, but, yes."

"Interesting."

Still close to laughing, he raised a hand. "Please. Don't be too interested."

I was pressing my luck, but I ventured to request even more details. "So, was Miss Flynt electrocuted? Or was she dead before that?"

Sometimes, when Jonathan didn't plan to answer me, he just . . . didn't. This was one of those times.

I could only surmise that he had a reason for keeping that sequence of events secret. I was also fairly certain that I wouldn't get any more information out of him that night. And since we'd both finished our drinks, I hopped off the stool, telling him, "Thanks for the coffee."

"My pleasure," he assured me, leading the way toward the door. "And thank you for the information about the manuscript." He looked over his shoulder. "But please don't go back inside Flynt Mansion, which is cordoned off as a crime scene now."

I didn't expect to return to the property, but I didn't want to make any promises either, so I stayed quiet until we reached the foyer, where a low, upholstered, steel bench was now the centerpiece of the space. "Before I go, can I ask one more question?" I requested. "Please?"

Jonathan nodded. "Yes. One more."

"What happened to the bear?"

I had hoped the majestic animal had been provided a decent burial. But that wasn't the case.

"I sold it to a hunting lodge in Colorado."

I reared back. "*Colorado?*"

"Elyse filmed a show there once," he explained. "Something about 'great inns of America.' She contacted the owner and convinced him the bear belonged in his lobby."

I felt my eyes widen. "Wow. Talk about selling ice to Eskimos!"

"Yes, Elyse can be very persuasive," Jonathan agreed, with a barely suppressed grin. "Now, I suppose we should check on the dogs. It's not like Artie to leave me alone for very long."

I'd almost forgotten that Socrates was outside with Artie and Axis, and I moved to grab the doorknob.

"But before you go. . ." Jonathan reached past me and rested one hand on the door, stopping me before I could open it. "I'd like to ask a question or two of you, with your vast knowledge of Sylvan Creek society."

He'd definitely grabbed my attention, and I looked up at him. "Yes?"

Jonathan grew thoughtful and spoke more quietly. "If Lillian Flynt was so rooted in Sylvan Creek, and the town was 'her life,' to use your own words, why was she selling her ancestral home? Why now? And where was she going?"

"I'm afraid I have no idea," I admitted. "And you should probably ask my mother those questions. She told me she didn't know much about Lillian's plans. But she might know *something*."

Jonathan was already shaking his head. "Your mother doesn't seem to know anything about Lillian Flynt's motives for selling the house. I get the sense that, once Miss Flynt agreed to put the mansion on the market, your mother cared primarily about the financial side of things."

"Yeah, that sounds like Mom," I agreed. Then I searched his eyes, trying to gauge his reaction when I asked, "Is my mother a suspect? Or Piper?"

"You know I can't answer that."

Yet, he already had. Jonathan was great at hiding his thoughts, but I'd glimpsed something in his eyes right before he'd responded. He definitely considered my mother, or Piper, or both of them, potential killers.

We stood staring at each other for a long moment. He was obviously well aware that he'd again revealed more than he'd intended, if only for a split second. And I hoped that *I* wasn't giving away too much, because sometimes, on those rare occasions when I stood close to Jonathan, like I was doing right then, I couldn't help but find him not only irritating, but very attractive.

Who *wouldn't?*

Unfortunately, we were complete opposites and would grate on each other like nails on a chalkboard.

As I was imagining that awful sound, I actually heard a scratching noise, caused by someone who was outside the door, trying to get in.

Jonathan and I had been staring pretty intently into each other's eyes, but we suddenly exchanged quizzical looks.

Then I opened the door—and gagged a little, into my hand.

Chapter 17

"I have no idea how Socrates managed to get 'skunked,' while Artie, who is usually—let's face it—a magnet for disaster, came away smelling perfectly fine," I complained to Moxie, whom I had on speaker phone. My cell was actually working after resting and charging all day, although I expected it to conk out at any moment. Probably before I had a chance to check several waiting voicemails, which were most likely from Detective Doebler. Taking a cue from my mother, I lit a scented candle while offering a very glum, chastened, and still somewhat stinky basset hound a sympathetic glance. Socrates was hunkered down in his favorite spot by Plum Cottage's arched stone fireplace, where a fire roared in the grate. The looming storm had finally hit during our chilly ride home from Jonathan's house, and by the time we'd reached Winding Hill, cold rain was driving in through the van's windows, which I'd had to keep open. Socrates *really* reeked. I placed the candle, which smelled like spicy sandalwood, on the mantel. "I wanted to let you know that your peroxide and vinegar mixture helped, though," I told Moxie, whom I'd consulted the moment we'd arrived home, after a wet, miserable walk through the woods. Now that the crisis had passed, I was calling again to thank her for giving me the recipe for a home remedy. "He's starting to smell marginally better."

"If there's one thing I know about, it's getting the stink out of dogs," Moxie informed me cheerfully. I could picture her in her cozy garret apartment on the top floor of the turreted Victorian building that housed Sylvan Creek's specialty bookstore, the Philosopher's Tome. It was getting pretty late, so she almost certainly wore one of her many pairs of vintage Doris Day–inspired pajamas. I had also changed into my jammies, a warm flannel pair, after bathing Socrates. "I once had to clean up a sheepdog that was playing off leash in Pettigrew Park," Moxie noted. "He somehow managed to roll in three different piles of—"

"No need to go into detail!" I interrupted, with a glance at Socrates, who cringed. "I get the picture." I suddenly recalled my interesting encounter near that same park, and I added, "By the way . . ."

I was about to ask Moxie if she'd seen anyone unusual lurking around town recently when all at once my phone died, just as a huge gust of wind slammed into the cottage and caused the plum tree outside to scrape against the already rattling window.

The coincidence was kind of creepy, and I looked nervously at the window, half expecting to see a ghostly figure hovering outside. But no one was there, and the spooky mood was quickly broken by the cheerful sound of a timer dinging in the kitchen.

I wore an oversized pair of fuzzy slippers that matched my pjs, and I shuffled across the wood floor to take a tray of Batty-for-Turkey Treats out of the oven before they burned, ruining them for the cats at Whiskered Away Home, who probably deserved a reward after spending time with Tinkleston.

Opening the oven door, I bent down and saw that the little bat-shaped cookies, made of ground turkey, Parmesan cheese and crushed crackers, were lightly browned, just like I'd hoped.

I removed the cookie sheet from the oven and set the treats on the counter to cool, next to an apple and cheddar pie I'd baked for myself earlier in the day.

Pulling open a drawer, I found a fork and dug right into the pie, cutting through the flaky top crust to reveal thinly sliced, tender Cortland and Granny Smith apples and sharp cheddar cheese. Then, while I savored a big bite, I picked up the can of Cleopatra's Choice Cuts cat food, which I'd also left on the counter to weigh down the extensive list of supplements Tinkleston was supposed to take. Squinting, I studied the label, turning the can so I could read the food's ingredients, which were printed in tiny type.

Corn gluten meal . . . soy . . . propyl gallate . . .

"What the . . . ?" I mumbled through my bite of pie. I furrowed my brow. "This is all junk!"

Confused, I kept staring at the list of fillers and artificial flavorings. Then I turned the can over, checking the bottom, and saw a price sticker that was nearly worn away. But I could still read that the food cost only forty-two cents.

"This makes no sense," I mused quietly, still holding the can, but digging my fork into the pie again. "Why would Lillian feed Tinkleston cheap, unhealthy food, when she was concerned enough to give him a bunch of expensive vitamins?"

All at once, my heart sank as I recalled that I'd taken more than just the supplements schedule and curious can of food from Miss Flynt's kitchen.

Dropping the fork, but taking the cat food and schedule with me, I hurried across the living room and climbed the spiral staircase up to my loft bedroom, where I tossed the can and paper onto the bed before dumping out a basket full of clothes that were waiting to be washed at Piper's house, since the cottage didn't have a washer and dryer.

Rooting through the pile, I located the skinny black pants I'd worn under my witch cape and dug through the pockets. I quickly found the note I'd accidentally removed from Miss Flynt's house, in all the confusion surrounding her death.

Climbing onto the bed, I sat cross-legged, smoothed out the crumpled paper, and reread the instructions for Tinkleston's care, although the awful penmanship was almost illegible.

> . . . *please feed the cat at least once a day and change the litter when necessary. . . . cell phone reception is poor where I'm traveling. . . . call a veterinarian. LF.*

"Something's weird about all of this," I said quietly, my gaze roaming from the cat food to the supplements schedule to the note. Above me, rain pelted the tin roof, so I could hardly hear myself whisper, "Something doesn't add up. . . ."

I'd thought I was talking to myself, until I caught a faint whiff of skunk. Looking up, I realized that Socrates had joined me in the loft. He was watching me with a look of concern, mingled with disapproval.

"I know I'm in trouble," I told him. "I'm starting to think the food and the papers might be clues—which means I *shouldn't* have taken them, and Jonathan Black is going to be furious when I turn them over."

Socrates sighed loudly and lumbered up onto his

purple, velvet cushion. Within minutes, he was sound asleep and snoring. Setting the can, the schedule, and the instructions for Tinks's care onto my nightstand, I checked my clock and realized it was nearly midnight. Yawning, I climbed under a down comforter Piper had given me as a cottage-warming gift. Just above my head, rain continued to clatter on the tin roof. But as the storm weakened, the sound grew soothing, and I soon found myself drifting off to sleep, too.

And as my mind relaxed, I finally realized what was wrong with the note *someone* had left on Lillian Flynt's counter.

"Jonathan is going to kill *me*," I grumbled, half asleep.

Then I burrowed deeper under the comforter and soon fell into a deep slumber. One filled with vivid dreams about dark, lonely lakes that were charged with crackling electricity, mysterious figures who moved through a haunted mansion late at night, and yowling black cats, trapped in cages.

I woke up at dawn, my eyes snapping open and the sound of those cats still echoing in my mind.

Sitting up, I looked over at Socrates, who was awake, too, and said, "I'm really sorry, and you're going to hate me, but I *have* to go get Tinkleston."

Chapter 18

The Whiskered Away Home cat shelter was housed in a sagging, gray barn that was tucked away in a wooded valley about five miles outside Sylvan Creek.

As my van bumped over the rutted, unpaved road that misty, chilly morning, carrying me deeper into the forest, I seriously considered turning back. The trees that arched overhead were already bare, and their naked, gnarled branches, which twined together across the narrow path, felt like fingers trying to trap and crush me. The woods smelled of decay, too.

Which was not half as bad as the odor that assaulted me when I got out of the VW.

My nose wrinkled as I caught a big whiff of cat urine.

Then I pulled the hood of my sweater up over my curls, tucked a container filled with Batty-for-Turkey cat treats under my arm, and tramped through a thick carpet of wet leaves to a door with a hand-lettered, sloppy sign that said CALL AHEAD TO SEE CATS!

I knew a thing or two about encouraging pet adoption, and I didn't think Bea Baumgartner was using quite the right approach. The shelter's name was cute, but I half feared someone was going to swoop down and "whisker" me away—to a shallow grave.

Which was probably why I nearly jumped out of my cowgirl boots when someone behind me snapped, "Step away from the door, missy. Or else."

Chapter 19

"I'm sorry, Daphne," Bea Baumgartner said, as she unlocked the barn door. "I didn't recognize you with your hood up. And living out here alone, I don't like trespassers."

"The mist is making my curls a disaster. . . ." I started to explain why I'd semiconcealed my identity when I glimpsed my van out of the corner of my eye.

Hadn't the pink VW with the misshapen dog—and *my name*—on the side given Bea a clue as to who was visiting? Hadn't she noticed my van when she'd stepped out of her trailer home, which was nearly hidden in a huge thicket of huckleberry about twenty yards from the barn?

"Your hair looks just fine," Bea assured me. She continued to fumble with padlocks. The shelter was sealed like Fort Knox. Wasn't she in the business of *giving cats away*? "You young girls all worry too much about how you look," she added, shaking her head and tsk-tsking.

I agreed, in theory, that people shouldn't put too much emphasis on appearance. But I thought Bea might want to worry a tiny bit more about how she looked. Her outfit that day consisted of gray sweatpants with dirty elastic around the ankles, a shapeless Sylvan Creek High sweatshirt that had seen better days, to put it mildly, and a knit cap with three large holes near its fluffy puffball top. All in all, Bea looked like she'd just come from playing a game of touch football at which she'd been attacked by moths.

"I suppose you're here for *Tinkleston*," she said, stepping aside so I could enter the barn first. "Or Sir Peridot Budgley . . . whatever *Lillian* called him."

I caught what sounded like a sneer in her voice when she said both those names. But I didn't check to see if Bea's expression matched her tone. I was too busy gawking at the barn's interior. Although the light that filtered through some high windows was dim and made hazier by floating bits of hay and dust, I began to locate cat. After cat. After cat.

They were hidden everywhere. I spied a calico behind a small tractor I'd probably be able to repair with the help of Mr. Peachy's old manual. A gray tiger sat upon a crossbeam, high above me. And three white kittens played in a stall that would've once housed cows or horses.

I started to set the container of treats on a messy desk that Bea must've used for the completion of paperwork, if any cats were ever really adopted, only to be startled when a fat orange tom rubbed against my knuckles.

Each time I blinked, I found more felines. It was like they multiplied in the moments I had my eyes closed.

"Wow, you've got a lot of cats here," I said, resisting the urge to cover my nose with my hand. The smell of urine that I'd noticed outside was almost overwhelming inside. Nearly as bad as the previous night's skunk smell. "A *lot* of cats."

"It's a shelter," Bea reminded me flatly.

Was it, really?

And had Dylan seriously thought this barn was a good place to drop off Tinkleston, whom I hadn't located yet?

I watched as the gray tiger trotted across the beam, which dripped with old cobwebs. For a second, I thought Bea had decorated for Halloween, then I shuddered as I realized the drifting strands were the real thing.

And the crowding.

Not to mention the *smell* . . .

The great German philosopher Immanuel Kant once said, "We can judge the heart of a man by his treatment of animals."

What did Bea's shelter say about *her*?

"Are you sure you want the Persian?" Bea asked, interrupting my thoughts. "He seems mean—like a lot of purebreds—and I have lots of other friendly cats you could adopt."

"I don't think purebreds are necessarily mean," I objected, turning to see that Bea was surrounded by felines. They twined around her legs like furry snakes. I loved cats, but the image was unnerving. "And I'm not *adopting* Tinkleston," I told her. "I'm just keeping him for a while. I feel responsible for him, for some reason."

"I don't know why so many people give preference to purebreds," Bea complained, misunderstanding my comments. "Lillian, who worked for every charity in town, wouldn't support Whiskered Away. I had to beg her for a few pennies, here and there, to support *non*-pedigreed cats. She had no time for us!"

I noted that Bea seemed to lump herself right in there with the cats. Clearly, she felt neglected, too.

"Lillian didn't like *anything* without a pedigree," Bea added, two little pink spots forming on her lined cheeks.

She was way too agitated, but I felt like I had to defend Miss Flynt. "I don't think that's true. Lillian was a great supporter of Fur-ever Friends. Most of the dogs who pass through there are mixed breeds and strays with no papers. But she was a huge advocate."

That was the wrong thing to say.

"Yes," Bea agreed, her mouth set in a firm line. "She did dote upon Fur-ever Friends—and earn a lot of recognition for supporting that more prominent organization. Otherwise, she was *obsessed* with bloodline."

I didn't believe that. I suspected that—like me—Lillian hadn't been sure if Bea was helping, or hoarding, cats.

"I tried to show her how desperate we are here," Bea noted, her voice rising again. "Pleaded for support, because this shelter is in trouble." That was obvious. I blamed poor leadership. "I told her that I was reduced to feeding the cats *this*!"

Bea bent down out of my sight for a moment. Then she hoisted a whole crate of cat food up from the floor and thudded the box down onto her desk, sending the orange tom running.

My heart jumped at the sound, too—and at the sight of eighty cans of Cleopatra's Choice Cuts.

Make that seventy-nine cans, because one was obviously missing. There was a hole in the plastic wrapping, and an empty spot in the cardboard packaging.

All at once, I got a tickly feeling in the pit of my stomach.

Just how much had Bea hated Lillian?

Enough to push her into a bathtub for refusing to support Whiskered Away Home?

And when, exactly, had Bea confronted Miss Flynt?

I was afraid to ask, because I could tell that, as Bea's anger faded, she realized that she'd just admitted to arguing with a murder victim.

We stood watching each other warily. Bea probably wondered if I'd share everything she'd just told me with the police, while I hoped she wouldn't silence me for good, right there in that barn.

"I'll get your Persian," she finally said quietly.

"Okay," I agreed, taking a step backward. Toward the door. "Thanks."

I didn't dare breathe until she tromped away from me through the hay, her heavy work boots thumping on the wooden floor.

"I'm afraid that I couldn't let him out with the others," she grumbled over her shoulder. "He's still in his crate. You'll have to clean it."

My hands were scratched up, but my heart suddenly ached, too, for a cat who might've had a bad temper, but who had to be confused and terrified, not to mention dirty after a night in a small, enclosed space.

Poor Tinkleston.

Was he really *that* bad, or had Bea taken her anger at Miss Flynt out on an innocent—okay, somewhat innocent—animal?

"Here he is," Bea said, emerging from one of the stalls, carrier in hand. Trudging back through the hay, she handed Tinks to me. "Good luck."

I accepted the crate and raised it as high as I could, so I could see inside.

Tinkleston was curled in a ball, so I couldn't see his unusual eyes, but I didn't think he was sleeping. Then, without warning, he erupted, rushing at the bars of the carrier, yowling shrilly and swiping his paws at me. I nearly fell over backward and barely managed to keep from dropping him.

"Good luck," Bea said again, deadpan.

"We'll be okay," I assured her, although I wasn't positive about that. I was certain that I'd done the right thing by claiming Tinkleston, though. Still, I wanted to be polite, and said, "Thanks for watching him."

Bea didn't say, "No problem." Or, "My pleasure." She didn't respond at all.

I moved toward the exit, backing up so I could keep an eye on Bea. Then I finally turned and pushed open the door, again noticing the note that warned people to call before visiting.

The handwriting was very sloppy.

Was there a chance it matched the scrawling script on the note in Miss Flynt's kitchen? The one I'd found under a can of Cleopatra's Choice Cuts?

I really didn't want to be murdered in a lonely barn, but my curiosity was so strong that I couldn't help but risk getting killed among cats. I paused, halfway out the door, then asked, as casually as I could, "So . . . did Lillian donate anything, the last time you talked to her?"

Because if she hadn't, Bea might've gone berserk. . . .

Bea gave me a funny look, like she didn't understand the admittedly nosy question, so I added, "If she didn't, and you're totally strapped for cash, I could bake and sell some pet treats, to help you raise money."

Bea still didn't respond to what I thought was a pretty generous offer, and I started to worry that she was about to reach for one of the many farm implements that hung on the barn walls. The shelter was filled with sharp, rusty, old things that I probably should've thought about, before provoking a possible killer.

Then all at once Bea answered, telling me, through gritted teeth, "No. Lillian wouldn't give me another dime—even though I threatened to finally tell the whole world that we were *sisters*!"

Chapter 20

"I hate to admit it, but I sort of miss you living in the farmhouse," Piper said, sitting down on my former bed, which was stripped to the bare mattress. Socrates also tried to make himself comfortable on a rug, in the absence of his velvet cushion. The bedroom where I'd "squatted," to use Piper's term, was nearly empty, with the exception of a few boxes of clothes, some of which I needed for my date with Dylan at the Wolf Hollow Mill that night. "It's very quiet here now," my sister added. "Especially since Artie is gone, too."

I was sweeping my hair up into a loose updo, but I turned from my intricately carved Thai mirror, which I also planned to take to the cottage, to smile at Piper. "I could easily move back in. Or I could bring Tinkleston to stay with you. He certainly livens up a room!"

"Umm, no," Piper objected, too quickly. "I'll get used to the calm soon. You just keep packing."

I wasn't sure which potential roommate she found more disagreeable—the ill-tempered cat or her own sister.

"How's Tinkleston doing?" Piper asked. "Is he settling in?"

Socrates answered that question before I could, with a barely audible, but low and menacing, growl.

"Can Socrates stay here while I'm out?" I asked Piper. I gave the disgruntled basset hound a worried glance. "I'm afraid to leave him alone with Tinks. So far, they aren't getting along."

"Sure," Piper agreed. "Even the most sedate dogs have been known to get aggressive when a cat encroaches on their territory."

"I'm actually afraid Tinkleston will hurt Socrates again," I said, slipping a wide, silver cuff around my wrist. I also wore a jewel-toned teal, velvet, sleeveless top that I thought went well with my grayish green eyes, and a long black skirt that was fitted through my hips but had an understated mermaid flare near the hem. I hoped the outfit was fancy enough for Wolf Hollow. "When I left Tinks, he was hunkered down on top of the icebox, and he had a funny gleam in his eyes. I think he's plotting revenge for the sponge bath I tried to give him."

"You did the right thing, removing him from Whiskered Away," Piper assured me. I'd filled her in on my strange encounter with Bea. "She couldn't keep him in that crate forever." Piper frowned. "Do you really think Bea is Lillian's sister? Or is Bea getting delusional, living alone out there with all those cats?"

I swept some blush onto my cheeks. "I'm honestly not sure. But it sounds like she tried to use her claim of sisterhood to *blackmail* Miss Flynt into supporting Whiskered Away. Then Bea started mumbling about that 'bloodline' thing again, which seems to be *her* obsession. . . ." I shrugged. "I have no idea if she was making sense. I just started moving toward the van, so I wouldn't end up buried behind a barn."

Piper's fingers flexed around the edge of the mattress.

"You don't really believe Bea could've killed Lillian, do you?"

I glanced at my sister again. "You didn't see how angry she got when she talked about Miss Flynt."

"Daphne . . ." I saw concern in Piper's brown eyes. "Please let the detectives solve this case. Don't go to cat shelters in the middle of nowhere and ask potentially unstable people questions that make them angry, okay?"

I was touched that she was worried about me. "I promise I'll stay away from cat shelters," I said, thinking that should be easy enough. There were plenty of other places to snoop around, if I felt the need. Then I finally spun away from the mirror, my arms outstretched for inspection. "So, how do I look?"

"Really nice," Piper said. "But aren't you a little overdressed for the Lakeside? Or Franco's, even?"

Franco's Italian restaurant, a former 1920s speakeasy that retained its ambiance and its collection of straight-from-the-Old-World recipes, was our other favorite Sylvan Creek hangout.

"Actually, Dylan's taking me to the Wolf Hollow Mill," I informed Piper. "Did you give him a raise or something?"

I'd been joking. Piper was more likely to fire Dylan than increase his pay. But my sister grew very serious. "No . . . No, I didn't do that."

"What's wrong?" I asked.

"Nothing," she said, with a smile that seemed forced. "I guess being involved in a second murder has me feeling unsettled."

"I really don't think you and I are *serious* suspects this time," I reassured her. Then I remembered that momentary, but telling, look in Jonathan's eyes when I'd asked him if my mother or Piper were under investigation. "At least, Jonathan hasn't said anything that gives me too much cause for concern."

Piper narrowed her eyes at me, with suspicion. "When did you talk to Detective Black?"

"I stopped by his house yesterday to tell him about some things that might be related to Miss Flynt's death." I didn't have time to explain everything, so I just said, "Stuff I found when I went to the mansion to pick up Tinks."

Piper and Socrates exchanged looks of mutual frustration. Then Piper said, "I am not going to lecture you again about the dangers of meddling in a murder investigation. But don't call me when someone threatens you with a hammer. Not that your cell phone will work!"

For someone who hadn't planned to deliver a lecture, she'd packed a lot of preaching into a few brief comments.

"Thank you, as always, for your concern," I said, because I knew that her annoyance was rooted in worry. "But I will be fine."

"I hope so," Piper said, sounding less irritated. She stood up and moved to the door, so I assumed our discussion was over. But before she left the room, she ventured, hesitantly, "Daph, I have to ask. . . . You're not *expecting* anything tonight, are you?"

I was opening a box that held a pair of black suede vintage heels Moxie'd loaned me, but I raised my face to give Piper a confused look. "What in the world are you talking about?"

She cleared her throat, then spoke more directly. "It's just that a lot of people get engaged at the Mill. And, in your own weird way, which I don't understand, you and Dylan have been together for a while. I just wondered if you might be hoping . . ."

Piper was somber, but I laughed out loud as I hopped around, trying to get my foot into Moxie's shoe. "No, Piper! I am not expecting—or hoping for—a proposal. Trust me!"

Was she crazy?

Had I not told her *and* my mother, many times, that marriage wasn't for me? Or Dylan?

"Okay," Piper said. She seemed relieved.

What was *that* all about?

Finally steadying myself on the heels, I looked at Socrates, who had also stood up, like he understood that we were all dispersing soon. "Would you mind giving him a snack in about an hour?" I asked Piper. "He likes something before bedtime. I left some Boo-Berry Biscuits in the kitchen for him."

Piper furrowed her brow. "*Boo*-berry?"

"They're made with blueberries, quinoa flour, and egg." I grinned. "I guess I'm getting into the holiday spirit with the name."

"You should consider selling your pet treats," Piper observed. "You really seem to like baking for animals. And you're good at it."

She sounded like Lillian Flynt. And she wasn't too far away from wearing old cardigans and sensible shoes, either. It wasn't even eight o'clock, and Piper was already in pajamas and thick, wool socks.

I knew she wasn't grieving the loss of her deceased ex-boyfriend, Steve Beamus, anymore, but was she starting to give up on her social life? Because I couldn't recall the last time she'd gone out to dinner, let alone had a date.

"Hey," I suggested, on a whim. "Why don't you come with me? Dylan won't mind. We'll have fun."

Piper's smile was definitely forced. "No, you go ahead. I have some work to do here."

That was the last thing I'd hoped to hear, but I knew better than to pressure my strong-willed sister.

"Well, if you change your mind, you know where we're at," I said. "And we'd love it if you'd join us."

"Thanks." Piper smoothed her hair, which was secured in a ponytail by an elastic band. Not exactly a glamorous look. She stepped into the hallway and started to walk toward the stairs. I barely heard her muffled promise, "I'll consider the offer."

No, she wouldn't. I knew her better than to believe that.

But as I hurried to my van and drove to Sylvan Creek's most romantic restaurant, I started to wonder just how well I knew Dylan.

Chapter 21

The Wolf Hollow Mill, which dated back to the Revolutionary War, sat just outside town on a bend in Sylvan Creek. As I stepped out of my van and approached the restaurant, I could hear water rushing over a large wooden wheel that still turned on the side of the stone building. The mill's original eight-paned windows glowed with muted, flickering light, and the small porch was framed by cornstalks and pumpkins. The cool night air smelled of sage, thyme, burning firewood, and the earthy scent of the surrounding forest.

Taking a deep breath, I smiled and went inside to wait for Dylan, whom I expected to be late.

But, for the first time I could remember, my date was already there, waiting for me on a seat at the bar.

And he wore a *suit*.

"You look great," I said, slipping up onto the tall, wooden chair next to his. He really had cleaned up nicely. I assumed that he'd borrowed the jacket and pants, but they fit him well, and his white shirt—probably also a loaner—was crisply ironed. I noted that he kept tugging at his tie, like it was a noose around his neck, but overall, he carried off his new look. Still, as we read the menu and placed our orders for drinks and food, I couldn't stop blurting things like, "I'm really shocked!"

Dylan merely grinned at my repeated exclamations of surprise. "You look gorgeous, Daph," he said, leaning back so the bartender could set two mugs of warm, mulled cider before us on the gleaming, reclaimed-pine plank bar. "And I'm *not* surprised, because you're always beautiful."

Dylan didn't normally say things like that, and I couldn't help blushing.

"Thanks," I said, taking a sip of the sweet, tart drink. Immediately, warmth spread right down to my toes, which were pinched into Moxie's shoes and had suffered during their ride in my poorly heated van.

Dylan took a moment to try the cider, too, and we both grew quiet until our appetizers were delivered a few minutes later. Warm goat cheese, drizzled with honey and served with toasted baguette slices for me, and butternut squash dip for Dylan.

The vegan selections at Wolf Hollow Mill were definitely a step above the Lakeside's burger garnishes.

When the bartender walked away again, I realized that I wasn't sure how to restart the conversation with Dylan, although I'd known him for over a year. It was like we'd changed clothes, and the clothes had changed us. Feeling awkward, I looked around the pub, which was a candlelit nook off the restaurant's main dining room. The small space was enclosed by thick stone walls, one of which featured a crackling wood fireplace. The oak mantel was decorated for the season with gourds, pumpkins, and branches of bittersweet.

Through a doorway surrounded by a wide, wooden frame painted a deep colonial red, I could see the formal dining room, where a much larger fire roared in a bigger fireplace.

And seated right in front of that, at a table for two, was Tamara Fox—and a "date" who *wasn't* her husband.

I forgot all about the strange vibe between me and Dylan, and I grabbed his arm, so he dropped a piece of crisp pita into his dip. "What is Tamara doing here with *Pastor Pete*?" I whispered, watching as she tossed her long, dark hair over her shoulder. The many rings she always wore glittered. Meanwhile, for once, Pastor Pete wasn't sporting his clerical garb. Like Dylan, he wore a jacket and tie. Pete and Tamara were deep in conversation, both of them leaning on the table, not even touching their food. I returned my attention to Dylan. "What is *that* all about?"

Dylan didn't seem as shocked as I was. He shrugged and fished the triangle of bread out of the creamy, bubbling blend of squash, sage and maple syrup. "They're probably planning their haunted hayride."

"How do you know about that?" I asked, because Dylan wasn't usually up on community events.

"Pastor Pete brought Blessing in for a worming this morning," he said. "He asked if I'd like to play a chainsaw killer. For charity."

So much about what Dylan had just said was wrong, including his mention of an unpleasant veterinary procedure while I spread velvety goat cheese, drizzled with sweet honey, onto fluffy bread with a perfectly crusty exterior. Talk about ruining a great cheese moment.

"Don't you think a haunted hayride, involving chainsaw murderers—"

"And killer clowns," Dylan interrupted. At some point, he'd loosened his tie. I had a feeling the next time I looked away, it would disappear. "That was the other character I could've been."

I wasn't sure that was important, and I continued with my original thought. "Don't you think terrifying children with gory sights is a strange way to raise money for a church?"

"I think a lot of things about organized religion are strange," Dylan noted, wiping his fingers on a cloth napkin. At the Lakeside, we were lucky to get a roll of paper towels. Yet I liked that place, too. "That's why I connect with a higher power on the waves, or by making music," Dylan added. "But I'm pretty sure Pastor Pete agrees with you about the hayride being weird."

I was about to take a bite of baguette, but I stopped with my hand in midair. "What do you mean?"

"I could tell he thought Tamara steamrolled the whole project the moment Lillian was dead," Dylan informed me. "He kept asking *me* if I thought they should've stuck with a bake sale at the Howl-o-Ween Parade to raise money for the church."

"What else did he say?"

Dylan shrugged again. "Something about Light-house Fellowship already having bad PR, but being broke, too." He shook his head and grinned. "I told him, 'Dude, I have no idea what you're even talking about. I'm just trying to worm the dog.'"

"Interesting. And please stop using the word *worm*, okay?"

Dylan laughed. "Sure, Daph. No problem."

"So, are you going to help out at the hayride?"

"No way."

The blunt, definitive response surprised me. Dylan was one of the kindest, most generous people I knew. He once literally gave a stranger the shirt off his back, when the other guy spilled coffee all over himself at the now defunct Espresso Pronto. *We'd* been forced to leave, then. No shirt, no shoes, no service.

"Why not play a clown for one night?" I asked.

"I'm all about giving back to my fellow man, nature, and the universe," Dylan assured me. "But organized charities can be *vicious*. I'd rather clip a rabid Great Dane's toenails than 'volunteer.'"

I worked with several great charities. But I had to admit that Dylan might have a point, since someone had murdered Sylvan Creek's most active volunteer.

Popping the warm bread with the cheese and honey into my mouth, I resumed watching Tamara and Pastor Kishbaugh. Their conversation seemed more intense at that point. The minister's bald forehead nearly bumped against the former cheerleader's bangs, and he repeatedly tapped the table with his index finger as he spoke.

Were they discussing where to rent deranged-clown costumes?

Or talking about funds that might be missing from church accounts? Because Tamara had likely jumped right in to take over Lillian's old bookkeeping job. If anything really was awry, as the rumors claimed, Tamara might've noticed and called for a meeting.

In the main dining room, Tamara finally sat back, removed her napkin from her lap, and shook out the crumbs, like she was done eating. And talking. There was something final about the way she crossed her arms over her chest.

I didn't think it was likely, but was there a *small* chance that pretty Tamara and the charismatic clergyman were involved in a *romantic* quarrel?

Wolf Hollow Mill was a very public place to have an affair.

Then again, there was that theory about hiding things in plain sight. . . .

"Daphne?"

The sound of Dylan's voice shook me out of my reverie, and I shifted on my chair to see that he looked almost somber, maybe for the first time since I'd met him. He hadn't removed his tie, like I'd expected, but his light blue eyes had clouded over while I'd been facing away.

He almost seemed worried.

Or nervous.

"You're not expecting *anything tonight, are you?"*

Piper's question replayed in my mind, and I got anxious, too. The last thing I wanted was for Dylan's and my relationship to change.

"Daph," Dylan said quietly. "There's something I need to tell you. And *ask* you."

He sounded so serious that all at once, my mouth got dry, and my heart started to race.

I knew I was being irrational. Dylan Taggart would never propose to me.

But he had grown more possessive lately. Especially around Jonathan Black.

What if he wanted, at the very least, a *commitment*?

Taking a shaky sip of my cider, I glanced at the main dining room, only to see that Pastor Pete and Tamara Fox were rising to leave.

I had no plan, yet I found myself standing up, too, and asking Dylan, "Would you excuse me, please? I *really* need to talk to Tamara Fox and Pastor Kishbaugh."

"But, Daph . . ."

Dylan started to protest, but I promised, "I'll be right back."

Then I hurried out of the pub and into the night, wobbling on Moxie's heels.

Only later did I realize that I could've just stood on the porch for a moment, gathering my thoughts in the bracing air before returning inside, instead of calling, "Pastor Pete! Tamara! Wait!"

Chapter 22

"Daphne? What are *you* doing here?" Tamara demanded, raising her chin in a snooty way and drawing a black shawl more tightly around herself. The wrap was like a higher quality version of my costume cape, and Tamara's comment was pretty witchy, too. She wasn't asking why I was stalking her in a parking lot. She was surprised that I was at an expensive restaurant at all. I could tell by the way she kept looking me up and down. "What do you want?"

I had no idea what I wanted, and thankfully, Pastor Pete was much kinder. He smiled at me. "How nice to see you, Daphne! Are you just arriving?"

"No, I was inside." I pointed to the mill, as if they wouldn't know what I'd meant by "inside." *Smooth, Daph!* I also realized I'd left my outerwear—a silk jacket I'd bartered for in Beijing—in the bar, and I wrapped my bare arms around myself. "I saw you both and wanted to ask you. . . ."

"What, Daphne?" Tamara prompted impatiently. "It's cold out here."

Tamara Fox wasn't normally a very nice person, but I sensed that I was also bearing some of the brunt of her anger at Pastor Pete. The tension between them was palpable, although Pastor Kishbaugh, at least, was trying to act like nothing was wrong.

"Well?" Tamara said, making a rolling motion with her hand.

I still had no idea what to say, so I went with the first thing that popped into my head. "I wanted to ask how Blessing's been, since the worming." Along with being unpleasant—really, another reference to parasites?—my comment was incredibly stupid, which only compelled me to explain further, "Piper was wondering how he's doing, and I'll see her later, if there's anything you can tell me. . . ."

Pastor Pete appeared confused, but he continued to be polite. "Blessing is just fine, Daphne. Thank you for asking."

"Really?" Tamara was justifiably incredulous. "That's what you wanted to ask?"

As Tamara had observed, the evening was chilly, but I started to get sweaty under her critical gaze, and I felt like I had to come up with something better than an inquiry about a dog's minor medical procedure.

Which is why I surprised everyone—including myself—by blurting out, "I also heard you need a clown for the hayride. I *really* want to volunteer!"

Chapter 23

"I can't believe I'm going to spend a whole night standing in an orchard, dressed like a homicidal clown," I grumbled, although there was no one to hear my complaint. I was driving home alone, after Dylan ended our evening early. He'd been aggravated with me, for the first time I could remember. It took a lot to get under Dylan Taggart's skin. I rubbed my cheek, where he'd planted a chilly good-bye kiss before climbing into his battered Subaru. "I really botched everything tonight."

Or had I?

Because my awkward conversation with Tamara and Pastor Pete had ultimately proven pretty interesting.

For one thing, I'd landed a pet-sitting job, watching Blessing while Pastor Kishbaugh went on yet another missionary trip, scheduled for close to Thanksgiving.

And Dylan had been right about Pastor Pete's reluctance to host a church-sponsored fright fest.

"While it's nice of you to volunteer, I'm not certain we'll be going through with the hayride," he'd informed me. Then he'd addressed Tamara. "We could just hold the bake sale. Honor Lillian's memory by doing things her way, one more time."

I'd been relieved, until Tamara had objected, firmly. "No. Lillian Flynt and I fought over this issue for years. Do you know how much money the hayride will bring in, compared to the sale of a few cupcakes? We will do this *my* way this year. The wagon is already rented."

Now *my* wagon was hitched to the hayride, too.

As I drove up Winding Hill, periodically patting the VW's dashboard to urge the old van along, I wondered just how often—and heatedly—Sylvan Creek's two "professional volunteers" had clashed. Because, at one point, Tamara had all but admitted that she was glad Lillian and her "antiquated ideas" were out of the way, so Tamara could move forward with her "progressive" plans for nearly every charity in town.

I thought back to the night of Lillian's murder, when Tamara had accidentally let Tinkleston escape. That meant Tamara had definitely been inside the house at one point. And she'd mentioned how Tinks had followed her around.

Had she, perhaps, ventured upstairs . . . ?

I was pondering all that when my headlights illuminated Piper's farmhouse and a vehicle that was parked near the barn.

Parking my van, too, I hopped out to greet the person who waited there, leaning against a shiny, black truck.

But before I could ask Jonathan Black what in the world he was doing at Winding Hill so late at night, a gleeful Chihuahua darted out of the darkness and launched himself at me. Artie was followed by Axis, who ran up and wriggled against my knees. Only one member of the welcoming committee didn't seem happy to see me: Jonathan, who greeted me with a dark look and a question I should've been prepared to answer.

"Did you take something from Flynt Mansion, Daphne?"

Chapter 24

"I have the note and the can of cat food," I assured Jonathan again. "I can show both things to you." I'd picked up Socrates from Piper's house, and the dogs, Jonathan and I were walking down one of the paths to my cottage. Although the night had grown colder, my cheeks felt warm. "And there's a list of supplements that Tinks is supposed to take, too."

"You took *three* things from a crime scene?" I couldn't really read Jonathan's expression in the darkness, but he sounded exasperated. "Between you, Elyse, and your mother, I think this might be the *most* disturbed scene I've ever dealt with."

"The scene's not as 'disturbed' as the clown I'm going to play," I muttered under my breath.

I'd thought my comment would be drowned out. Axis, Artie, and Socrates were romping noisily in the crunchy, fallen leaves that blanketed the woods beside the path. But Jonathan bent to give me a quizzical look. "What did you just say? About *clowns*?"

"Nothing," I said, trying to locate Socrates in the

forest. I had a feeling he was cutting loose more than usual on the assumption that I couldn't see him very well.

Actually, I couldn't see *anything* very well, and Moxie's heels made navigating the uneven trail even more challenging than usual.

"Ouch!" I complained, stumbling on a rock, twisting my ankle and nearly dropping the tin of leftover Boo-Berry Biscuits I had tucked under my arm.

Jonathan lightly grabbed my elbow until I could right myself again. Releasing me, he pointed at my feet. "Why are you wearing *heels*? In the woods?"

"They're Moxie's," I explained. "I was at Wolf Hollow Mill with Dylan."

"Oh." Jonathan took a moment to appraise me, to the degree that was possible under the canopy of trees. Then he offered me an actual compliment. "You look very nice with your hair up. And the jacket is unusual."

"Thanks." I peered up at him, trying to determine if he was making fun of my coat. But I didn't think that was the case. "I'm sorry again about taking so much stuff from the mansion," I added. "I didn't mean any harm, and I was going to turn everything over to you."

He didn't respond, probably because I'd already apologized several times, so we walked in silence for a few minutes, just listening to the breeze rattle the last of the leaves overhead and the dogs running around in the darkness.

"Do you always have to walk here alone at night?" Jonathan finally asked. He sounded concerned. "Isn't there an alternative?"

"Piper's going to run an access road from the

farmhouse," I told him. "But for now, yes. This is how I get to the cottage. It's pretty safe."

Jonathan opened his mouth, like he was about to remind me that Winding Hill had been the site of a homicide. But before he could mention that, I stumbled again. "Careful, there, Daphne," he said, catching me a second time.

"I'm fine," I promised, pulling away from him. "It's just these stupid heels."

We'd reached the cottage, and I bent down to take off the shoes. The ground was cold, but it felt good under my feet. As I stepped onto the porch, the dogs caught up to us and bounded up the steps, too, followed by Jonathan.

I opened the door, and Axis, Artie, and Socrates scrambled to get inside.

"You're *still* not locking your door?" Jonathan asked. "Don't you worry about yourself at all?"

"Not my possessions," I said. "If somebody needs my stuff badly enough to come here, break in, and take something . . . Well, they need it more than I do."

Jonathan shook his head. "Philosophy programs must be *very* different from the police academy."

"Are you coming in?" I asked, because he was lingering on the porch.

"No, I'll wait here while you get the note, the cat food—and the 'list' you mentioned."

"Oh, for crying out loud," I said. "Are *you* afraid of *me*? Do you think I'm going to get a hammer, like Mr. Peachy, and knock you out?"

"I think we've established that you're unpredictable," he joked. "And it's getting late."

"Just come in for a minute," I urged. "I want to give the dogs a treat. It won't take long. And I promise I don't bludgeon people—or bite."

He stood there for one more second. Then—right before I slammed the door in his handsome face—he agreed. "All right. But I can't stay long."

We followed the dogs inside, and I fumbled around for the lamp I'd placed near the door.

But before I could switch it on, Jonathan said, "Daphne . . . you might not bite. But something in here does. And I'd appreciate it if you'd *get it off me*."

Chapter 25

"I totally forgot Tinkleston was here," I said, joining Jonathan in the kitchen, where he waited on a chair at the spindle-legged table. My cottage felt even smaller since his arrival. He had a way of claiming space, and there wasn't much of that to claim in my house. It didn't help that three dogs were stretched out in the living room, munching on Boo-Berry Biscuits in front of the fire, and an angry Persian cat was on top of the icebox, sulking and watching Jonathan with evil intent. I set some antiseptic and a clean cloth on the table. "I'm really sorry you got hurt."

"It's not that bad." Jonathan removed the cap from the bottle of alcohol and poured some onto the rag. I winced, but he didn't so much as blink as he cleaned the scratches and bites Tinks had inflicted, before Jonathan could subdue him. Folding the damp cloth neatly, he placed it on the table. "Where are the cat food and the papers?"

I went to the counter and retrieved all those things, setting them on the table, too. But as I handed everything over, I was suddenly confused. "How did you know the food and the instructions for Tinks's care even existed?"

"I had a few more questions for your mother today," Jonathan informed me. "She mentioned the note, explaining that she had believed Lillian was away on a trip, not dead in a bathtub, as she prepared to show the house the night of the murder. And she remembered the contents of the message quite well, because Lillian's absence 'vexed' her, to use her own word."

I almost agreed that my mother had been very agitated that evening, then thought better of it. Instead, I asked, "Why were you questioning her again?"

"Just part of the investigation," he said vaguely, while scanning the list of supplements. His response wasn't cause for alarm, but it wasn't very reassuring, either. "Your mother also remembered that the message had been tucked under a can of cat food," he added, turning his attention to the container of Cleopatra's Choice Cuts. Frowning, he studied the label, like I'd recently done. "And she even recalled the brand. Apparently, Miss Flynt's messy kitchen was also a source of irritation for her that night."

I had a bad habit of speaking without thinking, but my mother didn't seem like she was being very prudent, either. Why would she keep telling a detective that she'd been upset with a murder victim?

"So what compelled you to take these things?" Jonathan asked, slipping the can and the papers into a plastic evidence bag he'd pulled from the back pocket of his jeans. Immediately forgetting his own question, he shook his head as he began to write on the bag with a Sharpie he'd also brought along. "I don't even know why I'm tagging these, at this point." Looking up for a moment, he held up the bag for my inspection. "I have to put *your name* in one of these boxes marked *chain of custody*. What's the first question even the most dim-witted defense attorney will ask, if these things are presented in court?"

"Umm . . . 'Who's Daphne Templeton?'" I guessed, filling the tea kettle and setting it on the stove.

Jonathan had insisted he couldn't stay, but I was going to be a good hostess anyway. Although that ship had probably sailed when I let him get attacked by a cat. Regardless, I dropped two teabags—I pegged Jonathan for an Earl Grey type of guy—into my favorite earthenware mugs, then placed those on the table, along with plates bearing big slices of pear-cranberry streusel I'd made that morning.

"I'm not staying," Jonathan said, pushing aside the tainted evidence and seeming to finally notice that he'd been served. "You didn't have to . . ."

I ignored him and sat down at the table, too. "You didn't let me tell you why I took the stuff from Miss Flynt's. Don't you want to know?"

Jonathan sat back in the chair again and studied me with his intelligent, sometimes impossible-to-read, blue eyes. "Yes. I am curious."

"The instructions for Tinkleston's care ended up with me by accident," I explained. "I was holding the paper when my mother ordered me to remove Tinks's litter box from the kitchen, and I crammed the message into my pocket, fully intending to put it back on the counter later. But then Tinkleston darted past me, and I followed him and found Miss Flynt's body."

"I suppose I can understand how you got distracted," Jonathan admitted, to my surprise. In fact, I saw a rare flash of sympathy in his eyes. Then he prompted, "And the other things?"

"I took the food and the list of supplements when I

retrieved Tinks from the mansion," I told him. The kettle finally whistled, and I rose to make the tea. "I thought he needed the food and might need the vitamins. It never occurred to me that two such little things could be evidence." I poured boiling water into the waiting mugs, then set the kettle back on the stove. "That is, until I read the ingredients in Cleopatra's Choice Cuts and studied the pet-sitting instructions again. Then I realized nothing added up."

"How so?" Jonathan asked, sounding somewhat intrigued. He picked up his fork and took a bite of streusel. When he'd swallowed, he explained, "Because I also think something is strange about all three of those objects."

My heart started beating a little faster, and I sat down across from him again. "Really? What bothers you?"

"The cat food isn't exactly made from 'choice cuts,'" he said, with a glance at the can in the plastic bag. "It's hard for me to believe that a woman who fed her pet a steady, regimented diet of supplements would buy such cheap food."

"I'm almost certain that Miss Flynt didn't buy that food," I told Jonathan. "I was at Whiskered Away Home today—"

Jonathan was about to take another bite, but he paused, fork in midair, and interrupted me. He sounded suspicious. "You went to Bea Baumgartner's . . . questionable cat shelter? Why?"

"To pick up Tinkleston, who was staying there temporarily," I said, looking around the kitchen for the Persian in question. Unfortunately, he had disappeared from the top of the icebox. That was worrisome. I returned my attention to Jonathan. "And when I was there, I saw a case of Cleopatra's Choice Cuts. And Bea admitted that she'd taken the food to Miss Flynt's to show her how low the shelter had sunk, in hopes of convincing Miss Flynt to make a donation to Whiskered Away."

I could tell that Jonathan was torn between chastising me for investigating and admitting that I'd uncovered a potential lead. "I'll talk to Bea again," he finally said. "Although, if you'd never taken the cat food in the first place, I would've made that connection, myself, earlier. I also saw the case of food when I visited Ms. Baumgartner at Whiskered Away Home, but had no reason to even think about it."

I felt my cheeks flush. "Sorry." Then I remembered something else that might be important. "Bea also told me that Lillian Flynt was her *sister.*"

Jonathan didn't visibly jolt, but I saw his eyes widen, just slightly. "Interesting," he conceded quietly. "She certainly didn't mention that to me."

I knew he'd follow up on that lead, too, and I glanced at the clear evidence bag, which held the instructions for Tinkleston's care.

. . . feed the cat at least once a day and change the litter when necessary. . . . If you have any trouble, please call a veterinarian. . . .

"The message is also strange," I noted. "Don't you think a woman like Lillian Flynt would give precise instructions for Tinkleston's care?" I saw another flicker of genuine interest in Jonathan's eyes, like—in spite of himself—he was enjoying our discussion. "Don't you think someone who typed up a schedule for her cat's vitamins would mention that, and leave the containers on the counter, in an orderly row?"

Jonathan nodded. "Yes. And if I'm getting an accurate picture of Lillian Flynt, she would've been particular about how often the litter box was changed, too. And she would've left contact information for your sister." He arched an eyebrow. "I'm assuming that Piper is Tinkleston's vet?"

"Yes." Looking around the kitchen, I finally located Tinks, who was hiding among the herbs I grew on my windowsill and observing us with narrowed eyes and his omnipresent scowl. He flattened his ears at me. Relieved to have him in my sights again, I returned my attention to Jonathan. "But why would someone leave a note with fake instructions?" I asked. "I don't get it."

"Maybe to buy time?" Jonathan surmised. He pushed his empty plate away. "Maybe the person who killed Miss Flynt knew that people would start looking for her. What better way to keep anyone from nosing around upstairs than to leave a note, supposedly from the victim, saying that she was away for a while—and out of touch?"

"Yeah, really." I'd also finished my streusel, and I pushed my plate aside, too. "Who can't be reached by cell phone these days?"

As soon as I said that, I realized I was often impossible to contact. Fortunately, Jonathan didn't mention that. He stood up and took his plate and mug to the sink, then he picked up the evidence bag. "Thanks for the dessert," he said. "You should forget amateur detecting and open a bakery."

"Thanks. You're not the first person to suggest that." I followed him toward the door. "And you have to admit, I gave you some good leads tonight."

"Please don't go looking for more," he requested, holding up the bag to remind me that I wasn't always the best amateur sleuth. "You've done enough."

As we passed through the living room, Axis and Artie stood up, shook themselves, and followed Jonathan. Socrates sat up, too. I thought he seemed sorry to see his friends go.

"Please, lock this door behind me," Jonathan added. He looked past me, toward the kitchen. "And good luck with the cat."

I turned around to see that Tinks had followed us. He stood just inside the living room, his tail twitching. "We'll be okay. I think," I said uncertainly. Then I reluctantly turned my back on Tinks and bent to pick up Artie, who wriggled at my feet. "Will you be taking Artie to the Howl-o-Ween Parade tomorrow night?" I asked, grinning at the little dog, whose eyes bugged out even more than usual, in response to being cuddled. "I'm sure he'd love to march through town in a costume!"

"Really, Daphne?" Jonathan said. He was trying to sound stern, but the corners of his mouth twitched with amusement. "You honestly think I'm going to put a costume on a dog?"

No, I didn't really expect that.

"I could walk him," I suggested. "Socrates doesn't 'do' costumes, either. He threw his wizard hat out the window the other night."

Once again, I'd said something that earned me a funny look from Jonathan. But he told me, "If you really want to walk Artie in the parade, it's fine with me. He probably would like to be the center of attention."

"He can stay here tonight, and I can figure out his costume tomorrow," I offered. "Socrates would love a sleepover. Axis is welcome, too."

"I'll take Axe with me." Jonathan reached down to rumple the Lab's ears, and Axis lifted his nose to gaze worshipfully up at the man who'd taken him in. Those two had definitely bonded. "But I suppose Artie can stay."

"That's great!" I set down the Chihuahua, and I swore he'd understood the discussion. He pranced back to Socrates's side, and the two dogs nudged each other in an almost conspiratorial way. "I promise I'll dress Artie tastefully," I added. "I won't subject him to anything *too* demeaning."

"He usually demeans himself," Jonathan observed. "I'm not too worried."

Then he opened the door, and we both noticed something on the porch. An envelope, tucked under a pumpkin I'd bought to carve before handing out treats with Moxie on Halloween night.

"Looks like you've got mail," Jonathan said. He stepped onto the porch, bent to retrieve the note, and handed it to me. "And again, please lock your door when I'm gone."

"There is no lock," I finally admitted. "The door dates back about a hundred years."

"They had locks then. . . ." Jonathan seemed to give up on arguing. He bent his head, rubbed his eyes, then told me, "*I* will come install a lock, all right? Something sturdy, with a deadbolt, which you should *use*, all the time."

I was touched that he was worried about me. But I was also distracted and hardly paying attention to his safety directives. My fingers were fumbling nervously to open the envelope, which was from Larry Fox, Esq., according to the return address.

Letters from attorneys? Not usually good news, for me.

Pulling out a crisp, white piece of heavy-stock paper, I unfolded and read the message, then frowned.

"What's wrong?" Jonathan asked.

"Maybe nothing," I said, confused.

Jonathan appeared puzzled, too, by my behavior. "Then why do you have that strange look on your face?"

"Because," I told him, "I've been summoned to attend the reading of Miss Flynt's *will*."

Chapter 26

"Maybe you're going to be a millionairess, Daph!" Moxie said, trapping some of my mother's hair between two fingers and neatly snipping off ends that already looked perfectly trimmed, to me. But Mom had burst through the door of Spa and Paw, insisting that she was "not presentable" and had to be "styled" immediately—during *my* scheduled appointment. After that, Moxie and I were going to shop for a costume for Artie. The Chihuahua and Socrates waited impatiently by the salon's door. "Maybe you're getting the whole Flynt fortune," Moxie added. "Maybe you're going to be rich!"

"Or, more likely, I'm getting Tinkleston, whom I already have," I said, worrying for a moment about the cat I'd last seen hissing at Socrates, then running under my bed. "Lillian knew that I care for pets."

"Daphne is probably right," Mom agreed. "I'm to be at the reading, too, and I doubt that I'm in line to inherit a million dollars."

I was sitting in Moxie's small waiting area, flipping through her unusual selection of reading material, which included three *TV Guide*s from 1953, lots of oversized books with pictures of hairstyles, and a stack of old Sylvan Creek *Weekly Gazette*s, but I paused to give my mother a quizzical glance. "Why are you invited?"

"Hopefully to learn that the sale of the house can go forward," Mom said. "Elyse is very eager to get her hands on the mansion, but we can't do anything until the estate is settled."

Moxie cut a big chunk of hair from Mom's head, then frowned in a way that would've alarmed my mother, if she'd been facing the mirror. "That's not the only thing Elyse Hunter-Black wants to get her hands on," she noted.

Mom turned slightly, risking another wayward snip. "What are you talking about?"

I shot my best friend a silencing look. I didn't want her to spread potentially unfounded rumors about Elyse and Jonathan, because I would probably get blamed for starting them. I'd already nearly lost Jonathan's friendship once for sticking my nose into his personal business.

Moxie understood my unspoken communication. "It's nothing," she told my mom. Then Moxie stepped back and observed her handiwork. "The cut is looking good. And whoever's doing your Botox does a great job, too. Where do you go?"

I stifled a laugh as Maeve Templeton sputtered and stammered, struggling for a reply. "Why, I never . . . ! Of course, I wouldn't . . . !"

I hadn't seen my mother show that much emotion since I'd brought home my fifth-grade science class's tarantula and promptly lost it in our house.

"Hey, Mom," I interrupted, thinking that she was going to be *really* unhappy when she saw what Moxie was doing to her hair. "Getting back to the will and Flynt Mansion . . ."

"Yes?" she asked, calming down now that the conversation had returned to real estate. Still, she reached out from under the black cape Moxie had draped around her shoulders and felt her hair, as if she realized things were going wrong. The corners of her mouth turned slightly downward. "What about those things?"

"Did you ever hear why Miss Flynt was selling the property? Or where she was going to live once the mansion sold?"

"As I told Detective Black, I honestly don't know," she said, twisting again in an attempt to check the mirror. Moxie shifted to block her view, then continued snipping. "I've no idea what her plans were. We didn't discuss them."

"That's too bad." I resumed perusing the *Gazette*. "I guess we'll never know, now."

"Unless it all comes out at the reading of the will," Moxie pointed out. "Those things can get crazy, you know."

I doubted that an event featuring old Larry Fox sitting at a desk, reading a legal document, would erupt into a rave with a mosh pit. Then again, I'd never been to a will reading before. I supposed things could get emotionally charged.

My mother moved to feel the back of her head again, but Moxie gently and firmly pushed Mom's hand down to her lap. "I just hope for good news about the house," Mom said.

"I wouldn't count on that," I noted, as I scanned an article in the *Gazette*. "I think you should be prepared for possible disappointment."

My mother spun around, and a big chunk of hair went flying.

Moxie looked alarmed, too. But not about Flynt Mansion.

"Daphne, what are you talking about?" Mom demanded.

I held up the newspaper, not that my mother would be able to read the article I was showing her from across the salon. So I summarized, telling her, "There's a story in here about how the Sylvan Creek Historical Society is counting on Flynt Mansion being deeded over to them in Lillian's will. Asa Whitaker says Miss Flynt promised that the society would get the house, upon her death."

"What . . . ?" My mom looked as ghostly as any spirit one might encounter in the mansion she so desperately wanted to sell. "What are you talking about?"

"The society might go under, without the mansion—which Asa says is supposed to be a museum someday. The plan is to sell the house's current contents, then move in a bunch of old junk from Sylvan Creek's past."

Asa Whitaker had used the words *artifacts* and *treasures*, but I imagined that most of the stuff that would be on display would come from Sylvan Creek's over-stuffed attics.

Mom didn't care about Asa's grand plans. She rested a hand against her throat, her eyes wide with concern. "What . . . ? But . . . ?"

I gave Mom, whom I'd never seen speechless, a moment to digest all that information, while I thought back to the night Lillian had been killed.

What if Asa Whitaker had learned that Mom was showing the house that night?

What if he'd confronted Miss Flynt about her apparent change of heart regarding her property's future—a decision that might bankrupt the historical society?

And if the will hadn't been changed yet, Asa might've had good reason to want Miss Flynt's demise to occur prematurely.

Heart thumping a little faster, I skimmed the story again and noticed two more things.

First, the article had a byline. *G. Graham.* I'd never seen that name before. In fact, I couldn't recall ever seeing any bylines in the freebie *Gazette.*

And there was something else interesting, too, right next to the story.

A small notice, alerting readers that Asa Whitaker would *not* be signing copies of *Sylvan Creek: A History* at the Philosopher's Tome that evening, as previously scheduled.

"Hey, Moxie?" I asked, creeping out of my chair with effort, because it was a midcentury modern egg. "Can you bring the dogs to meet me at Fetch! in about a half hour to get Artie's costume? I think I'll wait on my haircut." I looked at Mom, then addressed my friend again. "You seem to be having an off day, styling wise."

As my mother practically leaped out of the chair, lunging for a small mirror, and Moxie tried to reassure her that everything could be fixed with a little application of hair gel, I patted Artie, told Socrates I'd see him in a while, then left Spa and Paw, headed for someplace I'd never expected to go, in my entire life.

Stepping into the sunlight, I raised a hand to cover my mouth.

How could I be excited—and bored to the point of yawning—at the same time?

Chapter 27

The Sylvan Creek Historical Society was tucked away in a small, narrow building that used to house a bank, back at the turn of the twentieth century. As I pushed through a heavy brass door and entered the gloomy, musty space, my nose was assaulted by the distinctive smell of decaying documents, old printers' ink, and what I could only assume was *money*.

"Is anyone here?" I ventured softly, peering around the room, which seemed suitably trapped in time. I could almost see ghostly women in dresses with huge bustles floating toward spectral, eye-shade-wearing tellers, who waited behind the bank's long counter. It was also easy to imagine a portly banker emerging from the manager's office—a room now occupied by ASA WHITAKER, PRESIDENT, SYLVAN CREEK HISTORICAL SOCIETY, according to a plaque near the door. The far end of the room was dominated by an imposing, open safe. The metal door had to be at least three feet thick, and the locking mechanism—a jumble of gears and gizmos—reminded me of something out of Jules Verne. The vault's interior was pretty dark, but I could make out the outline of modern filing cabinets and cardboard boxes, which probably held historical records, photos, and the artifacts Asa hoped to one day display at Flynt Mansion.

Although clearly no one was around, I called softly again, "Hello?"

Nobody answered, and I began to wonder what, exactly, I'd hoped to find by going to the society's headquarters.

Maybe an old letter from Lillian Flynt, in which she promised her home to Sylvan Creek's keepers of history, upon her death?

Or a Post-it note on Asa's desk, with the reminder, *Turn self in for killing L. F.?*

Obviously, those hopes seemed misguided at that point.

I turned to go, only to hear something move behind me.

Far behind me.

In the dark vault.

I hesitated for a long moment. Then I walked reluctantly toward the small space and poked my head through the heavy door.

"Hello?" I ventured one more time, although I already felt claustrophobic. I had a very specific terror of being trapped in either an elevator, a restaurant walk-in refrigerator, or a bank vault. My fears were odd, but not as crazy as Moxie's horror of turtles. Regardless, I didn't want to give in to my phobia—my rational side knew the vault door wasn't about to shut behind me—so I took a step over the threshold. "Is anybody in here?"

Someone finally answered me with a soft "Mrrrow."

Blinking, I peered more closely into the gloom and found the source of the greeting: a small orange kitten, who was curled up inside an open cardboard box.

That very morning, I'd been ambushed by a black Persian who'd popped out from under the kitchen table, trying to sink his teeth into my calf and causing me to spill my morning tea. But the kitten was so adorable that I couldn't help approaching it.

"Hey, little one," I said, reaching into the box. I stroked her back as my eyes continued adjusting. The kitten purred loudly, a gratifying sound after my time with Tinkleston. I smiled down at her. "Are you the mascot here . . . ?"

My voice trailed off, and I stopped petting the cat, because I was finally able to see what she was sleeping on, in that carton.

Copies of Asa Whitaker's book, *Sylvan Creek: A History.*

The title lacked originality and was less than compelling, to say the least, but I picked up one of the volumes. Turning it over, I checked the price on the back cover.

"Eighteen dollars! Really?" I muttered, tucking the book under my arm. I had some money with me, but I planned to spend it at Fetch! to buy Artie's costume. However, I really wanted to read at least part of the history, to see if the contents matched the singed paper in Miss Flynt's fireplace, as I strongly suspected. I'd have to send Asa a check later. Or return the volume after I'd skimmed it, being careful not to break the spine. That was a more likely scenario. Still, I kept complaining under my breath. "This is priced like a bestseller!"

"Do you have a problem with the price—or the subject matter?"

The deep, male voice, coming from right behind me, nearly made me jump out of my skin, and I wheeled around, half expecting to find my imagined ghostly bank manager levitating at the door to the vault, right before he sealed me inside. Forever.

Fortunately, I'd been joined by a living human.

At least, I thought I was lucky, until Asa Whitaker stepped closer to me, blocking my exit and demanding, with a snarl, "Were you about to *steal* that?"

Chapter 28

"I honestly wasn't stealing the book," I told Asa, who glared at me, his thin arms crossed over his narrow chest and his goateed chin jutting. He'd turned on a light in the vault, and I could see anger in his bloodshot, pale blue eyes. He pressed even closer to me. Was it possible to smell like *tweed*? I stepped back. "I was going to send you a check. Or just borrow a copy for a few days."

"This is a historical society, not a library," Asa reminded me, still glowering.

"I thought most historical societies included small libraries," I said, with a nervous glance past him. I really wanted to get out of that vault, like the kitten had done. She sat calmly on the floor near Asa's office, licking her front paw and breathing the sweet air of freedom. "Don't they?"

Asa lifted his chin higher. "Yes," he admitted. "Most societies do have archives. But the materials seldom circulate!"

I felt a trickle of cold sweat run down my back. "Well, is it okay if I take a copy?" I asked. "I really will send you a check."

Asa remained suspicious. He continued to block my path and narrowed his eyes. "What do you really want, Daphne? And why did you come in *here*, unauthorized?"

"I didn't know I needed authorization," I said truthfully. "I just heard your kitten—"

"Himmelfarb," he interrupted.

For a moment, I thought he'd sneezed. Then I recalled from grad school that Gertrude Himmelfarb was an American historian. If I remembered correctly, she believed that chroniclers of history had the responsibility to pass moral judgments on the figures about whom they wrote.

Did Asa believe that, too?

If so, had he passed judgment on the past residents of Sylvan Creek—including, perhaps, someone in the Flynt family?

"I heard Himmelfarb in the vault," I continued. "So I went in to make sure she was okay." I held up the volume. "And I found her sleeping in a whole box full of your books. I'd read about the history in the *Gazette* and thought I'd check it out."

Some of Asa's anger finally seemed to drain away. I supposed if I'd invested years in writing a detailed history of a community, I'd be desperate to believe that someone honestly wanted to read my work, too.

"Really, Daphne?" he asked, uncrossing his arms and cocking his head. He sounded uncertain. "You . . . you really want to read the book?"

Maybe I wasn't interested in reading every single page, but I did want to compare the contents with the papers I'd found in the fireplace, and I wasn't lying when I assured him, "Yes. I really do."

"You're the first person to express interest," Asa admitted, growing wistful. "I canceled a book signing, because no one would commit to attending." His shoulders slumped. "No one seems to care about Sylvan Creek's past."

I hesitated for a long moment, looking around the vault, which still made my chest feel tight. Then I ventured, quietly, "Miss Flynt cared, didn't she? The society is set to inherit her house—and she read your manuscript, too, right?"

Asa Whitaker spent half his time in the windowless archives of the public library, and the other half in a bank vault, so he was already very pale. But when I mentioned Miss Flynt and the manuscript, he became more ashen than—well—the ashes I'd sifted through at Flynt Mansion.

"Who told you that?" he asked, his voice sharp again. "Who said she read the book?"

I took a step backward, although I wanted to go the other direction. "I don't know," I said, clutching the volume to my chest, like it was a shield. "Maybe I'm wrong."

Asa stared at me for a long time, then he finally said, softly, "Yes. I think you misheard. And I'm not certain the society will inherit the mansion. I understand that things may have changed in recent days. It's a topic I'd rather not discuss."

Although his voice had dropped to a near whisper, his tone was more threatening than soothing, and I felt another trickle of sweat roll down my back.

Like Jonathan, I hadn't really thought Asa Whitaker capable of murder, but as I looked into his eyes, which had grown cold, I could suddenly picture him arguing with Miss Flynt about her decision to sell the house to a private buyer. And then, when things had gotten heated enough to make her stomp away, he might've followed her upstairs, into the bathroom.

"I should get going," I said, using one hand to dig into the pocket of my jeans. It looked like Artie would have a homemade costume that year. Finding a twenty-dollar bill, I offered it to Asa. "Here," I said. "For the book." It nearly killed me, as surely as suffocation behind a three-foot-thick door, but I added, "And keep the change. For the society."

Asa's expression softened, just a tiny bit. "Thank you," he said grudgingly. He took the money from my hand. "Your donation is appreciated."

Then he *finally* stepped aside so I could hurry into the main part of the bank, where I took deep, grateful breaths of the musty air while Asa signed his handiwork. I supposed he assumed he wouldn't get many opportunities to do that and would grab the chance while he could.

A few minutes later, I was safely outside the old building, walking down Sylvan Creek's sunny main street and pondering two mysteries.

First, I kept trying to figure out why Asa wouldn't admit that Miss Flynt had read his manuscript. Because I was sure he'd been lying.

Second, I wondered yet again why, exactly, Miss Flynt had burned the book.

I checked the cover of *Sylvan Creek: A History*, fairly certain that the answer to that question was right in my hands.

I just needed to summon the will to dig through four-hundred pages of minutiae to find it.

Tucking the volume under my arm, I crossed the street, which was quiet that afternoon, and approached Piper's practice. Templeton Animal Hospital was housed in the oldest and prettiest building in town, and I paused for a moment to admire the many window boxes that Piper had filled with purple and yellow mums. The seasonal flowers contrasted beautifully with the structure's blue-green wooden siding and crisp white trim. My sister wasn't much for arts and crafts, but she'd also managed to carve very realistic silhouettes of a dog and a cat into two large pumpkins that flanked the door.

I bent to admire her handiwork, trying to figure out if she'd used a pattern or worked freehand.

Deciding she'd definitely used a pattern, I straightened again, finally noticing something new that was propped in one of the windows and partially obscured by a large cluster of purple mums.

A small red and white HELP WANTED sign.

Chapter 29

"Do you plan to help me at all?" Piper asked, waking me from a light doze. She was seated cross-legged on my living room floor and reached over to shake my shoulder. "Daphne!"

"I'm helping," I promised, struggling to sit up on the love seat. As I rose, I knocked *Sylvan Creek: A History* off my lap. The book thudded to the floor, startling Artie, who yipped and jumped. Socrates, lying by the fire, lifted one eyelid, then resumed pretending to sleep. I knew he was trying *not* to see his only real canine friend get sewn into a miniature clown costume, for the parade later that evening. I might've gone back on my promise to Jonathan about not demeaning the dog. Artie was going to wear a tiny polka-dot romper with ruffles on the sleeves and collar, and a pointed, polka-dot hat with a pom-pom on top. "I'm just trying to read about our town's history while we work," I told Piper, whose eyes were nearly crossed as she struggled to thread a needle in a room lit by two small lamps and the fireplace. "I think the book's going to get interesting, if I can just get past the part about the railroads."

Piper paused her sewing project to give my reading material a well-deserved skeptical glance.

"Why are you reading that?" she asked, pulling Artie closer to herself, setting the hat on his head, and adjusting an elastic strap under his recessive chin. The hat immediately slipped sideways, over his missing ear. "And why isn't Artie a witch? Aren't you supposed to match your pet with your own costume?"

"Actually, I'm going as a clown, too," I said. "I have to pick up my outfit at Lighthouse Fellowship before the parade."

"Why in the world . . . ?"

I could anticipate all of Piper's questions, and I interrupted to answer them. "I might've accidentally volunteered to play the part of a deranged killer clown at the church's haunted hayride fund-raiser. Tamara told me I can pick up the costume anytime, in the church. I figured I might as well get two wearings out of it."

Okay, maybe I hadn't answered all of Piper's questions. She still looked confused. "I don't know how someone 'accidentally volunteers.' And don't they lock the church?"

"No, I guess not," I said, with a glance at my own door. At some point, while I'd been out, Jonathan had made good on *his* promise by installing a shiny, new lock. Not that I was using it. Still, it was a nice gesture on his part. "Tamara—who's organizing the hayride—said the main areas of the church are always open," I added. "Something about 'offering a welcoming sanctuary for all who need one.'"

"Sounds like a welcome for *thieves*," Piper said, shaking her head. "Or vandals."

When Jonathan Black had first come to town, my mother had hinted that he'd be a good match for Piper. Sometimes I agreed.

My sister fluffed Artie's ruffles. "I also don't understand why a church holds a haunted hayride."

"Yeah, I don't get it, either," I agreed, trying to sit very still. Out of the corner of my eye, I'd spied a small, glum, black face, peeping up over the back of the love seat. Then I couldn't resist smiling at Tinkleston, which caused him to sink slowly back down into hiding. "It's Tamara's idea," I told Piper. "Dylan says Pastor Pete is worried it's going to be a disaster, and that Miss Flynt hated the whole plan, too."

"I think I agree with Lillian," Piper said. "The posters look terrifying."

All at once, I recalled the little sign in the window of Templeton Animal Hospital. "Speaking of posters, why are you looking for help at the hospital? Are you expanding? Or is somebody leaving?"

Piper gave me another quizzical look, then she averted her gaze, checking Artie's pom-pom to make sure it was firmly attached. "It's just time to add someone new," she finally said. Then she gave prancing, inordinately proud Artie a shove in my direction and changed the subject. "He looks pretty good, don't you think?"

"Yeah, he looks great. I knew we could make a clown costume!"

Piper was clearly incredulous. "Did you just say 'we'?"

Twisting and leaning off the edge of the love seat, I reached down to pick up *Sylvan Creek*, which was still on the floor. The book had fallen open to Asa's inscription, which read, *Best wishes. Asa Whitaker.*

Originality was *not* his thing.

As Artie trotted over to nudge Socrates out of his false slumber, in a doomed attempt to show the basset hound his costume, Piper stood up and gestured to the book. "You never said why you're reading that."

"Oh, yeah." I held up the history for her inspection. "I think Asa Whitaker might've killed Miss Flynt—that is, if Tamara or Bea didn't do it—and that there might be a clue inside these hundreds . . . and hundreds . . . and hundreds . . . of pages."

Piper rolled her eyes. "Seriously, if you get threatened with a hammer again, do *not* come running to me."

"I really don't think that's going to happen," I informed her, tossing the book onto the steamer trunk coffee table, so I could use the narrative to put myself to sleep later that night. "And there's no time for a lecture, right now. The parade starts in an hour."

Piper bent to tidy up her sewing materials. "I'm not going this year, Daph."

I couldn't believe my ears. My sister would know every pet in the parade. "Why not?"

She shrugged, her shoulders drowning under a big sweatshirt. "I'm just not interested this year. I feel kind of tired."

My sister *was* withdrawing in the wake of Steve Beamus's death. I couldn't let that happen. Piper Templeton had never given up on anything in her life. She couldn't give up on life itself and become a sweatshirt-wearing recluse like Bea Baumgartner.

"Aw, come on, Piper," I cajoled. "I need you to watch Socrates while Artie and I march in the parade."

Piper glanced at the basset hound, who continued to keep his eyes tightly closed, while Artie danced around him on excited little feet. "Socrates isn't walking with you? Not even just as a . . . dog?"

"Can you really imagine him in a parade full of costumed animals? It is so beneath him!" I shot Artie an apologetic look. "Sorry."

Artie wasn't insulted. His bulging eyes glowed, and he offered me a happy, "Yip!"

I turned back to Piper, clasping my hands. "Please? For me? And Socrates? Because I'd rather not leave him here with Tinkleston, who is still trying to scratch him, sometimes. And he'll be scarred for life in a different way if he has to be a canine float in a parade."

"Can't Socrates just stay at the farmhouse with me?"

That was an option. I decided to be direct. "You need to get out more, Piper. Do you want to end up like Bea Baumgartner, living alone in the woods?"

Piper opened her mouth to object, then her shoulders slumped under her shapeless shirt. "Fine. Let's go."

I hesitated, then pressed my luck by asking, tentatively, "You *are* changing, right?"

Piper pulled at her sweatshirt, examining it like she was seeing it for the first time. "I wasn't going to . . ."

"You know, I think Bea was wearing that same shirt when she showed me her barn full of cats," I observed, waving to Artie, who hurried to the door. Socrates must've grasped that he wouldn't have to march or wear any kind of costume, because he opened one eye, then fake yawned and stretched, rising to his feet. "Or, at the very least, Bea's outfit was similar."

"Okay, okay!" Piper raised her hands, a sign of surrender. "I'm changing!"

"Just make it snappy," I urged. "Don't forget, I still

need to hunt for a creepy clown costume in an empty church."

Piper looked concerned for me, and at first I didn't understand why.

Then I mentally replayed the last thing I'd just said.

Why hadn't that sounded like a scary prospect, until it came out of my mouth?

Chapter 30

Sylvan Creek's main street was crowded with pets and people by the time Piper, Socrates, Artie, and I arrived for the parade, which was one of the community's biggest annual events. All of the local benevolent societies, such as the Elks, the Moose, and the Masons, chipped in to decorate, so the many trees that lined the route were strung with tiny orange lights. The globes on Sylvan Creek's iconic, three-armed lamp-posts were temporarily replaced with glowing orange jack-o'-lantern faces. Dangling, jangling skeletons and cackling witches riding brooms were suspended from storefront canopies, and real flickering jack-o'-lanterns sat on every stoop. Vendors representing local charities pushed carts selling warm cider, hot chocolate, spiced nuts, and cones of pumpkin-spice ice cream, for those who didn't mind the chill in the air. Of course, there were pet treats, too. In fact, I had made a batch of Pumpkin-Peanut-Butter Ghosts for the volunteer fire company to sell, to raise some money for their retired dalmatian fund.

I would've also made something for Lighthouse Fellowship, but nobody had asked that year. Apparently,

Pastor Pete had decided to let Tamara have her way entirely, and the church wouldn't be selling any baked goods.

"I have to admit, I'm glad I got to see the town looking so festive," Piper said, as we all backed up against the Philosopher's Tome to make room on the sidewalk for Little Miss Muffet, who led an adorable miniature pony dressed like a spider, with googly eyes on his halter and eight legs dangling from a blanket. "You know, Lillian usually coordinated everything. I thought things might not run smoothly this year."

I bent to pick up Artie so he wouldn't get crushed under hoof, foot, or paw. "I wonder who's in charge. Do you know?"

The question was barely out of my mouth when Tamara Fox interrupted our conversation, just like she'd done at Flynt Mansion. Apparently, she had to be involved in literally everything.

"*I* took over for Lillian this year," she smugly informed me and Piper. She smiled at my sister. "I'm glad you like it."

I turned to see that Tamara was dressed as Raggedy Ann, which was disconcerting, and not only because she was an adult in a flouncy dress, striped tights, and a red yarn wig. She also looked odd because she'd used makeup to create the illusion that her eyes were big, black buttons. Only the whites gave away her actual, naturally dark eyes.

In her arms, she carried her white Maltese, *named* Buttons, who wore a vest covered with . . . buttons. And a big button cap.

I was starting to see the theme.

At my feet, Socrates whined softly on Buttons's behalf, although the Maltese looked as proud as Artie. The two smaller dogs were straining to see each other, their bodies wriggling and their tails wagging. I nearly dropped the Chihuahua.

"Watch for some minor changes this year," Tamara added. "And more dramatic improvements next year. I really see the potential to make this event great."

"It's already great," Piper said. "Perfect!"

I could tell she thought Tamara was disrespecting Miss Flynt's memory, and I agreed. The poor woman wasn't even buried yet. Plus, there was nothing wrong with the parade.

"Yeah, I don't see the need for big changes," I added. "What would you want to do?"

"There's no need to go into all of your many, many plans, dear," someone said, in a deep, weary-sounding voice. "This is neither the place nor the time."

I saw a flash of irritation cross Tamara's face, even as she politely said, "Piper, you remember my husband, Larry."

I hadn't even noticed Larry Fox, Esquire, although he stood out in his own way, by looking completely normal. He wore a gray suit, a dark tie, and still had a leftover summer tan that I guessed came from lots of time spent on golf courses. I had seen Larry around town, but I'd never met him. Up close, the age gap that separated him from Tamara seemed wide and deep. His face was lined, more than I'd expected, and his gray eyes looked tired. His hair, although thick, was snow white.

"Nice to see you, Larry," Piper said, smiling and shaking his hand.

Although Tamara hadn't even acknowledged me, I smiled, too, and stuck out the arm that wasn't cradling Artie. "I'm Piper's sister, Daphne," I introduced myself. "Nice to meet you."

Larry didn't exactly greet me, either, although he

did shake my hand. His grip was firm. "I understand you're to be at the reading of Lillian's will tomorrow," he said. "Please be there—and be prompt."

Apparently, my reputation for forgetting things and being late preceded me.

"I'll do my best to be on time," I promised.

Tamara tugged her husband's sleeve, signaling that it was time for them to move on. "We'll see you all later," she said, waggling her fingers. Then she lost her fake smile and addressed her husband. "Come along, dear. The parade's starting soon."

"You know I don't really like animals," Larry said, frowning at Buttons. "I'm heading home."

Tamara playfully smacked her husband's chest, then told Piper and me, "He's just kidding. He loves pets."

No. He obviously didn't.

"Come along now, Larry," Tamara repeated more firmly. "Let's get you a good spot along the route, so you won't miss Buttons and me."

Larry Fox was a high-powered attorney, but he caved and did as he was told. He shuffled along after Tamara in his Oxfords, not bothering to say good-bye.

I watched them walk away. "They're great at parties, I bet."

Piper frowned. "Larry's usually a *little* more animated."

"Really, because . . . ?" I was about to express my skepticism—and tell Piper that I still wondered if control-freak Tamara had killed Miss Flynt—when I heard a voice from on high.

"Hey, you guys!"

All of us, including the dogs, looked up to see Moxie waving at us from a small balcony that extended off her top-floor apartment's living room, under one of the

Victorian building's peaked eaves. It was a prime spot from which to watch the parade.

"Hey, Moxie," I called. Then I bent my head back farther, trying to see her better. "Who are you supposed to be now?"

I was surprised she'd dressed up, since she didn't have any pets. And she once again denied that she was in costume.

"I just got out of the shower," she said, pulling a fluffy bathrobe more tightly around herself. It looked like her hair was still blond, but it was hard to tell, since it was wet and plastered against her forehead. "I'm not dressed up."

"Why are you holding a butcher knife, then?" Piper inquired, tilting her head way back, too.

"Oh, this?" Moxie looked at the large implement in her hand, like she'd forgotten she had it. "I decided to do some post-shower pumpkin carving."

Moxie couldn't keep from grinning when she said that. She *knew* she was dressed like Janet Leigh, in *Psycho*, and was just messing with us, at that point.

"You know the character of Marion Crane gets stabbed in the movie," I reminded Moxie unnecessarily, because she knew way more about fifties and sixties films than me. "She doesn't do the stabbing."

"Well, without a prop, I just look like a person in a bathrobe," she pointed out. "That's not very interesting."

Socrates whined, like he couldn't understand why anyone who didn't have to wear a costume would ever do it.

"Have fun watching the parade," I said, because I needed to get going. I was also getting a crick in my neck, and some people were starting to glance nervously up at the woman holding a knife. "I've gotta go get dressed."

"See you," Moxie said. "You guys have a good time, too."

She withdrew, so we couldn't see her anymore, and I told Piper, "I really do have to get moving. Are you okay with the dogs for a minute? I'll come back for Artie when I'm in costume."

"Yes, we're fine," Piper promised, accepting Artie from me. "I'll get them some of those treats you made for the fire company, to fuel Artie for the half-mile route."

Artie's remaining ear drooped, as if he'd suddenly realized he was going to have to walk a fair distance.

"Don't worry," I reassured him. "I'll carry you most of the way."

His eyes lit up, and he barked approval.

"You'd better hurry," my sister urged, checking her watch. "You're going to miss the whole thing."

That was not true. I had at least a half hour to find my costume and get dressed. But I started to thread my way through the crowd toward the Lighthouse Fellowship Church, which was located about two blocks away, down a side street.

All around me, people were making last minute adjustments to their pets' costumes.

Bea Baumgartner, dressed even more raggedly than usual, wrestled with a whole wagon full of cats that wore what looked like shredded strips of fabric. At first, I thought they were supposed to be mummies, until I saw a hand-lettered poster, in Bea's sloppy writing, attached to the back of the cart. The sign read, PLEASE ADOPT AN 'ORPHAN' FROM WHISKERED AWAY HOME CAT SHELTER. CALL FIRST!! SHELTER IS ON PRIVATE PROPERTY!!

Bea *really* needed a lesson in public relations.

I also saw Tom and Tessie Flinchbaugh—owners of the Philosopher's Tome and Fetch!—double-checking the cherry on top of their ancient poodle Marzipan's suitably sweet cupcake costume. Luckily for Marzipan, the Flinchbaughs planned to pull her in a cart, too.

Noticing me, Tom and Tessie, who looked *interesting*— to put it kindly—in their own sprinkle-covered cupcake outfits, complete with cherry hats, both waved.

Pastor Pete, struggling to affix angel wings and a halo to Blessing, was a few feet away from the Flinchbaughs, and he paused to greet me, too, with a wan smile. Although normally cheerful, he didn't look like he was having fun. And Blessing's silky ears were also pinned back. Maybe the poor retriever had been cast in that heavenly role one too many times. Pastor Pete, who hadn't even bothered to add wings to a white robe that I was pretty sure had come from his church's acolytes' collection, definitely wasn't thinking outside the box.

Raising a hand, I waved back to all of them. And because I wasn't paying attention to where I was headed, I bumped right into none other than Martha and Asa Whitaker, who were accompanied by their bloodhound, Charlie, and the little orange kitten with the mouthful of a name, Himmelfarb.

"Daphne, please watch where you're going," Martha said, tugging lightly on Charlie's leash, as if he might dart away. Which was unlikely. I walked Charlie—who was dressed as literary figure Sherlock Holmes, in a deerstalker hat—and it was a struggle to keep him awake.

I thought of Artie and Marzipan.

Weren't there any pets in Sylvan Creek who could complete a half-mile walk without collapsing?

"Daphne," Martha said, sounding more severe than usual. "Aren't you going to apologize? You nearly ran down Charlie."

"I'm sorry," I said, not sure why she was so cranky on

such a festive night. I looked her up and down. "Are you *Watson?*"

That was an honest question. I didn't know what Watson looked like.

Martha acted insulted, though. "Of course! Who else would be paired with Holmes?"

I wasn't sure. I hadn't read Sir Arthur Conan Doyle's works in a long time.

Hoping to redeem myself, and change the subject, I smiled at Asa. "I'm really enjoying your book. It's got me on the edge of my seat."

That second part was true. I'd recently tumbled off my love seat while reading *Sylvan Creek: A History,* because, as usual, I'd fallen asleep.

Asa watched me carefully. "You're really enjoying it?"

"Sure." One more well-intentioned fib to make him feel good about his book couldn't hurt. Then I reached out to scratch Himmelfarb under the chin. The cat was adorable in a tiny top hat and cravat. She purred, and I smiled, asking, "And who are you supposed to be?"

Asa pulled the kitten back to his chest, protectively. "Himmelfarb is dressed as Elijah Cortland. And I am Jedediah Cortland."

I hadn't even realized Asa was in costume. He wore a suit jacket and an ascot, but I hadn't found the outfit too out of the ordinary. At least, not for a historian.

Regardless, it must've been obvious that I didn't recognize the names.

"You do know, from reading my book, that the Cortland brothers *founded* Sylvan Creek?" he asked, studying me closely and suspiciously again.

"Oh, yeah." I felt my cheeks growing warm. "I guess I didn't get to that part yet."

"It's all in *Chapter One,*" Asa said evenly.

Both he and Martha stared daggers at me, while I

slowly backed away, telling them, "I love your costumes. All of them!"

When I couldn't take their accusing gazes anymore, I spun around and resumed hurrying toward Lighthouse Fellowship, which occupied an imposing, spire-topped brownstone building on quiet, otherwise residential Acorn Street.

The brownstone—the tallest building in town, if its sky-stabbing spire was taken into account—had been constructed decades ago by Lutherans. But something had happened in the fifties to cause that congregation to break apart, and the abandoned church had undergone many incarnations over the years. When I'd been about seven years old, it had served as a dance studio. I'd taken three disastrous tap lessons there before realizing that a klutz like me shouldn't make my shoes slippery on purpose.

As I made my way down Acorn Street, under a canopy of old oak trees, the noise of the parade faded away, replaced by near silence. Most people were on Market Street, and before long, I could hear my own breathing and the faint sound of leaves rustling overhead in the evening's light breeze.

The only light came from street lamps on the corners, and they did little to dispel the gloom. Most of the houses were dark and empty, too. And the "sanctuary for all," which I was approaching, was, ironically, the least welcoming place on the block. The side entrance that Tamara had promised was always unlocked was hidden under an arch that cast the door in a deep shadow.

The entrance looked so unwelcoming that I could hardly believe the door wasn't locked up tight. Which was why I nearly fell backward when I yanked on the handle, and the glass door swung open.

The church's foyer was dark and eerily quiet, and I almost turned around without getting the costume.

Then I pictured Artie's eager, bulbous eyes and recalled how he'd been abandoned by no fewer than three families, somehow losing an ear along the way, and I couldn't bear to disappoint him again.

Taking a deep breath, I stepped inside—and let that breath out in the form of a short, sharp scream that echoed all the way to the church's impressive vaulted ceilings.

Chapter 31

"Stupid clown outfit!" I grumbled, my fingers still shaking a little as I tried to button myself into a big yellow and red jumpsuit.

In what I assumed was an effort to be helpful, Tamara had hung the costume on a coatrack just inside the door, so I'd come face to face with the leering rubber mask the moment I stepped inside the church.

At least, I hoped Tamara had tried to be helpful. I hoped she hadn't deliberately tried to scare me to death.

"I'm going to give you the benefit of the doubt, Tamara," I said softly, as I struggled to pull on the oversized red rubber shoes she'd left neatly side by side under the nylon suit. The shoes fit tightly and awkwardly over my favorite cowgirl boots, but I managed to get them onto my feet. Then I picked up the mask, which I'd torn off the costume during a one-sided struggle with what I'd momentarily believed to be a real clown. Tamara had pinned the hideous face to the fabric, along with a sheet of paper. I took a second to study the clown's expression again. He was smiling, but too broadly, in an evil way, revealing sharp, yellowed teeth. "I really don't think this is right for a kids' church event," I muttered. "And I am not wearing the mask tonight. It'll scare the dogs!"

Tucking the rubber face under my arm, I next unpinned the paper from the costume. Squinting, I was able to see that I held a sign out sheet. A sticky note in Tamara's handwriting told me to sign and date the line next to "Killer Clown," indicating that I'd taken possession of the suit. There was a spot to initial when I returned the outfit, too.

I had to admire Tamara's organizational skills. I probably would've just let the volunteers take the costumes home and ended up costing the church money for rentals that were never returned.

I wanted to help Tamara keep track of things. However, I didn't have a pen, and I wasn't sure where I was supposed to leave the sheet once I did sign it.

Taking another moment to think, I looked around the church and noticed a very faint light glowing at the far end of a hallway that ran behind the sanctuary.

I suspected that the light came from a computer monitor, maybe belonging to a church secretary or Pastor Pete, and I shuffled down the corridor in my clunky shoes, hoping to find a pen and a desk upon which I could leave the paper.

And, sure enough, the room was someone's office.

Poking my head inside, I flicked a switch on the wall to turn on a brighter light—and immediately saw something that might help me solve, if not a murder, at least a mystery that surrounded Pastor Pete.

Chapter 32

"Where have you been?" Piper demanded, when I finally found her at the end of the parade route in Pettigrew Park, where everyone who'd marched, and half of the spectators, as well as all of the vendors were gathered. The parade always became something of an outdoor costume party. But Piper wasn't having fun. She crossed her arms over her chest, and I saw two small red blotches on her cheeks, a telltale sign that she was angry. "I had to walk in the parade—without a costume. And so did Socrates. It was really embarrassing!"

If Piper was mad at me, Socrates was *furious*. He wouldn't even look at me. He sat with his butt planted on the grass and his face turned resolutely away.

Only Artie didn't seem to care that I'd missed the parade. He was running pell-mell through the park, his clown hat missing and his costume in tatters.

I followed his path through the crowd and saw that Elyse Hunter-Black had taken part in the event with her two greyhounds. Elyse might've been new in town, but she was commanding a small audience, which was fitting, because she was dressed as an icy, imperious queen in a silver gown that looked like it came from a boutique on Park Avenue, as opposed to a costume shop. The tiara tucked into her sleek, blond hair didn't look like plastic, either. And the dogs at her sides were regal princesses in jeweled collars and their own matching crowns. I wasn't sure how Elyse kept the pretty, lacy circlets on Paris and Milan's narrow heads, but every crystal was in place.

Artie darted past my oversized shoe, and I saw that he'd drooled so much that the ruffle under his chin had completely collapsed.

"Are you going to explain yourself?" Piper prompted, snapping me back to our conversation. "I would really like to know how I got stuck walking Artie in a pet parade!"

"I'm really sorry," I told Piper—and Socrates, who was finally looking at me. He didn't hold onto anger, and he would accept a logical explanation, if I had one. I wedged the rubber mask further under my arm. "I thought I'd be back from the church in plenty of time. But I found some interesting things in Pastor Kishbaugh's office, and I had to check everything out."

Socrates no longer seemed angry about the parade, but he furrowed his already wrinkled brow, as if he disapproved of my snooping.

Realizing that I'd probably said too much about my investigative efforts, I gestured to my feet. "And then it took forever to walk back in these big, red, floppy boats."

"Why didn't you just *take them off*?" Piper suggested, although she sounded more irate than helpful. "You are wearing shoes underneath them!"

I looked down at my feet. "You can't believe how

much effort it took to put these things on. I would've wasted more time. . . ."

I sensed that Socrates understood the dilemma I'd faced, but my sister wasn't even listening. Her attention—and mine—had been drawn to a man who was tapping Piper's shoulder, indicating that he wanted to speak with her.

"I don't mean to interrupt, Piper, but would you like to get some cider?" the man asked, smiling.

I had no idea who he was, or how he knew my sister's name, but she seemed very pleased to see him. She smiled brightly, too, so it was almost difficult to believe she'd just been scowling. I exchanged quick, confused glances with Socrates, who obviously didn't know the guy, either. Then Piper *blushed* and tucked some of her hair behind her ear in a gesture that could've been considered nervous. Or *flirtatious.*

I couldn't ever recall Piper acting coy, and I took a moment to size up the stranger, who was about Piper's age and kind of good looking, in a conservative way. He had neatly cut brown hair and wore a red fleece jacket, a plaid shirt, and khaki pants.

"Aren't you going to introduce . . . ?"

My request fell on deaf ears. Piper totally ignored me.

"I'd love something to drink, Roger," she said, still smiling. "Thanks for offering."

I watched them walk away. Then I looked down at Socrates.

"Who, exactly, is 'Roger'?" I asked. "And how does Piper know him?"

Socrates lifted his eyebrows, like he had no idea, so I resumed observing my sister and her friend as they threaded their way toward the cart that sold hot cider. And while I was distracted, I felt a tap on *my* shoulder, right before someone observed drily, "This costume is even better than 'boxing witch.'"

I turned around to see that, in spite of his deadpan tone, Jonathan Black was laughing at me. And Socrates made a snuffling sound, too. I took his amusement to mean that all was forgiven.

"This is a costume, right?" Jonathan added, giving my nylon jumpsuit a skeptical once over. Axis, who stood at Jonathan's side, cocked his head, like he wasn't sure about my getup, either. Then Jonathan finally succumbed to the urge to grin. "You're not trying to make some unusual fashion statement, are you?"

"Very funny," I said, fighting the urge to kick his shin with my big shoe. "You know I'm dressed for the parade!"

"And yet, you didn't march with Artie," he pointed out, reaching down to scratch Axis behind the ears. He next lifted Artie, who'd bounded over to greet his family. While slightly irritated to be the object of Jonathan's mirth, I was pleasantly surprised by his show of affection for the little dog. Then Jonathan set Artie down before the excited Chihuahua could cover his face with kisses. Still, they'd come a long way. "You're the one who was supposed to walk the canine clown, right?" Jonathan asked me. "Not Piper—who, for some reason, *carried* a perfectly able-bodied animal for a half mile, while the person who insisted that pets need to march in parades didn't show up at all."

Wow, he packed a lot of criticism into a few short sentences.

I wanted to fire back with some clever retort about his appearance, but, as usual, Jonathan looked just fine in a black down vest, a gray Henley, and jeans.

Actually, he looked way more than just fine.

"For your information, I missed the parade because I was at Lighthouse Fellowship Church," I informed him, earning a low, cautionary whine from Socrates. I ignored the warning and told Jonathan, "I think you'll want to know what I found in Pastor Pete's office, too, because I'm pretty sure he really should be in jail."

Chapter 33

"Why in the world were you at Lighthouse Fellowship *tonight*?" Jonathan asked. He was clearly skeptical about my recent visit to the church, but kindly buying us both Mexican hot chocolates from a cart operated by one of my favorite Sylvan Creek establishments, Casita Burrito. He pulled his wallet from his back pocket while I accepted two paper cups from a young man in a T-shirt that advertised the restaurant. However, a sign on the cart said the sale of each beverage and sugary churro would benefit a local charitable organization, which was identified only by an odd symbol that I didn't recognize. That seemed like poor advertising to me. "Please tell me you were authorized to be in the building," Jonathan added, putting away his wallet. "So I don't have to worry about whether *you* should be in jail."

"First of all, thank you for the drink," I said, handing him one of the cups as we walked away from the cart, followed by Axis, Artie, and Socrates. The dogs were sticking close to us, probably because Jonathan had also purchased some of the Pumpkin-Peanut-Butter Ghosts I'd baked to support the retired dalmatian fund. "And

I don't deserve jail time. Tamara Fox can attest to the fact that she told me to pick up my clown costume at the church whenever I wanted."

Jonathan looked askance at me. "The *church* rents evil clown outfits?"

"I'm playing a diabolical killer clown for them in a few days," I explained. "At their haunted hayride at Twisted Branch Orchard."

"Ah, yes." Jonathan was obviously starting to put the story together. "The hayride that Tamara and Lillian Flynt argued about." Resting his free hand on my elbow, he guided me toward a bench that overlooked Sylvan Creek. Then he frowned. "And now you're involved."

I drew back and raised my hands, nearly spilling my drink. "Just as a volunteer ghoul," I assured him. "And only by accident. I don't even want to do it."

Jonathan didn't seem convinced that my involvement in a controversial event spearheaded by one of Miss Flynt's foes, who'd been at the mansion the night of her death, was purely innocent.

He didn't say anything more, though. We sat down on the bench, so I finally had a chance to sip my dark, rich hot chocolate, which was enhanced by hints of vanilla and nutmeg and finished off with a kick of cayenne pepper. The night was chilly, but I immediately began to feel warm inside. Jonathan sampled his drink, too, then took the dog treats out of his pocket and handed out three to the waiting canines. Socrates, Artie, and Axis quickly settled down to eat their snacks, which were made from pumpkin puree, peanut butter, eggs, and a touch of cinnamon.

We all got quiet for a while, just enjoying the view of Sylvan Creek, which was illuminated by a huge, nearly full moon. Wispy, spooky clouds swept across the sky, and a rising wind plucked the last of the leaves from trees that arched over the water, which ran black and silent at our feet.

The peaceful spell cast by the night seemed to have affected even Jonathan. He sounded more curious than accusing when he finally shifted slightly to ask me, "So. Why, exactly, were you in Pete Kishbaugh's office? And what did you find?"

"I didn't really intend to go near his office," I explained. "I needed a pen to fill out a form before I took my rental costume, so I followed the glow of a computer monitor down a hallway. I was trying to follow Tamara Fox's instructions when I found the office."

Jonathan smiled wryly. "Yes, I know you're a stickler for paperwork and would never wander off without completing a required form."

I could tell that he thought I'd wanted an excuse to nose around. Which, in retrospect, might've been partly true.

"Anyhow, I went into the room, which turned out to be Pastor Pete's office. And, right there, out in the open"—meaning tucked along with some other documents under a glass paperweight etched with the Ten Commandments—"was his passport."

I was getting excited, but Jonathan seemed baffled, and far from certain that I'd found anything worthwhile. "I have no idea where this is going," he admitted, setting his hot chocolate on the bench and pulling a paper cone from the pocket of his vest. When he opened the top, I recognized the distinctive, delicious smell of cinnamon-and-sugar-roasted nuts. He held out the cone, and I reached in and grabbed about five still warm pecans. "What is so significant about a passport on a desk? Especially since Pete Kishbaugh travels frequently, by his own admission."

I tossed the pecans into my mouth and took a second

to savor the sweet, salty snack. Then I explained, "The stamps were all wrong. *At least* three separate times, over the last few years, Pastor Pete wasn't where he was supposed to be—"

Jonathan spoke a little sharply. "*You looked in the man's passport?*"

"I didn't think it was a big deal," I said, defending myself. "It's not like a journal or a diary. It's a government document, filled with nothing but stamps."

"Yet you felt compelled to open it."

"Yes," I said. "I just had this hunch. . . ." I couldn't exactly explain why I'd been drawn to read the history of Pastor Pete's travels. Especially not to a logical person like Jonathan Black. "The point is, I found several inconsistencies."

Jonathan leaned forward, the better to see my face. "What do you mean by 'inconsistencies'?"

"Times when Pastor Pete wasn't where he should've been," I said. I had Jonathan's full attention, and I set my nearly empty cup on the bench, too, so I could list the discrepancies on my sugary fingers. "First, the summer before last, when he was supposedly in Guatemala, helping orphans, he was in *Italy*. Then, last May, when he was 'building a church in Haiti'"—I air quoted—"he was really in France. And just six weeks ago, when he was supposed to be distributing food to poor people in Sierra Leone, he was living it up in Switzerland. On his parishioners' dime."

My sense of betrayal on behalf of Pastor Pete's parishioners had grown as I'd outlined the minister's obvious indiscretions, but Jonathan's confusion had kept corresponding pace.

"And you know about these discrepancies because . . . ?"

"I sit for his golden retriever mix, Blessing," I said,

with a glance at our very patient dogs, who lay quietly in a row, watching the creek. Even Artie was relatively still, presumably caught up in the hypnotic spell cast by the black, slow-moving water. I returned my attention to Jonathan. "And when he goes away, Pastor Pete *always* makes a point of letting me know, in his 'humble' way, about the good works he's doing in the world's poorest places. He also mentions how grateful he is for his 'flock's' generous support, which pays for his travel."

All at once, I felt personally betrayed. I'd given Pastor Kishbaugh a discount on my already low fee, as my way of contributing to his charitable acts.

He'd cheated me, too.

"You're sure about this?" Jonathan asked, watching my face carefully, even as he popped a few pecans into his mouth. I reached into the cone again, too. "You're absolutely positive that you have your dates right? Because—no offense—but you are not the most organized person."

That was true, but I knew what I was talking about, this time.

"I know for certain that he was supposed to be in Haiti in May," I said. "I tested a new Cinco de Mayo treat recipe on Blessing, and he spit up the Cheese Enchi-paw-da all over Pastor Pete's rug. I had to use most of my already discounted fee to rent a carpet cleaner." I hung and shook my head, growing even more disappointed with a certain swindling minister. "He should've told me, at some point, that Blessing was lactose intolerant."

I looked up to see that Jonathan had a grave expression on his face. "These are serious allegations, Daphne."

"There's more."

Jonathan's eyes kept searching mine, like he was

trying to figure out if I was a brilliant ally, or a crazy pain in the butt. Then he said, "Go ahead."

"Pastor Kishbaugh has one of those big blotter-style desk calendars," I said. "The kind that cover the whole top of the desk."

"Yes, I've seen them."

"Even though October's not over yet, that page was already gone. Completely missing!"

"Maybe he spilled coffee on it," Jonathan guessed, refusing to get swept up in my excitement, which was increasing again. "Or his lunch. There's a good chance he just made a mess and cleaned it up by getting rid of a calendar page that's almost outdated, anyhow."

"Oh, I think Pastor Pete might've made a *big* mess, but not with his lunch," I said. "Because when I dug through the recycling bins behind the church, I found the missing page."

Jonathan rubbed his temples. "While I banish the image of you crawling into a trash bin in a clown suit, please tell me that you didn't take anything."

I was so proud of myself that I nearly burst my over-sized buttons. "No, this time I left everything just like I found it."

"Not *exactly* like you found it," he reminded me. "Or how it would've been, if you'd left things alone."

"And yet, I think you might be interested to know what I learned." He didn't respond, so I told him, with a hint of triumph in my voice, "On the date of Lillian's murder, he'd written, *Meet LF—house—5 o'clock.*"

Jonathan did a good job of hiding his thoughts, but he drew back slightly, and I *knew* that meeting must've been set for close to the time of Miss Flynt's death, as established by coroner Vonda Shakes. But he would never share that with me, so I forged ahead, adding, "Lillian was treasurer of Lighthouse Fellowship. What if she'd figured out the same things I did, about Pastor Pete's travels? Or maybe knew worse things? Like the fact that he's probably been cooking the books, too, if Moxie's gossip mill is right. As it usually is."

Jonathan still didn't say anything. He sat back, taking a moment to reflect on everything I'd just told him.

"Well, you have given me a lot to consider," he finally admitted. Handing me what was left of the nuts, he pulled his cell phone from his pocket and tapped the screen. "I'll need to get Doebler over to the church before the recycling's taken away. Luckily, there's no need to get a warrant to search outdoor garbage bins."

I was not surprised that Jonathan was assigning his older, but subordinate, partner to dig through the trash.

"What about Pastor Pete's passport?" I asked.

"I need to think about that," Jonathan said, still tapping the screen. "You shouldn't have touched it, and I'm not sure, at this point, how to explain that I need a warrant to search his office." He looked up at me again. "I'll think of something, though." Hesitating, he stared hard into my eyes. "If you're *sure* about those dates."

"I'm positive," I promised him.

Jonathan put away his phone and grew even more serious. He didn't say anything for a long minute, and I thought I was in for my usual lecture about interfering in his investigations. Then he said, more quietly, "I can't condone your amateur detecting, and I do worry that your curiosity is strong enough to be dangerous, but I have to admit that you have some good instincts."

I was so surprised that for once I didn't say anything. I didn't even thank him for the compliment, for fear of prompting him to offer some sarcastic, distancing remark. Instead, we sat quietly again for a long time, the dogs still watching the creek, and Jonathan and I studying each other. I got the sense that we were trying to figure out a relationship—or lack of a relationship— that sometimes confused me, and probably him, too.

Then I finally broke the silence by asking some questions that had been on my mind since I'd first met him. "What brought you here, Jonathan?" I inquired softly. "How does a Navy SEAL end up in Sylvan Creek, Pennsylvania?"

I expected his eyes to close off, like they usually did when I asked him anything personal, but that didn't happen.

"As you guessed, I have my own share of long stories, and to trace my route here would take hours," he said. Then he smiled, but faintly. "I think what you're really asking is, why did I leave the military?"

I would've liked to hear the entire tale of his adult life, including the stories about his time in Afghanistan with his canine partner, Herod. But he was right about my biggest question. Because, although my peacenik self didn't know much about the Navy, I'd always thought that SEALs were SEALs for life.

"Without going into too much detail," he continued, "I had to leave when I couldn't meet the physical demands of the job. When it just wasn't realistic anymore."

I didn't understand what he was saying. I'd never seen anyone in such peak physical condition.

My confusion must've been obvious, because he added, more directly, "I got very sick, Daphne. Was sidelined for months while I underwent chemotherapy. And, while I'm healthy now, there's no guarantee that I'll stay in remission. It wouldn't be fair to my team to ask them to wait while I went through treatment again. Mine wasn't a job you can drop in and out of. So I—reluctantly—dropped out."

"Wow." I sucked in a deep breath, and my stomach twisted on Jonathan's behalf. Then I glanced at Socrates, who had turned to face us, appearing stunned for the first time I could ever recall. I was shocked, too, by Jonathan's confession. The news itself, and the fact that he'd told me something so personal. "I'm so sorry."

"Thanks, Daphne, but I'm honestly fine." He smiled again, more genuinely. "You were right when you said, months ago, that you have a gift for making people confide in you." Then he also looked at the dogs before turning back to me. "Not to mention a way with animals. I wouldn't be surprised if you even get the cat to come around, at some point."

I didn't want to talk about Tinkleston. I had a million more questions about Jonathan. But before I could even open my mouth, I heard the grass rustling behind us, and a moment later, someone rested two hands on the back of the bench and greeted us in a singsong voice that tried to sound chipper, but somehow fell short.

"Well, well, well . . . Don't you all look cozy!"

Chapter 34

Jonathan and I had moved close to each other while he'd confided in me, and on instinct, we both pulled away quickly when Elyse Hunter-Black and her ghostly greyhounds joined us in the park.

"Elyse . . . ?" Like me, Jonathan seemed caught off guard. But only for a moment. Then he regained his composure and stood up, while Artie and Axis bounded over to sniff Paris and Milan, a ritual that Socrates decided to forgo. In fact, he turned his head away and resumed studying the creek.

"How'd you like the parade?" I asked Elyse, rising, too, and smoothing my crumpled nylon outfit, which I'd nearly forgotten I was wearing. However, as I stood across from a beautiful woman in a silver gown, I started to feel somewhat self-conscious. Still, I smiled and said, "You look really nice, by the way."

"Thank you." Elyse looked me up and down, and I thought she was trying to find something kind to say about my outfit. Then she gave up, smiled at me and Jonathan, and came around to our side of the bench. Paris and Milan, who'd endured the sniffing ritual with about as much enthusiasm as Socrates, followed on her heels, trying unsuccessfully to distance themselves from Artie. "As for the parade," Elyse added, "it's just the type of thing viewers will love. I'm sorry I couldn't have a crew in place here in time to get footage for *America's Most Pet Friendly Towns*."

"So you're really going to feature Sylvan Creek on the show?" I asked, still not sure how I felt about that prospect. I kind of agreed with Moxie that the town didn't necessarily need national exposure.

But apparently we were getting that, whether we wanted it or not.

"Yes," Elyse said. Her gown shimmered in the moonlight. "I imagine we'll have cameras here before Christmas. There *will* be holiday events, right?"

I suspected that a successful TV producer would've already researched Sylvan Creek's annual Run, Rudolph, Run, a fun, dog-friendly 5K, in which both people and pets wore antlers and glowing red noses. She probably also knew about the Bark the Halls Holiday Ball, which was a fancy dance attended by humans and canines, who all donned their finest attire. So all I said was, "Oh, yeah. We do a few things differently from most other towns, I guess."

"I can hardly wait." Elyse continued smiling, mainly at Jonathan. "I hope to have most of the renovations to Flynt Mansion completed by then, so I can throw my own holiday open house and get to know some of my new neighbors."

"Are you sure the sale will be able to go through?" Jonathan asked. I got the sense that he was both curious about whether Elyse would really buy the mansion, and wondering if there was some news about Miss Flynt's estate that might be pertinent to his murder investigation. "Have you heard something?"

All at once, I nearly panicked. "I didn't miss the reading of the will, did I?"

"No, that's tomorrow," Elyse reassured me, just as I recalled that Larry Fox had already told me that, earlier that night. She absently stroked one of the greyhound's heads, while Artie continued to dance around the dogs' feet in a desperate attempt to regain their attention. "But I feel confident that things will work out."

"I guess you'll know soon," Jonathan noted, with a glance at his wristwatch. "And, speaking of time, I need to get going." He was all business again. "I'm meeting Detective Doebler over at Lighthouse Fellowship in fifteen minutes."

"Oh, really?" Elyse sounded disappointed. "You're working tonight?"

"Yes, I have some information I need to follow up on," he said, looking at me. His expression was neutral, and I wasn't sure if I'd messed up his evening or made his day by potentially helping him solve a murder. He addressed Elyse again. "But I'll walk you and Daphne to your cars."

"Thanks," I said. "But I've got to stick around for a few minutes."

"Why?" Jonathan sounded concerned, like he feared I might do more investigating.

"Somewhere between the hot chocolate cart and the bench, I lost my mask," I told him, patting myself down, as if I might somehow be harboring a big, rubber clown face. "And if I don't find it, I'm pretty sure Tamara Fox will make me reimburse the church. I am not eager to give them more money right now."

Jonathan looked around the park, and I noticed that most people had left by then. "Are you sure you don't want to come back in the morning? There's a killer out there somewhere."

Elyse rested one hand on Jonathan's arm, a gesture that would've made Moxie's eyes light up with interest. To be honest, I stared, too, for a second.

"I'm sure she'll be fine, Jon," Elyse said. "She has a dog with her."

"And I can take care of myself," I added.

Jonathan still hesitated, as if he wasn't convinced that Socrates offered much protection. He was probably also thinking about my propensity for getting into trouble.

"Honestly," I said, shooing him and Elyse away. "I'll be okay."

Jonathan gave me one more uncertain look, then he agreed, "All right. But be careful."

A few moments later, he and Elyse were walking across the park, trailed by four dogs. Artie looked back once to yip a farewell to Socrates, who'd come to my side.

"Well," I sighed, looking down at him. "I guess we better start looking around."

I'd promised Jonathan that I would be okay, but as I searched everywhere for the mask, and the park emptied out completely, I did start to get a little edgy.

Still, before I resigned myself to the fact that I'd have to pay for the missing part of the costume, I made one last trip back to the bench near the creek, just to make sure the rubber face hadn't fallen through the wooden slats.

Bending down, I felt around under the seat, only to hear a noise, close by.

I froze in place, then whispered, "Who's there?"

Nobody answered. But Socrates, at my side, *growled*. That almost never happened.

Rising slowly, the back of my neck prickling and my blood running cold, I ventured again, "Who's there?"

The words were barely out of my mouth when I caught a glimpse of white, moving behind a tree near the creek, and although I should've run away, I called, "Stop! Why are you spying on me?"

Then, as the person who'd observed me once before in that same park ran off into the night, I lurched forward in my big shoes—only to tumble headlong toward the water.

Chapter 35

"Are you okay?" Dylan asked. At least, I was pretty sure I'd heard him right. I was using Mr. Peachy's old landline phone, located in the bedroom loft, and Dylan's cell was a cheap, prepay thing from a discount store. "You could've drowned, Daph. Those shoes could've dragged you down. Sylvan Creek looks lazy, but it has some deep spots."

"I'm fine," I promised him, snuggling under my down comforter as the wind whistled around Plum Cottage's windows, rattling the panes right over my head. The temperature outside was dropping, but thanks to extra blankets and a roaring fire downstairs, I was finally starting to get warm after tumbling into the creek, hauling myself out, trudging shivering and bedraggled back to my van, and driving home without benefit of a heater. I really needed to get that fixed. "I probably have near hypothermia, but I'm alive."

Alive and humiliated. Not that anyone but the mysterious person in white had seen my accident. Thankfully, Jonathan, who had a way of witnessing all of my shoe-related mishaps, had already left for

Lighthouse Fellowship when I'd tried to chase after the young woman who seemed to be stalking me.

Who was she?

And what did she want with me . . . ?

"Daph? Are you there?"

"Oh, yeah," I said, shaking my phone, although I was pretty sure that was fine. The wires in my *head* had momentarily disconnected. I sat up just enough to reach for my mug of steaming hot, soothing chamomile tea with honey and lemon. Taking a quick sip, I snuggled back under the blankets, starting to feel the warmth reach my toes, which were tucked inside heavy, soft socks. "What were you saying?"

"We really need to talk."

I'd been getting sleepy, but my eyes flew wide open, and I glanced down at Socrates, who lay on the floor on his purple, velvet bed.

He lifted his head, just slightly, and shook it.

I took that to mean he agreed that midnight on an already disastrous night was a bad time to undertake a discussion that started with that ominous sentence.

Although those words were often prelude to a breakup, I didn't think Dylan was going to say that he didn't want to see me anymore.

I was starting to fear quite the opposite.

"Umm . . . I think our connection is getting worse," I told him, shaking the phone again. I wasn't being entirely untruthful. When the wind blew, the old lines that ran from the cottage to who knew where sometimes shorted out. "Can we do this some other time?"

There was a long silence, during which I thought one or both of our phones really had died, completely. Then Dylan agreed. "Sure. How about Casita Burrito? Thursday?"

"Okay," I said, but reluctantly.

Dylan and I had decided early on that we didn't want to have a relationship that required a lot of heavy, ponderous conversations about us.

Ideas, yes. We could dig into those for hours.

But us . . . ? No.

"I'll see you at the restaurant," I added, right before we both hung up.

A few minutes earlier, I'd been close to dozing off, like lucky Socrates, who was already snoring. But Dylan's request had disturbed that peace.

Sighing, I pulled myself upright and reached to my nightstand again, this time for the world's most effective sleep aid: *Sylvan Creek: A History*. If Asa Whitaker ever decided to market the book as a nonnarcotic, certainly nonaddictive, alternative to sleeping pills, he'd make enough money to buy Flynt Mansion outright for his historical society and support his dream museum for years to come.

"Let's see," I muttered, trying to find the last passage I'd read. I never stayed awake long enough to slip a bookmark between the pages. "Old barn burns down . . . volunteer fire company formed . . . men leave for World War Two . . ." At least I was getting somewhere. I hadn't read about the railroad in ages. I flipped one more page—and found myself plunked right down in 1963, as Sylvan Creek residents grappled with the Kennedy assassination.

"What the heck?" I scooched myself up straighter, wriggling against four down pillows to get comfortable. "Where's Moxie's favorite era?"

Thumbing back and forth through the book, I tried to figure out if I'd somehow missed the fifties. I couldn't imagine that Asa, who'd spent nearly twenty pages on the less-than-riveting year of 1905, alone, would skip an entire decade. Surely, something—a tornado, a department store opening, a minor car crash—had occurred *sometime* in those ten years.

But I couldn't find one reference to poodle skirts, the Cold War or Elvis Presley, as they'd impacted Sylvan Creek.

"That's really odd," I mused aloud.

I thought I was talking to myself, until I looked down at the foot of my bed, where a dark little ball of fur lay curled on the comforter.

At some point, Tinkleston had arrived, in his ninja way.

Not wanting to disturb him, I quietly replaced the book on my nightstand, crawled deeper into the nest of blankets again, and turned out the light.

In the darkness, I could hear the wind whipping around the cottage, Socrates's gentle snoring, and the crackling fire downstairs. Gradually, my mind began to settle again, and to wander, first to another fireplace, where I'd seen a charred manuscript, a page of which had included the cryptic words and numbers, *Benedict Flyn . . . 195 . . . congregation . . . scandalo . . .*

Was that the start of a date?

A year in the 1950s, when something "scandalous" had happened, involving a congregation and someone named *Flynt?*

Curling into a ball, like Tinks, I drew my blankets closer to my chin, thinking about Lighthouse Fellowship, too. And the Lutheran congregation that used to call the building home . . . until the 1950s.

Was there a connection?

If so, my brain was too tired to make it, and before long, I'd drifted into a deep and dreamless sleep, only to be awakened in what seemed like minutes by a paw tapping on my face and the shrill sound of the telephone ringing right next to my head.

Carefully edging away from Tinkleston, who looked like sleep had restored his devilish side, I picked up the phone and said, "Hello?"

"Daphne!" the caller snapped, in a voice as harsh as the ring. And before I could even guess why my mother was angry with me, she ordered me, in no uncertain terms, "Get over here right now! We are all waiting for you!"

Chapter 36

I'd never been to the reading of a will before, but apparently these events started right on time, as Larry Fox had warned me. And if my first experience was to be trusted, will readings were also formal affairs. Unfortunately, no one had told me that. As I opened the door to a conference room at Larry's practice, which was located in a stately old brick building just off Market Street, I discovered that everyone was staring at me, impatiently. And I was the only person in jeans.

Asa Whitaker, who fidgeted on one of the metal folding chairs that had been set up to hold the small crowd, looked professorial in a tweedy suit. By his side, his wife, Martha—presumably there on behalf of the library—wore a shirt embroidered with autumn leaves and the slogan, *Fall Into Books!* But she'd paired that with a black skirt and pumps.

Two rows ahead of them, I spied Pastor Pete Kishbaugh, who hadn't been arrested overnight. He sat like a black hole in the middle of the room, tugging at the collar of his clerical shirt. Meeting my gaze, he waved. I was still upset with him, but I waved back, on the presumption that, in spite of the evidence I'd found, he was innocent until proven guilty in a court of law.

A few chairs over, Tamara Fox, who was probably representing every other charity Miss Flynt had once had a hand in, kept alternately checking a gold wristwatch, flipping her long, dark hair, and sighing, like she had a million other will readings to attend.

I looked between Pastor Pete and Tamara, recalling how they'd argued, heatedly, at the Wolf Hollow Mill.

Did Tamara know anything about Pastor Kishbaugh's travels?

Had she ever gone with him to Paris or Rome . . . ?

I couldn't ponder those questions right then. I needed to take a seat, and I edged past a bunch of people I didn't know—maybe Miss Flynt's out-of-town, distant relatives?—and Bea Baumgartner, whom I hadn't expected to be there. She wasn't exactly dressed like a Talbots model like Tamara, but she had donned dark pants and a conservative, if rumpled, shirt that buttoned down the front.

I still considered Bea a strong suspect in Lillian's murder, and I didn't appreciate how she'd pointed a gun at me, but I greeted her, too, as I moved farther into the too silent room, heading toward my mother, who sat in the front row, glaring at me.

Needless to say, Maeve Templeton was dressed in a smart, navy blue suit. The day's silk scarf, which I knew she would've liked to twist around my neck, was pale green and white. And her hair . . .

"Wow, that is an interesting cut," I whispered, sliding into a seat next to her. "Yikes."

Even the numbing treatments that I *knew* my mother indulged in couldn't keep the corners of her mouth from turning downward. "Don't make this worse, Daphne," she warned me, lightly and self-consciously touching the back of her hair, which was clipped short, while the front was rather long. I'd seen similar cuts before, but Mom's was *very* dramatic. "I am not happy with you—nor Moxie—right now."

"I actually like it," I said honestly. "It takes ten years off your face. And Moxie didn't even use needles!"

My mother didn't appreciate the joke. She got a thunderous look in her eyes, and she opened her mouth. But before she could reply, the door at the back of the room opened again, and everybody swiveled around to see that Larry Fox was joining us.

"I understand that we're all assembled," he said somberly, while shooting me a very dark look. "Everyone is in attendance?"

I had no idea if everyone affected by the will was there, and I was too distracted to even nod, because, while I'd been ill-advisedly teasing my mother, two other people had slipped into the room.

I first noticed Jonathan Black, who stood against the back wall, leaning casually against the oak wainscoting. I knew that he was very alert, though, and wouldn't miss a thing.

Then I spied a pale young woman, who lurked in the far, back corner of the room, her arms folded around herself, like she was trying to blend into the woodwork.

Gasping, I clutched my mother's arm, which was also the wrong thing to do.

"Daphne," Mom snapped, but quietly. She tried to peel my fingers off her suit jacket. "Get a hold of yourself! You're making a scene!"

"I'm sorry," I said, releasing her. She clearly wasn't in the mood for more drama, but I couldn't help confiding softly, "I think my *stalker* is here!"

Chapter 37

It was very difficult to concentrate on Larry Fox's sonorous reading of Miss Flynt's last will and testament. As he droned on about "probate," "residual estates," and "lapsed gifts," I kept sneaking peeks at Jonathan, who never seemed to lose focus. His posture remained relaxed, but I could tell that he was following every word and simultaneously watching all of us potential inheritors.

I tried to catch his eye, so I could silently urge him to notice the young woman in the corner of the room, but his attention remained trained on Larry, and he wouldn't even look at me. So I had to check in with her now and then myself, usually to discover that she was observing me.

As Larry flipped yet another page, still not getting to the actual dispersal of property, I risked my mother's censure and turned around one more time, just as the younger woman quickly looked away, pretending like she was staring at something out the window.

I took the opportunity to study her again, as I'd done the night of the Fur-ever Friends gala. Only this time, the light was better, and I could estimate her age at about twenty-five or twenty-six. She was pale, as I'd judged before, and her complexion was washed out more by an old-fashioned ivory blouse with a lace collar. Her gaze darted nervously around, and she kept playing with a lock of her curly, shapeless, brown hair.

She seemed awfully timid, for a stalker. . . .

"Did you hear me, Miss Templeton?"

"What?" I asked, spinning around, because apparently Larry Fox had addressed me. He sat behind a gleaming mahogany desk at the front of the room with the will in one hand, his reading glasses pushed up into his thick, white hair, and a deep, disapproving scowl on his tanned face. "I'm sorry," I apologized. "What did you say?"

I expected him to tell me to face forward and pay attention. He seemed to be taking his job very seriously.

Instead, he slipped the glasses back onto his nose and resumed reading on behalf of Miss Flynt, telling me and everyone else, in a voice much deeper than Lillian's, "And to Daphne Templeton, I leave my beloved Persian cat, Budgely's Sir Peridot Tinkleston, trusting that she will care for him until his natural demise."

"Yes, I saw that coming," I whispered to Mom, who turned to me and made a shushing motion, with one finger to her lips.

Assuming that my part in the proceedings was done, and that the reading would go on for a long time, I started to stand up and make a discreet exit. I also hoped that the young woman in the corner would follow me, so I could ask what the heck she wanted with me.

Then my butt plopped back down onto the metal

chair when Larry Fox added, "I also bequeath to Daphne Templeton the oil painting entitled *Woman in Red Three*, with faith that she will intuit and fulfill my wishes, regarding that piece."

"No . . ." I was pretty sure Martha Whitaker launched that soft protest. Apparently, she'd hoped for the painting. Maybe to display it in the library?

I, meanwhile, was baffled. It probably wasn't proper protocol, but I couldn't help breaking into Larry's narrative to ask, "What does *that* mean? What are her 'wishes'?"

My mother had discouraged me from grabbing her, but she squeezed my arm so hard that I was afraid I'd get a bruise.

She was silencing me because, in her opinion, I was once again making a scene. But she was also trying to hear Larry, who ignored me and forged ahead, reading, "And I leave my ancestral home, located at 2331 Wallapawakee Vista Drive, to the Sylvan Creek Historical Society, for the property's maintenance, in perpetuity, as a museum dedicated to the history of the community I so loved. . . ."

Behind me, I heard Asa Whitaker hiss, "Yesss!" I could imagine him doing some sort of historical version of a fist pump, whatever that might be.

Was that wise, given that his wife had just been disappointed by the inexplicable bequest to me?

Was Asa in for another tongue-lashing from Martha, like he'd experienced the night of Miss Flynt's murder?

Whatever fate he was destined to suffer, it probably wouldn't compare to the fury my mother was about to unleash on Larry Fox.

Maeve Templeton didn't like outbursts, and she

didn't often show emotion, but more than anything, she hated being cheated out of a million-dollar real estate deal, and she nearly pushed me off my chair as she leaped up to her feet, roaring, "No! This was NOT Lillian's intent!"

Chapter 38

"Maeve, please calm down," Larry urged, raising one hand. "I promise you, the will represents Lillian's final wishes, and it is duly witnessed."

"Of course it is," Asa Whitaker interjected. I turned to see him half rising from his chair, but Martha pulled him back into his seat, with a strong arm and a sharp, silencing glance.

"I want to see those signatures," my mother demanded. I'd seen her scrappy side before, many times, but I'd never seen her in full fight mode. The sight was quite impressive. Grabbing her tote bag from the floor, she slung it over her shoulder and stormed up to the desk, her Ferragamo pumps clicking on the hardwood floor. "I want to see the date—and the time, if possible—that this document went into effect!"

"The time is not available," Larry said. "You know that, Maeve. You deal with many legal documents"

"Show me the date, then," Mom repeated, thumping her tote bag down onto the desk. I wasn't sure why she was carrying that along everywhere, but I assumed she had her reasons. She glared at Larry Fox,

Esquire, like he was the cause of the mix-up. Which was possible. He *was* in charge of the estate. "Now, Larry."

I glanced over my shoulder to see how Jonathan was reacting to the type of drama Moxie had warned me might break out, but he maintained his SEAL composure and observed impassively.

Then I looked to the other side of the room, trying to keep tabs on my stalker. But she was gone.

I didn't know what to make of that, and I faced forward again, in time to see Larry flip through the entire will, to the last page, which he spun around so my mother could read the signatures, right side up.

The whole thing wasn't really my business, but I drifted up to join my mom, reading over her shoulder.

Then my eyes got huge, because if the date written in Lillian's handwriting, and affixed again by her witness, Larry Fox, was correct, the will had last been updated the *day of Miss Flynt's death.*

That had to mean something. And my mother didn't miss the significance, either, although she wasn't interested in catching a killer. Just reeling in a big sale.

"I have a listing agreement dated from the morning of that same day," Mom said, dumping the entire contents of her tote bag onto the desk. She wasn't normally a disorganized, flustered person, but there was a lot at stake, and she let everything tumble out of the bag—including a bunch of stuff she'd taken from the mansion when she'd swept it clean prior to Elyse's arrival. As usual, she hadn't returned the clutter. A few pens and a paperback novel skidded across the shiny desktop, followed by a wadded up ball of fabric. "Lillian Flynt committed to selling her house—in writing," Mom insisted, locating a paper she'd kept tucked in a black folder. She held the document up for Larry's inspection. "Like her will, my listing agreement is valid under Pennsylvania law. It is a contract between Lillian and myself, which could not be voided without her written consent. Which she *did not* give me."

Mom had a decent point, but I was only half listening by then. My attention had been drawn to the pile of fabric, which looked like a *jacket*.

As Larry and Mom argued over which document took precedence—a fight that I could imagine going all the way to a real courtroom—I unfolded the windbreaker, which smelled musty and felt damp, like it had been crumpled up while wet.

The beige jacket was nondescript, except for an insignia on the chest. The small symbol, which incorporated a bird flying out of a burning book and an old-fashioned pen, looked vaguely familiar to me.

I was trying to place where I'd seen that mark when someone reached past me and took the garment from my hands.

Jonathan Black studied the jacket, too, for quite a long time. Then he interrupted the ongoing argument between realtor and attorney by asking my mother, quietly but firmly, "Is this yours, Ms. Templeton?"

I wasn't sure why he seemed so deadly serious, until I recalled that whoever killed Lillian Flynt had almost certainly gotten wet in the process.

Looking at the jacket again, I also finally noticed something that Jonathan had probably spotted right away.

A few small specks, near the left cuff, that looked a lot like dried blood.

Chapter 39

"I'm not surprised that you were remembered in Lillian's will," Piper said, as she rode with me, Moxie, and Socrates to Flynt Mansion the day after the fiasco at Larry Fox's office. Piper was in the backseat, by choice. She wasn't a fan of my driving and would've insisted that we take her Acura to go check out my inheritance, if the sedan hadn't been in the shop—not because something was broken, but for preventative maintenance, in anticipation of winter. My sister always kept her car in tip-top shape. "Lillian always spoke very highly of you," Piper added. "She admired your work with rescue dogs, in particular, and told me several times that *you* should run Whiskered Away Home."

"Really?" I asked, turning onto Lakeshore Drive. The surface of Lake Wallapawakee was churning that day, the water gray under an equally leaden sky. "Because she usually treated me like an intern. I didn't expect to inherit anything but Tinkleston. And I don't understand why she didn't leave detailed instructions about the painting. How am I supposed to know what to do with it?"

"Maybe she just wants you to hang it over your

mantel," Moxie suggested, leaning forward, because Socrates had somehow nudged her out of the front passenger seat, so she was riding in the back, too. "That's possible."

"I don't think so," I said. "I got the sense that Miss Flynt had bigger plans for the *Woman in Red Three.*" I met Piper's gaze in the rearview mirror. "Seriously, don't you think the whole thing is a little strange? And—again—why me?"

"Lillian was eccentric," Piper reminded me. "And she saw something in you. Some promise that, let's face it, I don't always see. Especially when I'm riding in a van that might not make it up a small hill, thanks to your neglect, while I'm seated on a 2012 calendar so I don't get poked by the spring that is sticking up out of the backseat."

I grinned at Socrates, who was enjoying riding shotgun. He looked almost happy. "I knew that calendar was in here somewhere!"

"I can't believe you're getting a painting *and* a cat," Moxie noted, dropping back against her seat again. "It's like winning the lottery, only sadder. And a little scary, if you don't like being pounced on."

Moxie had visited Plum Cottage that morning and, while Tinkleston was warming up to me, he'd attempted his trademark refrigerator launch on her. Fortunately for Moxie, the icebox was only about four feet high, and he'd slammed harmlessly into her shoulder before plopping to the floor and running away. Still, I apologized again. "Sorry about that. I'm pretty sure that happened to Mom once, too."

"Do you think she's really in trouble over that jacket?" Piper asked, sounding concerned. Of course, I'd filled her and Moxie in on everything that had happened at the reading of the will. "Surely, Detective

Black doesn't believe that Maeve Templeton would own, let alone wear, a cheap nylon windbreaker. She dragged him all over creation to look at houses. He must've noticed that she never wears anything without a designer label."

"I'm not sure," I said, pressing the gas pedal, because we'd turned onto the hilly road leading up to Flynt Mansion. Ahead of us, the house loomed ominously against the dark clouds. "He seemed pretty grim."

"Where did your mom get the jacket, anyhow?" Moxie asked.

"She snatched it off the floor, from behind a chair near the back door, when she did her last minute, preshowing straightening at the mansion," I explained. "She jammed it into her tote and promptly forgot about it."

"Sounds like the jacket might belong to the killer, huh?" Piper ventured. "If, of course, the spots really were bloodstains."

"Jonathan said it'll take a day or two for the lab to determine if the stains are blood, and—if so—whether the blood is Miss Flynt's," I said. "In the meantime, Mom's not supposed to leave Sylvan Creek."

"I remember getting that order," Piper said glumly.

"Let's not get too worried yet," I urged, parking the van in front of the estate's high iron gates. Then I got out and helped Socrates hop down from his seat. Now that the car ride was over, he didn't seem excited to return to the mansion that had yielded Tinkleston. His tail hung lower than usual.

Moxie, meanwhile, couldn't get inside the house fast enough. "Can we please get going?" she requested.

I turned to see her warily scanning the sky, her hand over her head. She wore a white wool coat with wide

lapels that were pulled up around a black turtleneck.
Her hair, now an even lighter shade of platinum blond,
was drawn back into a sleek helmet. I recognized Kim
Novak's character, Madeleine Elster, from the classic
Hitchcock film, *Vertigo*.

"What's the rush?" I asked.

Moxie kept her eyes trained upward. "Ever since the
Fur-ever Friends fund-raiser, with all the creepy crows,
I've really started to dislike birds. They're the turtles of
the sky!"

"You might want to stop channeling Hitchcock's
muses soon," Piper observed. She must've watched
Vertigo, too, at some point. And she'd seen Moxie's
Tippi Hedren getup at the gala. "You can carry these
things too far, you know."

"You might be right," Moxie admitted, nevertheless
wrapping her coat more tightly around herself and
hurrying to the covered porch.

Socrates and I joined her, followed by Piper, who
lagged behind. She was skeptical about the adventure,
although I'd assured her that, as a bona fide heiress to
at least a tiny part of the Flynt estate, I had every right
to check out my property, now that the house was no
longer surrounded by crime scene tape.

"How are we going to get inside?" Piper asked,
glancing around, as if we might get arrested at any
moment. "Do you have a key?"

"No, but the lock is faulty and easy to spring," I informed her. To prove my point, I rattled the knob, then
turned it and swung open the tall, wooden door. "See?"

Moxie ducked into the foyer, followed by Socrates,
while Piper grabbed my arm, holding me back. "I don't
know about this, Daphne. Did you actually hear Larry
Fox authorize you to do this?"

Had I implied that I had *official* permission?

Because that would've been a slight exaggeration.

I was just about to tell Piper that if she was really concerned, she should follow her conscience and wait on the porch—when Moxie called to us, her voice practically quivering with excitement: "Please, please tell me you inherited the *Tuttweiler*!"

Chapter 40

"The what-weiler?" I asked, joining Moxie and Socrates in the mansion's parlor. Piper had succumbed to curiosity and reluctantly come inside, too. Moxie stood in front of the painting of the woman in the red dress, appraising it with one gloved hand resting under her chin. She looked very elegant as Kim Novak, and if I hadn't agreed with Piper that my best friend might be carrying her "homage" phase too far, I would've suggested she keep the look. "What is a Tuttweiler?"

"Only a painting by one of the best portrait artists of the 1950s!" Moxie informed me. She really knew that decade inside out. I sometimes wondered if she'd been reincarnated and maintained some knowledge from a past life. "His work is very sought after!"

"Really?" Piper asked. She cocked her head, just like Socrates was doing. I recalled that he'd studied the painting before, in a similar way, no doubt recognizing its quality, if not its pedigree. He was more discriminating than I was when it came to art. "It just looks like a regular old portrait to me."

"Oh, no," Moxie objected, stepping closer to the painting and pointing to the woman's severe eyes. "See

how he used impasto to make her look so angry?"
Moxie shook her head and sighed, in a bemused way.
"Classic Tuttweiler!"

"He used *pasta*?" I asked. "Like a kid in preschool,
making *macaroni art*?"

Moxie, Piper, and I went back a long way, and we
normally had what I considered to be set roles in our
relationship. Piper was the sensible, smart one; I was
the carefree adventurer; and Moxie was the lovable
ditz. But when it came to art—and the 1950s—Moxie
was the expert. Now that those two things were inter-
secting, she sounded like a genius to me.

"Impasto is a painting technique," she said. "It's all
about using thick paint to create texture and mood.
Davis Tuttweiler had a unique way of incorporating
impasto into portraits. That's how he got her to look so
pretty, but mean."

"How do you know all this, Moxie?" Piper asked. She
was also clearly thrown off, to be supplanted, even temporarily, by a new "smart one." "Where did you learn
about art?"

Moxie beamed proudly. "I took oil painting lessons
at Perfect Palette before I worked on Daphne's van. I
learned all kinds of techniques, and ate some really
good tapas, too."

If only the people who ran the little art store on
Market Street, where tourists and locals could take
workshops accompanied by gourmet fare and wine,
had taught Moxie to paint a realistic dog.

At least she'd learned something, though.

"Are you *sure* it's a Tuttweiler?" I asked her.

She pointed at the bottom of the portrait. "Well,
even if I didn't recognize his style, his signature is
right there."

"Oh, yeah." I had definitely assumed the "ditz" role.

I hoped this version of *Freaky Friday* wouldn't last too long.

"Do you have any idea what it's worth?" Piper asked Moxie.

She shook her head. "No clue. Who can put a monetary value on art?"

"Umm . . . lots of people," Piper reminded her. "They're called art dealers."

Okay, things were getting back to normal.

"I wonder who she is," I mused aloud, studying the woman's face. The longer I looked at her, the more I judged her to be striking, as opposed to classically beautiful. Her jaw was a little wide, her dark eyebrows were a bit thick, and her eyes were . . . *familiar*, somehow.

Piper apparently agreed. "You know, there's something about her," she observed quietly. "I feel like I recognize her, but I can't say why, exactly."

"I don't know who she is," Moxie said, rubbing her arms like she'd suddenly gotten cold. She looked around the room. "But I bet she's the ghost who haunts this place."

My pragmatic, logical sister snapped out of her reverie. She moved toward the staircase. "That's just an old story. There's no such thing as ghosts."

"Where are you going?" I asked.

"I really need to use the bathroom, if you must know," Piper said. "There must be two upstairs, right?"

"Probably," I said. I knew that she didn't want to disturb the room where Lillian had died, not because she was afraid, but because, in spite of the lack of crime scene tape, the police might still be investigating. "Although, I didn't open every door."

Piper wasn't listening. She was halfway up the stairs.

When she was out of earshot, Moxie said, "I don't care what Piper says. I can feel the spirit of the woman in the painting in this room, right now. And she's still angry about something."

I was open to the possibility of energy that lived on after we died, and I trusted Moxie's paranormal instincts.

Sensible Socrates disagreed. He finally dragged his attention away from the portrait so he could roll his eyes at us.

"I wonder what made her so mad," I mused aloud, ignoring Socrates and meeting the woman in red's gaze. It felt like she was staring right back at me. Davis Tuttweiler really must've been a master of his technique. "It's like a mystery within a mystery." I faced Moxie again. "I almost feel like her story is linked to Miss Flynt's murder."

"Maybe we should hold a séance," Moxie suggested, growing excited, even as Socrates whined softly. He clearly thought that potential activity would be pure folly. Moxie ignored him, too, adding, "We could try to talk to *both* of them!"

"First of all, you two are not breaking in here again," Piper said. I hadn't even heard her rejoin us. "And, second, this place isn't haunted by ghosts. A *living, breathing* human being is staying here!"

Chapter 41

I had tons of questions churning around in my brain, which felt like the choppy waters of Lake Wallapawakee, and I moved restlessly around Plum Cottage after dropping off Piper and Moxie.

I couldn't even concentrate on the Scrumptious Salmon Dinner I was making for Tinkleston, who'd found a comfortable spot among the herbs on the kitchen windowsill. Crouched down behind the rosemary and thyme, he looked like a miniature wildcat, spying on me from the jungle.

"Did Lillian ever talk to you?" I asked him, while I mixed up canned salmon, mashed broccoli and carrots, some whole wheat bread crumbs, and a few pinches of brewer's yeast, for an extra nutritional boost. "Did she tell you any of her secrets?"

Tinkleston yawned, which was better than hissing. But that response didn't answer my queries.

Absently stirring the bowl of food, I stared out the window, hardly even noticing the red, gold, and orange leaves falling from the trees.

What does Lillian want me to do with the painting?

Who's the strange woman who seems to be following me?

Why was the shower wet, when Piper used the spare bathroom at Miss Flynt's?

What's the insignia on the jacket mean?

Why is a decade missing from Asa Whitaker's history?

Will Moxie ever be able to go outside again, without worrying about birds?

WHO THE HECK KILLED LILLIAN FLYNT?

The questions kept swirling around in my mind, randomly, and I finally realized that I needed to take some kind of action to solve at least a few of those puzzles.

Leaving the salmon on the floor for Tinks and filling Socrates' special bowl with his homemade dog food, too, in case he woke up from his postadventure nap while I was gone, I pulled on my boots and my denim jacket. Then I stepped out into the chilly afternoon, headed for the one place that might be able to provide me with some answers.

If I didn't get arrested the moment I walked in the door.

Chapter 42

The Sylvan Creek Public Library was located in a refurbished 1850s Italianate house on the edge of Pettigrew Park. The elegant yellow building—surrounded on all sides by a wide porch and topped with a square, four-windowed cupola—always reminded me of a wedding cake. When I was a child, I used to love exploring the many sun-drenched rooms, all filled with tall shelves overflowing with books, like a maze within a maze. Sometimes I'd hide from my mother, forcing her to search all three floors for me before I'd allow myself to be dragged home.

I had given up that game long ago, but I still hoped no one would find me as I sat behind a computer monitor in the library's only dark room, which was set aside for the few of us Sylvan Creek residents who didn't have Internet access, maybe related to problems with a cell phone or a move into a cottage that had no Wi-Fi.

Not surprisingly, I was alone, but I worked quickly in hopes of avoiding a certain librarian, whom I'd sneaked past once already on the way in. Fingers flying, I did a search for biographies of artists, which led to a site called *americanartists.com*. Moments later, I found a page dedicated to Davis Tuttweiler, and I scanned the text.

> *American painter . . . 1927–2010 . . . Much sought after portrait artist in the 1950s and 1960s . . . mercurial personality . . . distinctive brushwork . . . impasto . . . Many works considered missing . . . likely forgotten in attics, their value unknown . . . one surviving daughter, Fidelia, from a late in life fifth marriage, quickly annulled . . . works valued from two hundred thousand to three hundred thousand dollars . . .*

I reread that last part, once I got my eyes popped back into my head.

Was "my" painting worth that much?

Was that really possible?

I didn't think so, and I refused to get excited until I had the portrait evaluated. For all I knew, someone else had painted *Woman in Red Three* and scrawled *Tuttweiler* on the bottom. Moxie wasn't *really* an expert on art. Although *impasto* had turned out to be a real thing.

I also didn't know if I was supposed to sell the painting. And if I did, I wouldn't keep the money. I seriously doubted that Lillian's intent was to make me rich.

"Moving on," I said softly, clicking off that page and returning to the search engine. Typing rapidly again, I tried different combinations of the keywords *bird, flames, pen, book,* and *insignia.* But nothing came up. At least, nothing relevant. I did learn that the Alpha Sigma Pi fraternity at the University of Akron, Ohio, had a phoenix on their crest, but the bird looked nothing like the one on the jacket Mom had found at Flynt Mansion.

"Interesting, if uninformative," I said, sitting back and moving to shut down the browser for the day.

Then I glanced at the clock on the bottom of the screen and decided I had a few more minutes to spare, not to mention curiosity to burn.

I probably could've done some more investigating related to the murder while I had Internet access, but on impulse, I returned to the search engine one more time and did some research on another topic that would probably meet with Jonathan Black's disapproval.

Fingers hesitating just one extra second above the keyboard, I typed in *Elyse Hunter-Black*.

Chapter 43

It was late afternoon by the time I logged off as a guest user on the library's computer, and I hurried through the stacks toward the exit, hoping that Martha Whitaker was on a break, or better yet, gone for the day.

I was also taking stock of everything I'd learned about Elyse Hunter-Black, who was all over the Internet. I'd seen pictures of her air-kissing her sorority sisters at a Harvard homecoming, more traditionally kissing Jonathan at a fancy party at her parents' house in the Hamptons, and even receiving one of those Daytime Emmy awards that nobody hears about, but which is still an Emmy.

Even Elyse's home was successful. Her sleek, modern Manhattan loft had been featured in the August 2015 edition of *Fine Living* magazine.

All at once, I stopped short, recalling how Elyse had pressed for the inclusion of the Tuttweiler painting in the sale of Flynt Mansion, even though all of the artwork in her apartment was abstract and angular.

I could hear Elyse's rationale, and it didn't ring true. *"I believe it just* belongs *with the property. . . ."*

I resumed creeping through the shelves, whispering

under my breath, "'Belongs,' my foot. I bet she knows the painting's value."

Then I stopped talking, because I'd reached the building's grand foyer, which now served as the library's lobby.

Bending slightly, I peeked around a column, trying to see the counter where Martha Whitaker usually stood, checking out books and collecting fines.

Fortunately, she wasn't at her post, and I quickly tiptoed across the gleaming parquet floor, wishing I'd worn different shoes. Maybe my moccasins.

However, even with my boots on, it seemed that I was going to escape.

I reached for the knob to open one of two massive, arched doors—the last things standing between me and freedom—only to hear Martha calling, way too loudly for a library, "Daphne Templeton! Stop right there!"

Chapter 44

"You should know that the computers are for patrons *in good standing*, Daphne," Martha informed me. Scowling, she lowered the reading glasses she kept on a chain around her neck. Her expression was at odds with her black shirt, which featured a cute, green alien holding a book and the slogan, *Take Me to Your Reader!* "You are not to use the Internet if you have outstanding fines!"

"How did you know I was using a computer?" I asked. I didn't like the idea of her spying on me. "Were you *watching me*?"

"Yes," she said, sounding smugly proud of herself. Then she pointed to a monitor on a desk behind the counter. The image on the screen changed every second or so to reveal a different part of the library. "Of course, we have security cameras everywhere. People are always trying to sneak in beverages."

Jeez, I'd almost done that, too. I liked to stay hydrated while I conducted research.

"I'm sorry, Martha, but my fines are at least a decade old," I reminded her. "At least! I don't think I've had an overdue book since I was a teenager!"

And I hardly ever went to the library anymore. I got

all my reading material from the Philosopher's Tome, where Tom Flinchbaugh allowed me to borrow anything I wanted, without ever levying a fine if I kept something too long.

He might not have had a degree in library science, but Tom had the true heart of a librarian. Martha Whitaker was more like a parody, always shushing people and nagging about fines, like she was doing right then.

"We maintain records for *thirty years*," she advised me, pulling a keyboard closer to herself and tapping rapidly on the keys. She stared at her computer screen, but continued lecturing me. "Funding for public libraries is limited and growing more scarce, thanks to government cutbacks. We can't afford to let *scofflaws* abuse the library and its holdings."

I was pretty sure I'd just been insulted. "Hey, I was just a kid . . ."

Martha wasn't listening. She continued typing and shook her head, talking more to herself than me. "Now that Lillian is gone, I intend to pursue every last dime. *She* refused to be aggressive. Said the library should be a *welcoming* place. Well, a shuttered, empty, bankrupt building isn't very welcoming!" Still shaking her head, she began to mutter, clearly forgetting that I was even there. "We've already lost the archives, thanks to Lillian and her policies and her *will*. The whole research wing will close next month. Not that Lillian cared!"

Martha had drifted into her own world, and I held my breath, hoping she'd keep typing and oversharing.

But she suddenly caught herself, and all the color drained from her face as her head jerked up and she met my gaze again. For once, she didn't seem to know what to say. "I . . . I . . ."

I took advantage of her uncertainty. "Why did you

mention Miss Flynt's will?" I asked, hoping she was unnerved enough to actually answer me.

But she averted her eyes. "No reason."

"Did Lillian promise *you* the painting?" I pressed. "For the library? Because I heard you gasp when Larry Fox announced that I was getting the Tuttweiler."

Martha's cheeks flushed, and I saw a glint of anger in her steely gray eyes. "Lillian did mention that she might donate the portrait to the library, upon her demise. But apparently, she changed her mind."

No wonder Martha was practically attacking me over some ancient fees. She probably hated me, right then. I was about to take possession of an object that might've been able to save the archives, if the portrait really could be sold for several hundred thousand dollars.

All at once, I jolted.

What if Martha—who obviously hated Lillian—had tried to secure her expected "donation" early, and save her precious archives? Which would also save her husband's job?

In fact, the library would probably become Martha's fiefdom, now that strong-willed Lillian was out of the way, no longer able to impose her ideas on the board of directors.

Martha and I were staring at each other, and I swore she understood exactly what I was thinking. Her eyes got hard and cold again, and she swung the monitor around so we could both see it.

"You have nearly forty dollars' worth of outstanding fines, Miss Templeton," she told me, in a low, even, almost threatening voice. "Were you aware of that?"

"No . . ." It was my turn to feel unsure and somewhat chastened.

Martha seemed to grasp that she was regaining the upper hand, and she grew more composed, turning the monitor back toward herself. "Let's see," she said, her eyes sweeping back and forth as she scanned the screen. "Titles you were late to return include *A Pony for Tessie, Mr. BeeBop's Circus Adventure,* and *Little Kitty in the Big City*"—she lowered her glasses for a moment to give me a scathing glance—"which you never brought back." Then she pushed the glasses back up on her nose and resumed reading. "And, more recently, you have accrued debts for *Tennis for Dummies, The Care and Feeding of Tarantulas,* and *What's Happening to My Body: A Guide to Puberty.*"

I reared back, confused.

I knew why I'd borrowed the book about spiders in fifth grade, and why I'd needed help with puberty. My mother hadn't given me much information on that second topic. But when had I ever expressed any interest in tennis?

"Would you like to pay by cash, check, or credit card?" Martha asked, holding out her hand.

I had only a few dollars in my pocket, and I started digging for them. "I'll pay cash, but I only have—"

But before I could explain that I would need to return with a check, someone slapped a wallet down on the counter next to me and said, "Please, let me make a down payment on Ms. Templeton's fines, as a show of good faith, until you two can work out a plan for reimbursement."

I turned slowly to see who was coming to my aid and immediately knew that the kind offer would have strings attached.

Big, tangled strings.

Chapter 45

"How much of my conversation with Martha did you hear?" I asked Jonathan, when we were outside the library, strolling through the park toward Market Street. The sun had come out, and Sylvan Creek's small commercial district was busy with shoppers, dog walkers, and folks in town for homecoming at Wynton University. The air was crisp, and I wrapped my jacket more tightly around myself—sort of shrinking into it, too. I was pretty embarrassed. "Did you hear the actual roster of books . . . ?"

I didn't have to finish the question. Jonathan's grin gave me my answer, before he informed me, "I heard enough."

I felt my cheeks getting hot. "I needed a book! Can you imagine talking with Maeve Templeton about puberty? She told me it was something not to be discussed, then gave me some money to buy—"

Jonathan cleared his throat loudly, cutting me off. "For once, I think your mother is right. Let's change the subject. Please."

"Fine," I agreed, as we turned onto Market Street. I had no idea where either one of us was headed. My van was back at the library. "But did you hear the stuff *before* the embarrassing revelations about my childhood reading habits—which have definitely evolved." I had to insert that quick defense of myself. I didn't want him to think I was still reading about Mr. BeeBop's adventures at the circus or, heaven forbid, how to score a tennis match. "Did you hear everything Martha said about hating Miss Flynt? And how much she wanted the painting I inherited?"

"No, I missed all that," Jonathan said. "But I already know about their feuds."

"Well, did you know about the portrait? The Tuttweiler? And how Martha thought Miss Flynt was going to leave it to the library? Which would've allowed Martha to keep the archives open—and save Asa's job?"

"Could you go back a few steps, please?" Jonathan requested. "And go more slowly. You lost me at 'Tuttweiler.'"

He'd stopped walking, right in front of the Kind Cow Creamery, which had a window open to the sidewalk, like gelato shops in Italy. As I waited, he ordered two cones of Pumpkin Spice Cheesecake. But before he could pull out his wallet again, I found the ten-dollar bill in my pocket and quickly handed it over to the kid behind the counter.

"Thank you," Jonathan said, smiling as I accepted my change. He offered me one of the cones. "I didn't expect that."

"I really do want to start paying you back," I said, taking a big bite of the custard, which was swirled through with actual sweet and tangy cheesecake. As I wiped my mouth with my sleeve, I recalled two times I'd walked out of restaurants, leaving Jonathan to foot the bill. "For the meals you've bought me. The lock for my door—which was very kind of you. And the loan at the library. Everything."

"Repay me for the lock by using it," Jonathan suggested, still grinning. "And buy the library a new copy of *Little Kitty in the Big City* before you give me another dime." He resumed walking. "Now, getting back to the portrait—and the library . . . ?"

"Oh, yeah." I took one more quick lick, then told him, "I was at the library to learn more about the painting Miss Flynt left me—"

"Yes," Jonathan interrupted me. He wrapped a napkin he'd grabbed from a dispenser at the creamery around his cone before it dripped. "That was a strange bequest. People don't usually ask heirs to intuit their intentions."

"I know, right?" I agreed. "Anyhow, Moxie recognized the artist's name and style."

"So the painting dates to the fifties or sixties?" Jonathan guessed.

"Yes," I told him, not surprised that he recalled Moxie's interest in that era, which had helped to solve the last murder we'd been tangled up in together. "So I went to the library, and I learned that portraits by Davis Tuttweiler—the artist—can sell for several hundred thousand dollars."

Jonathan's dark eyebrows shot up. "That's quite a bit. Congratulations."

I shook my head. "No, no. I don't think Miss Flynt wanted me to hang the painting or sell it for personal gain. I think she had something else in mind. Maybe something charitable?"

"Wow."

I looked up to see Jonathan watching me with something like admiration in his eyes.

"What?" I asked. "Why are you looking at me like that?"

"I've seen people commit murder for less money," he said. "I'm impressed that you aren't running over to Flynt Mansion, snatching up your inheritance, and selling it to the highest bidder."

I shrugged. "As Democritus once wisely said, *Happiness resides not in possessions.* I guess money's not my thing."

"No, I don't think it is."

He was teasing me again, because I owed him so much.

"Anyhow, I'm pretty sure Martha expected the library to get the painting," I said, overlooking his comment. "Then she could've sold it and used the money to save the archives, which are scheduled to be shut down. And when that happens, Asa will be out of a job."

We were strolling past Templeton Animal Hospital. The purple and yellow mums in the window boxes were thriving under Piper's care—and the HELP WANTED sign was still in the window.

Maybe Asa could apply there, depending on who was leaving. . . .

"Daphne?"

I realized I'd gotten distracted, and I turned to see that Jonathan was offering me a napkin.

"What? What's wrong?"

He pointed to my chin. "You have some ice cream . . ."

"Oh." I accepted the napkin and wiped my face. "So, like I was saying, I think Martha might've been desperate enough to try to get her inheritance early."

But Jonathan shook his head. "I don't think so, Daphne. The library's security cameras prove that she was in the library at the time of death."

Stupid cameras!

They'd ratted me out to Martha and ruined my theory, too.

"Well, I'm still not convinced," I said. "Security footage can be altered, you know."

"That's true," Jonathan agreed, tossing the last few bites of his cone into a trash can. I would've finished the cone, if he'd offered, because I was almost done, too, and still hungry. "I learned all about security camera footage," he added. "At the police academy."

I also ignored his usual reminder about my lack of formal law enforcement education. I could see his truck, which was parked in front of the Philosopher's Tome, and I had a few more questions to ask. Including a big one that might affect my mother. I looked up at him again. "Did you learn anything about the stains on the jacket?"

"No," he told me. "The lab results aren't in yet."

"What about fingerprints?"

I knew my mother's prints would be on the windbreaker, but maybe somebody else's were, too.

Jonathan didn't seem hopeful, though. "It's difficult to lift those from any fabric," he informed me. "Let alone from nylon that's been wet and crumpled in a bag for days. I'm not saying it's impossible, but it will take some work, and may not pay off."

"Well, is there any news on Pastor Pete?" I asked quietly, because we were passing a group of people in Wynton University sweatshirts. They were probably in town for homecoming and wouldn't know Pastor Kishbaugh from Adam, but I still thought discretion was in order. "When are you going to arrest him?"

"I'm a *homicide* detective," Jonathan reminded me. "I only investigate murder. Financial crimes are handled by an entirely different unit." He hesitated, like he was weighing whether to tell me more, then said, "I can say that he's been advised not to use that passport any time soon." Jonathan must've seen me getting excited, because he raised one finger. "That's not information to be shared with Moxie Bloom or anyone else."

"You can trust me," I promised, making a motion like locking my lips. Then I threw away the imaginary key—and immediately opened my mouth again, to pop in the very last bite of my ice cream cone. And as I chewed, I gradually realized that Jonathan's arrival at the library was a little too well timed. I eyed him suspiciously. "Why were you at the library, anyhow? Huh?"

"I read," he said. "Quite a bit, actually. You saw my bookshelves. I could tell you wanted to snoop around them."

I wasn't buying it. "Yes, I did see your collection. But book *borrowers* don't have huge personal libraries. You strike me as someone who would buy all the books you want to read."

"That is an interesting observation—and accurate," he conceded, grinning at me again. "I don't borrow many books."

"So why were you there?" I asked again.

We'd reached his truck, and we stopped in front of it. He ran one hand through his thick, dark hair, looking almost guilty. Then he admitted, "To be honest, I was walking past the park and saw your van at the library. Given that the head librarian was at the scene of Lillian Flynt's murder, I immediately wondered what you were up to. I have decent instincts, too, and they—along with your history of meddling—told me it was likely no good."

"I could've just been checking out some books."

He arched his eyebrows, and I saw that he was laughing at me. "Really, Daphne? I was also fairly certain that you'd have been blacklisted from the library years ago, for unpaid fines." He nodded, gesturing to the store right behind us. "And you haunt the Philosopher's Tome. That's your library."

My shoulders slumped, to think that I was so predictable. "Yeah, I had to sneak in past Martha. And Tom rarely makes me pay for books. I guess you have me pegged."

Jonathan moved to open the door of his truck. "Oh, I don't think I'll ever have you completely 'pegged,' Daphne Templeton. In fact, I don't think the best FBI profilers could ever assemble a complete picture of you."

He was the master of ambiguous compliments.

"Keep your doors locked if you take that painting home," he added, growing more serious. "People *will* kill for that type of money." A shadow of concern darkened his eyes. "Maybe someone already has. Maybe possession of the portrait *is* part of the motive, even if Martha Whitaker seems to be ruled out as a suspect."

He didn't wait for me to tell him that I did intend to take the *Woman in Red Three* to Plum Cottage soon, so I could take my time studying the painting. I hoped that closer inspection might yield clues to Miss Flynt's intentions for the portrait—and help to solve her murder. Jonathan probably suspected that I wouldn't leave the painting alone, and he didn't want to get dragged into a debate about the soundness of my plans. He got into his clean, black Ford F-150 and turned over the engine, just as I realized, too late, that I should've asked for a ride back to my van. Although the library was only a few blocks away, Jonathan and I had spent quite a bit of time ambling through town, talking. The

sun was sinking, and I needed to return to Winding
Hill, change clothes, and grab my clown suit before
meeting Dylan for an early dinner at Casita Burrito.

I'd also forgotten to tell Jonathan that Piper thought
somebody might be staying at Flynt Mansion. That
could be important.

Raising my hand, I tried to signal Jonathan, to get
him to stop, but he was already driving away, and I
ended up waving to someone who stood across the
street. A person who had no doubt been observing me
and Jonathan.

Elyse Hunter-Black, who stood next to her sleek,
silver BMW, shopping bags dangling from her arms
and an unhappy expression on her pretty face.

Chapter 46

Casita Burrito was a little hole in the wall, tucked away in a narrow building and marked with only a small, wooden sign, but it was one of my favorite restaurants in Sylvan Creek. The food, which was conjured up from chef and owner Sofia Medina's grandmother's recipe book, was practically magical. And the atmosphere was enchanting, too. The thick plaster walls, the color of desert sandstone at sunset, were lined with hand-forged, wrought-iron sconces Sofia had brought from her native Mexico, and the rustic, terra-cotta floor tiles were authentic to that nation, too. In honor of the upcoming Day of the Dead, Sofia had strung skeleton-shaped lights all around the tiny room, and each table was decorated with a candle flickering in an elaborately painted ceramic skull.

Sofia was also celebrating the holiday with special menu items, including the Ghost Pepper Salsa that Dylan and I were enjoying with freshly baked, blue-corn tortilla chips—all vegan, for Dylan. As she'd set the salsa on our table, the gray-haired, spunky chef had promised us, with a wink, that we'd feel the lingering spirit of the fiery blend of tomatoes and peppers long into the night.

"Wow, that is really good," Dylan gasped, waving one hand in front of his mouth and reaching for a tall glass of ice water. His blue eyes were watering. "I think that could bring the dead back to life!"

I dunked a tortilla into the small, glazed cauldron that held the salsa and swirled the chip around. "Yeah, I wish."

"Something wrong?" Dylan asked. His cheeks had a faint flush under his tan. My face was probably beet red. "Because I was just joking, Daph. Although, I do find the idea of reincarnation really cool. I've been reading about it in the Bhagavad Gita." He shook his head. "Heavy stuff."

I admired Dylan's spiritual curiosity and his willingness to tackle a pretty weighty sacred text of India. We definitely shared an interest in exploring life's mysteries and the secrets of the universe.

"So, what's up?" he asked again. "You're awfully quiet tonight."

Part of me was worried about whatever topic Dylan wanted to discuss that evening. But I had other things weighing on my mind, too. Namely, Lillian Flynt's murder, and the jacket that was keeping its own secrets.

"I keep thinking about Miss Flynt, and who might've killed her," I told him. "It's bugging me."

"You don't have to solve another murder, Daph," he reminded me. "Like I told you when Steve Beamus got killed, trust karma to do its job and mete out justice."

I'd eaten more of the Ghost Pepper Salsa, and I quickly dunked a second chip into some creamy, cool, house-made guacamole, in a vain effort to soothe my tongue. Then I abruptly started coughing and slammed my hand against my chest.

I wasn't choking on a tortilla chip or overcome by the intense heat in my mouth, although the chunky blend of tomatoes, onions, and Scoville-scale-busting peppers was still making my eyes water, too.

No, I'd suddenly remembered where I'd seen the strange symbol with the bird, the flames, the pen, and the book.

I turned to Sofia, who was at that moment approaching our table, carrying a tray laden with vegan-friendly butternut-squash-chipotle chili for Dylan and her special cheese enchiladas for me.

"Thofia!" I said, too loudly. I also lisped, because I couldn't feel my tongue. I raised one finger, asking her to wait a moment while I took a sip of water. Then I asked, more calmly and clearly, "What charity did you sponsor, with your hot chocolate cart, the night of the Howl-o-Ween Parade?"

Chapter 47

"I'm sorry, Daphne, but I don't really know which organization we sponsored this year," Sofia said, setting Dylan's bowl and my plate on the table. My mouth started to water at the sight of melted cheese, bubbling up from under deep red enchilada sauce. "Lillian Flynt—God rest her soul—always assigned each participating business a charity," Sofia continued. "You could object, if you didn't like the cause, but I think most of us always trust that the groups are legitimate and worthy of support." Wiping her hands on her white apron, she gestured around her restaurant, which only had about seven tables. But all of them were occupied, and there was no waitstaff. "As you can see, I am very busy this time of year. I didn't even think to ask questions."

"It's okay," I said with a smile, although I was disappointed that she didn't know more. "Thanks, anyhow."

A shadow crossed her lined face. "Is it important? Did I sponsor some objectionable cause?"

"No, no," I assured her. "At least, not that I know of."

She didn't seem completely reassured, but she patted my shoulder with a grandmotherly hand. "If I think of anything, I will tell you." She smiled at Dylan. "And if you two need anything more, please call for me."

"Thanks," we both said, as she returned to the kitchen. When she was out of earshot, Dylan asked, "What was that all about?"

"My mother found a jacket at Flynt Mansion, the night Lillian was killed. It was damp—which means someone might've worn it when he or she pushed Miss Flynt into the tub—and it had a weird insignia on it. A logo I *thought* I'd never seen before, until I remembered spotting it on Casita Burrito's hot chocolate cart, at the parade. Proceeds from the sale of each drink and churro benefited whatever group the symbol represents."

"Interesting," Dylan noted, scooping up a big spoonful of chili. I could smell earthy chipotle and cumin, herbaceous cilantro, and a hint of cinnamon. I almost wished I'd ordered the same thing, although I was also very happy with my gooey, melty mix of sharp Manchego and salty *queso fresco*, oozing out of rolled up corn tortillas. "I know a little something about iconography," Dylan added. "Maybe we can decipher the logo?"

I hadn't known he was interested in the study of symbolic representation.

I liked that topic, too. As an undergrad philosophy student, I'd taken an elective class on Eastern European iconography and nearly ditched school to spend a semester in Slovakia, so I could check out the Byzantine churches firsthand.

Maeve Templeton had put a stop to that.

"Why don't you draw the insignia?" he suggested, sliding a napkin across the table. Since neither of us had a pen, he tapped the person sitting right next to us in the cramped room and a moment later handed me a ballpoint, too. "What's it look like?"

I wasn't much of an artist, and I really wanted to dig into my enchiladas, but, setting pen to paper, I did my best to recreate the open book, the flames, and the bird with the pen in its beak.

When I was done, I slid the napkin to the center of the table, so Dylan could check it out.

"Not bad," he said. "I totally see the hermit crab."

The sad thing was, I could see it, too, so I pointed out each of the various components I'd *tried* to execute. When I was done, we both sat back, and I noted that Dylan didn't compliment me again.

"That's, like, the definition of ambiguous," he observed. "I could see that being used by all kinds of groups."

I agreed, but I was interested in what he thought. "How so?"

"Well, flame is often used as a religious symbol," he said. "Like with Moses and the burning bush." He turned the napkin slightly and bent his head, looking more closely at my artwork. "The book could also be a Bible, or just a book that might represent teaching or libraries. Meanwhile, the bird could be a dove of peace, or a phoenix, representing something or somebody soaring upward after a bad crash. Lots of groups, like the Alpha Sigma Pi brothers, at the University of Akron, use the phoenix. I think it's because they lost their charter once and had to earn it back."

I was impressed by his analysis. I was also curious about how the heck he knew about the fraternity I'd run across while doing my Internet search.

"Did you attend college in Ohio?" I asked, thinking maybe I didn't know Dylan as well as I believed.

"Nah. I just crashed at the Alpha Sig house for a

couple weeks on my way to California, a few years back." He crumbled some tortilla chips into his chili. "Nice guys."

I did know him. I'd expected an answer like that.

"What about the pen?" I asked, tapping the napkin. "You didn't mention that."

"That could also have a ton of meanings, don't you think?" he pointed out. "Although the first thing that comes to mind is writing and writers. I could imagine some sort of writers' group or book club using the pen as a symbol."

"So, basically, you're saying that the jacket might've belonged to someone in a religious organization. Or to a writer. Or to somebody who belongs to an association of teachers or librarians."

"Lots of charities help lift people upward, too," Dylan added. "Pretty much any charitable group could use a rising bird as a symbol. It's trite, actually."

Sitting back, I sighed. If Dylan was right, the windbreaker could've belonged to almost any one of the people I suspected of killing Miss Flynt.

Asa Whitaker was a writer, while Martha was a librarian.

Pastor Pete was a man of the cloth.

And Tamara Fox probably got freebie T-shirts and jackets all the time, for her work with "uplifting" charities.

"Well, that wasn't very helpful," I said, crumpling up the napkin. I was getting tired of looking at the hermit crab I'd drawn. I was also grateful that at least the symbol didn't contain a cat. Bea Baumgartner was probably off the hook, if the jacket really was the killer's.

Then Dylan, a thrift store shopper like Moxie, had to burst that bubble.

"You know, whoever owns the jacket might not even

belong to the group," he noted. "I see windbreakers like that all the time at Goodwill. Eagles, Elks, Moose jackets . . . They always end up at thrift stores."

I pictured Bea's outfit when I'd seen her at Whiskered Away Home. Her holey knit hat had featured a logo for a distant city's sports team, and her sweatshirt had celebrated a high school she hadn't attended for forty years. She probably wasn't picky about the symbols on her windbreakers, either.

"Yeah, you're probably right," I agreed. "The logo might seem like a huge clue, then mean nothing. Maybe Miss Flynt just kept an old windbreaker by the door, for taking out the garbage on rainy days. The 'blood' could turn out to be ketchup or something."

I said that, but those instincts Jonathan had complimented me on told me that the jacket was important.

Then I glanced out the window and realized how dark it had grown while I'd been decoding symbols that might be meaningless.

"Oh, my gosh," I said, standing up. "I've got to go."

"But we didn't get a chance to talk." Dylan sounded uncharacteristically frustrated. "And you hardly ate anything, Daph."

"I'm really sorry," I said, although part of me felt relieved. Of course, another part was disappointed to leave so much of my dinner behind. I had to get going, though. "I'm pretty sure I'm running late for this thing I have tonight."

Dylan was skeptical. "What thing?"

"I've got to practice scaring innocent children," I said, digging into my pockets and placing some money on the table. "We'll talk later, okay? I promise."

Then I hurried out into one of the darkest nights I could remember, feeling a tiny bit guilty, because I might've been able to stay just a few minutes more. However, I wanted to make two quick stops before I "haunted" an orchard.

And the first place I needed to visit?

A rumored-to-be-truly-haunted *house*.

Chapter 48

"I'm telling you, I really do think there's something creepy about Flynt Mansion," I told Socrates, who was strapped into the front seat of my van. "I felt like I was being watched, the whole time I was getting the painting." The road to Twisted Branch Orchard was narrow and winding, obscured by fog, and slick with fallen leaves, but I dared to glance at him. "Maybe Piper was correct about someone staying there. Or Moxie's right, and there really is a ghost lurking around."

Socrates again rolled his brown eyes, indicating that he agreed with Piper about the existence of spirits, so I returned my attention to the road, wishing I could go faster. It had taken forever to lug the huge portrait down the path to Plum Cottage, then drag a reluctant basset hound in the opposite direction, back to the van. It didn't help that I'd taken time to don my clown costume, including the big shoes—but minus the mask, which I'd never found. I was going to be incredibly late for the hayride rehearsal. But I didn't feel like I could increase my speed by even a few more miles per hour. The night was moonless, and although both of my temperamental headlights were working that evening, they barely penetrated the mist that swirled across the road.

Leaning forward, I used my sleeve to wipe away some condensation that was forming inside my windshield, too, just as I spotted the sign for the orchard. Turning the wheel sharply, I steered us onto the last, rutted path through the trees. The VW jolted, and I looked at Socrates, who swayed back and forth on his squat legs, trying to keep his balance. "I wish I hadn't agreed to this."

There was no question that Socrates also thought I'd made a poor decision in the heat of the moment, back at Wolf Hollow Mill.

Leaning forward over the steering wheel again, and pushing the fluffy, orange wig I'd added to the costume off my forehead, so I could see, I spotted about ten cars parked near the orchard's rustic cider house. That was reassuring. There was also a fire burning in a barrel that was surrounded by some hay bales. I assumed there'd been a meeting of the costumed ghouls before everyone had disappeared into the acres and acres of apple trees.

At least, I thought no one was around, until I maneuvered the van into a rutted spot next to an old truck, and a chainsaw-wielding person in a blood-spattered lab coat stepped right in front of my headlights.

Chapter 49

"Wow, Tamara," I said, still pressing my hand against my thumping chest as I tried to help Socrates out of the van. He eyed Tamara Fox warily and hung back, like he didn't want to get down off his seat. Although I knew he wouldn't be happy, I finally lifted his entire wrinkled body and set him onto my oversized shoes, by accident. Straightening, I added, "You are one terrifying doctor!"

"And you are *late*," Tamara complained. Now that my headlights were off, I could barely see her, but I could tell that she was looking me up and down with a critical, better adjusted eye. She handed me a flashlight. "And where is your mask? Who told you to add a—not scary at all—wig?"

"There was a problem with the mask. . . ."

Tamara shifted the chainsaw in her hands, and I recalled that a small part of me believed she might've killed Miss Flynt.

Silently vowing to visit a costume shop as soon as possible, I hung my head and promised, "I'll be in a mask tomorrow."

"Yes, you will," she said evenly.

She was in an extremely foul mood, and I was short on time, but I wasn't sure when I'd get a chance to talk with her again, and I ventured to ask her one quick question.

"Before I run to my spot, can you tell me what group Casita Burrito's hot chocolate cart sponsored at the parade? It was an organization with a weird symbol, with a bird flying out of a burning book. I thought you might know, since you took over for Miss Flynt."

Tamara's *eyes* looked ready to shoot flames. "There's no time for this! And Lillian coordinated all the carts and charities this year. It was one of the last things she did, before she died."

"But you must've distributed the money raised. . . ."

She hoisted the chainsaw, adjusting it in her hands, and took a step closer to me. "No, I haven't yet. There's a lot to sort through, now that Lillian *is gone.*"

Tamara Fox's voice was normally high and feminine. But right then, she sounded like Freddy Krueger.

"Okay, thanks anyhow," I said, backing up a few steps. Socrates stepped back, too. "Where do we go . . . ?"

"Your spot is six rows of trees over, to the west," she directed me, using the toothy tool to point through what looked like a wall of gnarled apple trees. I could smell fruit that had fallen to the ground and been left to rot. I could also hear the low, muffled rumble of a tractor, moving in the distance. Peering in that direction, through the fog, I saw headlights shining dimly through the trees. "And hustle, so you're in place when the tractor goes by," she added. "You'll find a shed there, where you can hide."

"We'll hurry," I promised, adjusting my wig again. Switching on the flashlight, I looked down at Socrates, who shook his head in protest. I also wished we could hop back into the van, but I told him, "Come on. Let's go."

He whined softly to express his misgivings, then he stood up and followed me, with his head down and his ears dragging.

"Make sure you turn off the flashlight when you're in place, and act scary!" Tamara called after us. "Just like you will tomorrow, when the kids are here—and you *wear your mask!*"

I turned to see her standing by the flaming barrel, and my blood ran cold.

Tamara Fox was intimidating enough when she was just her normal self. Add a few bloodstains and a chainsaw, and she was downright terrifying.

What had I gotten myself into?

I couldn't back out, though, and I assured her, "I'll do my best. Don't worry."

"I'm serious, Daphne," Tamara warned me. "When I realized you were late, I had to assign you the very last spot, long after the other characters have jumped out. Most kids will think the ride is over. Your scare is *the* grand finale."

"Great."

I wanted to sound enthusiastic, but my response rang weakly in my ears.

Was I really going to be separated from the other volunteers and stuck waiting alone inside some creepy shed?

And, seriously, what type of person was so eager to frighten church kids?

"Let's go," I told Socrates again, bending down to tromp through the trees. Even though I stayed hunched over, my wig kept getting caught on the low-hanging branches, so I felt like hands were grabbing at me. The smell of decay intensified, too, when my oversized shoes squished the rotting fruit underfoot.

With each step we took farther away from the fire and the safety of my van, I felt more uneasy. The trees, illuminated by the shaky, weak beam of the flashlight, seemed to be closing in on us, and the fog was growing thicker. I rubbed the back of my prickling neck, trying to dispel the eerie feeling that we were being followed.

"There's no one behind us," I told Socrates, while silently reminding myself that I'd felt the same sensation at Flynt Mansion. Maybe I was getting paranoid after seeing that young woman at the park twice and once at the reading of the will. However, I hadn't spotted her since, and I reassured Socrates—and myself—again, "This place is supposed to be spooky!"

But I could tell he shared the feeling that we were being followed. He kept looking behind himself, the deeper we went into the orchard.

That bothered me, because he had good senses and wasn't normally fearful.

Stopping for a moment, I straightened, trying to decide if we should go forward to the shed, which might offer some protection if something bad really was happening, or turn back, even if that meant facing Tamara's wrath.

Then I stiffened in place, and what felt like a ball of ice formed in my stomach.

"Socrates?" I whispered. "Did you hear that?"

Chapter 50

Socrates wasn't built for running, but on that terrain, his low-slung body and short but powerful legs allowed him to travel faster than I could. The beam from the flashlight moved jerkily as I stumbled forward, so I caught random views of dead leaves and knotty roots and murky, ominous spaces between the trees, but I was able to keep him in sight, just ahead of me, while I struggled to keep up, hampered by my big shoes. My wig got torn off by a branch, and my one sleeve was ripped, too. I didn't really care. We just had to keep moving.

Behind us, I could distinctly hear the sound of footsteps snapping small branches and crashing through the fallen leaves.

"Leave us alone!" I begged, daring one glance over my shoulder. I couldn't see anything, though, except my wig dangling spookily in the fog. I spun around again, yelling louder. "Help! Somebody!"

Nobody answered, though. I couldn't even hear the tractor anymore.

"Faster, Socrates!" I urged, finally spotting the shed that Tamara had mentioned. It sounded like the footsteps were drawing closer. "Run to the shed!"

The gray, tilting outbuilding looked menacing itself, but it was the only refuge around, and I made a final, headlong dash toward the crooked door. Clutching the flashlight, my only potential weapon, I used my free hand to lift a wooden latch, my fingers shaking like crazy.

Hauling open the door, I let Socrates run inside first, then I followed and slammed the weak barrier behind us, blocking it with my body and dropping the flashlight, which went out as it hit the floor.

Then I braced myself, fully expecting someone to come crashing against the warped, wooden panels, knocking me forward.

But the strange thing was, that didn't happen.

Suddenly, there was just . . . quiet.

Standing in the dark, listening to my ragged breathing and Socrates' shuffling feet, I realized that I couldn't even say, for sure, when whoever *had* been behind us had given up the chase.

I continued to drip cold sweat, and my chest was tight with fear, but gradually my breathing slowed. Sliding quietly down the door, with my back against the splintery planks, I fumbled for the flashlight. Locating it, I flipped the switch.

To my surprise, the bulb hadn't broken, and we had feeble light again.

I first found Socrates, who seemed to be growing calmer, too.

Then I swept the beam around the shed, illuminating dusty, gray nets of gauzy cobwebs dangling from the rafters; some wooden barrels, presumably for cider; and . . .

"Pastor Pete?"

I heard the confusion in my voice, to discover the founder of Lighthouse Fellowship sitting on a crate in a corner, while he had a haunted hayride to coordinate with Tamara.

For a split second, I thought maybe I was in the wrong shed. Or Pastor Kishbaugh had misunderstood and thought he was the hayride's grand finale.

He certainly looked scary enough.

"Umm . . . Pastor Pete? Are you okay?"

He didn't answer, and I stepped closer, training the weak beam from the flashlight onto his face.

His eyes were blank, his jaw was slack and his skin was more pale and rubbery looking than any mask I'd seen at a costume shop.

Swallowing hard, I turned to Socrates and whispered, in a voice tight with real horror, "I'm pretty sure he's . . . *dead*!"

Chapter 51

The fire that continued to burn in the rusted barrel did little to dispel the gloom as I sat huddled under a blanket, waiting with a mummy, a werewolf, and a bunch of random ghouls while Jonathan, Detective Doebler, coroner Vonda Shakes, and a lot of uniformed officers traipsed in and out of the trees, which were splashed with red and blue lights from squad cars and an ambulance.

"I've sent for coffee," Tamara announced, jolting us all out of a grim, chilly reverie. She was treating the murder investigation like yet another event that needed coordination, stalking around in her bloody lab coat and making calls on her cell phone. "The caterer should be here soon."

As she paced by me, her eyes trained on her phone's screen, I looked more closely at her white doctor's coat.

Might some of that blood be *real*?

Then I glanced around at the various grave robbers and zombies who ringed the fire and realized that pretty much all of us were blood spattered.

"You're the only one who doesn't look like he committed murder tonight," I whispered to Socrates,

who sat next to me on a hay bale. He'd refused my
offer to share the blanket and was staring at the fire,
meditating like he did when he needed to center himself again.

I didn't want to disturb his peace, so I resumed
gazing at the flames, too, trying not to recall how Pastor
Pete had tumbled stiffly forward when I'd shaken him.

I'd been angry, to think that he'd scammed his
parishioners—and me, to some extent—but he hadn't
deserved to be killed. . . .

"Daphne?"

I nearly jumped at the sound of my name, then relaxed when someone placed a reassuring hand on my
shoulder.

Twisting, I looked up to see that Jonathan stood
behind me. I was pretty sure, from the serious, official look on his face, what he wanted with me, but I
ventured, "Yes? What's up?"

"Come on," he said, releasing my shoulder and stepping back. "It's your turn to answer a few questions."

Nodding, I rose and followed him to the cider house,
which was serving as a makeshift command center. Although Jonathan hadn't summoned him, Socrates
shook off his reverie and hopped awkwardly off the hay
bale, joining us.

Jonathan held open a squeaky door, allowing Socrates and me to pass through first. Then he closed the
door behind us and gestured for me to take a seat at a
rickety table.

"Where's Detective Doebler?" I asked, looking
around the spare pub, which was open only on fall
weekends. Although Twisted Branch only sold hard
cider and soft, warm pretzels, the place was always
packed with folks who gathered around the mis-
matched, wobbly tables to hear local country bands

play acoustic music. There was no electricity in the building, only a brick fire pit, which someone— probably Tamara—had lit for the investigators. I normally enjoyed a visit to the orchard when the leaves started to change, but that night I felt nervous. "Isn't your partner supposed to be here?"

Jonathan spun a chair around and sat across from me, resting his arms on the back of the seat, while Socrates plunked down at our feet with a heavy sigh, like he knew the discussion might take a while. "It's late, and we're trying to move things along," Jonathan explained. I noticed that he wasn't in his usual suit, probably because he had to tramp through an orchard full of mushy apples. But he was still dressed for work in a gray sweater, a collared shirt, and a tie. "Doebler's questioning a mummy right now."

"Oh."

I wished that Jonathan's sandy-haired, middle-aged partner could've been there to advocate for me. Detective Doebler wasn't nearly as intense as Jonathan during an interrogation.

However, to my surprise, Jonathan didn't immediately press me for details about my discovery of Pastor Pete's body. His first question was, "Are you okay?"

I was still wrapped in the blanket, and I pulled it more closely around my shoulders, although the fire was warming the room. "Yeah. I'm fine. A little shaken up. And not just because I found Pastor Pete—"

"*Another* body," Jonathan interrupted, rubbing the spot on his jaw where he had that scar.

"I can't help it," I said, my voice rising slightly. "I keep ending up at the wrong place, at the wrong time—"

"Because you *put yourself* there, Daphne."

"Not this time," I argued. "I just volunteered to help

out at a hayride. Then someone chased me through the trees!"

Jonathan had been growing frustrated with me, but he sat back, clearly surprised. "Someone chased you?" Before I could even nod, he asked, "Who?"

"I have no idea," I said. "I was walking to the shed, where Tamara had told me to wait for the tractor, and I heard footsteps behind me." I nodded to the basset hound who lay at my feet, watching the discussion with an alert expression on his long face. "Socrates heard them, too. We started running and hid in the shed. That's when we found Pastor Pete."

Jonathan glanced at Socrates, then returned his attention to me. "Can you tell me anything else?"

"Tamara was acting strangely," I said. "She kept pointing her chainsaw at me, and she practically growled when I tried to ask her about the symbol on the jacket."

"You don't need to ask anyone about that," Jonathan said firmly. "I've got it covered."

"Really?" I shrugged off the blanket. The fire was burning higher and the room was warm. Jonathan looked briefly at my clown outfit, but I didn't see the faintest hint of amusement in his eyes. He met my gaze again as I asked, "Can you tell me—?"

"What else can *you* tell *me*?" Jonathan inquired, overriding my question. I wondered if he had already figured out what the bird, flame, and pen represented, or if he meant that he'd eventually identify the logo. His phrasing was ambiguous. "Do you recall anything more about finding Pete Kishbaugh?"

"No," I informed him. "The shed was dark, and as soon as Socrates and I realized he was dead, we ran for help." I hesitated. "I should tell you that tonight wasn't the first time I've been followed, though. Someone has been sort of trailing me for a while."

"Who?" Jonathan spoke sharply, but I knew he wasn't angry. Just curious and worried about me.

"A young woman you might've seen at the reading of the will," I told him. "She was standing opposite you, in a corner."

"I recall her," Jonathan said. "She seemed awfully timid. Are you *sure* she's followed you?"

"Not exactly," I said. "But I saw her twice at Pettigrew Park, watching me, when nobody else was around. Including the night of the Howl-o-Ween Parade. After you and Elyse left."

He was *definitely* worried on my behalf. He spoke more softly, and I saw concern in his eyes. "Why didn't you tell me this before?"

I shrugged. "I didn't know if it was important."

Jonathan continued to study my face by the flickering light of the fire, then he asked, even more quietly, "Where's the painting, Daphne?"

"At Plum Cottage," I admitted. "I took it there this evening."

He obviously thought I'd made a mistake. I could tell by the way he rubbed his eyes and groaned. Then he looked up at me again. "You should sleep at Piper's tonight. Or, better yet, at your mother's house."

Talk about scary ideas. "I don't think so! Not at my mother's!"

Jonathan rose. I couldn't believe my interrogation was already over. I still had questions for him. How could he be done with me?

"Please, stay with Piper, then," he urged, spinning the chair back around. "At least until I can put locks on your windows, too. Or *I* catch a killer."

"I'll consider it," I said, standing up, too, along with Socrates, as Jonathan moved toward the door without another word.

I would probably never understand how he could dismiss me like that, when we *were* friends. He was afraid that I was in danger, and he wanted to keep me safe. Yet he didn't offer to call me every five minutes, like Moxie always did when she was worried about me. Nor did he give me a reassuring hug, like Dylan would have done before leaving.

Then I considered what I knew about Jonathan's past. I'd never seen *anyone* die, let alone friends. I might very well close myself off, too. Maybe lecturing me about safety, installing locks for me, and showing hints of concern were all he could do at that point. Maybe he needed to protect *himself* in a way I couldn't fully understand, any more than he could grasp why I didn't fret excessively about locking my doors or changing the bald tires on my VW.

"Jonathan?" I called to him before he could leave.

He turned to me. "Yes?"

"I really will think about staying at Piper's, okay?"

"Thanks," he said gruffly, reaching to push open the door.

"Wait!" I said, stopping him again. I hurried across the cider house, with Socrates close on my heels. "Can you at least tell me how Pastor Pete died? He was just sitting there. . . ."

Jonathan paused, like he always did when considering whether to give me any information. Then he said, "There's a reporter for the *Gazette* here, so I suppose most of this will be public tomorrow."

That was the first time I'd ever heard of a journalist actually producing news for the *Gazette*. And I'd seen that byline, too, on the story about the historical society.

G. Graham.

Was there some new reporter in town? Someone who dug for information?

I wanted to ask Jonathan, but he was answering my other question, so I stayed quiet.

"We found a rusted old pair of pruning shears, tossed aside in the woods, with some blood on them," he informed me. "You probably didn't see the wound on Kishbaugh's back, because his shirt is black."

"So the weapon probably came from right on the property?" I ventured. "This *is* an orchard."

"I don't think so," Jonathan said. "The tools here are all clean and locked away. This place may look rustic, but it's a commercial establishment."

He must've seen the strange expression on my face, as a thought crossed my mind. He'd again moved to push open the door, but he lowered his hand. "What is it? What are you thinking?"

"I was just at a place that was *filled* with rusted old tools," I said softly. "I kept looking at them, hanging on the walls, because they seemed like a safety hazard."

"I think I know where you mean," Jonathan said, taking a step toward me. "But why don't you tell me, anyhow. Just in case I'm guessing wrong."

He'd probably noticed the dangerous-looking tools, himself, and made the same connection that I'd just made, yet I still felt guilty when I admitted, reluctantly, "Bea Baumgartner's cat shelter."

Chapter 52

I ultimately chose not to sleep at Piper's farmhouse the night of Pastor Pete's murder, but I did lock my door. And I slept fitfully, too, on the love seat, under the imperious gaze of *Woman in Red Three*.

I'd dozed off while studying the portrait, searching for an answer to Lillian Flynt's challenge to me. And when I awoke, I found myself face to face with the nameless, scowling lady.

It was almost as if she was disappointed in me for not understanding what Miss Flynt wanted me to do.

Nor could I figure out why the woman in the portrait seemed familiar.

Sitting up and stretching, I saw Socrates dozing by the door instead of the fire, like he'd also been watchful.

I swung my feet off the love seat, moving quietly so as not to disturb him, only to hear a faint yowl.

Looking down, I found Tinkleston sitting in one of my slippers, reminiscent of the first night I'd found him under Miss Flynt's bed.

I was grateful that Tinkleston's teeth weren't sinking into my ankles, but a new, nagging feeling gnawed at me. I couldn't quite put my finger on what bothered me, either, though, so I tried to shake it off.

"Happy Halloween," I told Tinks, recalling that the spooky holiday had arrived. "This is kind of your day, huh?"

Tinkleston didn't attack me for greeting him. He merely stared at me glumly, so I dared to bend down and tentatively stroke his back, only to be rewarded with a swipe from his pom-pom paw and a deeper than usual frown on his pushed-in face.

That was okay. At least he wasn't a constant ball of fury anymore.

Over by the door, Socrates snuffled grumpily in his sleep.

I could live with taciturn animals.

I couldn't live with so many questions, though, so I got dressed and fed Tinks and a groggy Socrates breakfast. Then I retrieved my VW from its spot next to Piper's barn and drove to Sylvan Creek to confront a murder suspect in a place that made me want to hyperventilate, just to think about it.

Entering the Sylvan Creek Historical Society through the heavy brass door, I first glanced nervously at the open vault, which still gave me nightmares. Next, I leaned over and stroked Himmelfarb, who'd run to me the moment I'd stepped into the former bank lobby.

"Hey, there," I greeted her, stroking her back. She blinked up at me and purred gratefully. "I have to admit, it's nice to see a *sweet* cat today."

Then I straightened and marched directly to Asa Whitaker's office.

As I rapped on the open door with my knuckles, I saw that he was seated at his desk and wearing an antique eyeshade, which made it difficult for me not to laugh when I gave the little speech I'd prepared.

"I could waste a lot of time digging through all the dusty, old files you keep here," I told him. "Or you could just tell me about the scandal that Benedict Flynt was involved in, in the 1950s. Because I know something happened—and that Miss Flynt made you keep it quiet."

Asa raised his head, so I could see his eyes under the visor, and I lost the urge to chuckle.

He stared at me for a long time without speaking.

Then he pushed himself upright with his long, bony arms, and said, in a soft tone that somehow didn't reassure me, "Fine, Miss Templeton. If you *insist* upon digging up that particular aspect of the past, I have a few things I can show you. In the vault."

I'd spoken brashly when I'd marched into his office, but my throat tightened and my voice got squeaky. "Umm . . . What sort of things?"

He spoke even more quietly. "Things that will prove Lillian wasn't the first woman murdered in Flynt Mansion."

My pulse started to race with excitement and fear, but I kept my voice calm and even. "Is this stuff you can bring out here?" I requested, my gaze darting to the open but dark chamber. "Or maybe we could go to a coffee shop . . . ?"

He was already stepping around the desk, though, and taking my elbow into his hand, which was unexpectedly strong.

"No, Daphne," he said. "We don't need to go to a coffee shop. Everything you need to see is *in the vault.*"

Chapter 53

Maybe if Moxie sat in a room full of turtles, she'd get over her phobia. It only took me about a half hour of listening to Asa Whitaker ramble on about the entire history of the Flynt family, while I sat on a storage box in the vault, before my heart rate slowed to a snail's pace and my chin began to repeatedly bump against my chest.

"Daphne, are you listening?" Asa asked. "What are you looking at? The cat?"

My head bobbed back up. "I'm listening," I promised, petting Himmelfarb, who was sound asleep on my lap. Lucky kitten. "You were talking about the Flynts. And things that happened to them. In the past."

"I was trying to tell you that Lillian's father, Benedict Flynt—the last Lutheran minister at the church on Acorn Street—had an affair in the early 1950s with a *harlot* from Philadelphia. The woman in the painting *you* inherited."

Finally, things were getting interesting. Shaking the cobwebs out of my brain, I sat up straighter and leaned forward, being careful not to wake Himmelfarb. "And . . . ?"

"It tore the congregation, and the Flynt family, apart. But Benedict didn't care. He was obsessed, and he flaunted his lover in front of all of Sylvan Creek. Went so far as to push his wife out of the mansion, so the 'other woman' could move in. And to the family's horror, he had that painting commissioned and"—Asa lowered his voice—"he swore that, if anyone ever removed it from the house, even after his death, the 'woman in red' would haunt the place forever!"

That was very dramatic, but I had to point out, "Everyone says the woman haunts the house anyhow. Even though the painting was never removed."

Until now. By me.

Asa's eyes had a feverish gleam. "It's said that she haunts the mansion because, in a fit of rage, Benedict *strangled* her."

I rubbed my throat, which felt constricted again as I also got caught up in the story. "Why?"

"He learned that she was unfaithful to him. And he couldn't bear the thought of sharing her with—or losing her to—another man."

"Is that true?" I asked. "Miss Flynt really wasn't the first person murdered at the mansion?"

"It's never been proven," Asa admitted, losing some of his fervor. "But about six months after Benedict's paramour mysteriously disappeared, a decomposed female body washed up on the shore of Lake Wallapawakee. The corpse was impossible to identify back then, before DNA testing, but no one else had gone missing recently. And the family withdrew from society for many years. Lillian was the first Flynt to take a role in the community since the 1950s."

"Wow."

"There was a child, too," Asa added, softly. "But the little girl also seemed to disappear, with her mother."

Cradling the kitten, I leaned further forward, starting to understand how small-town history could be riveting. "Was *she* murdered, too?"

Asa didn't answer my question. Instead, he told me, "Benedict's scandalized congregation split apart for good and abandoned the church, which, as you know, has undergone many incarnations since that time."

Yes. The building was currently occupied by Lighthouse Fellowship.

What would happen to *that* congregation, now that Pastor Pete was probably leaving?

"Why did you remove all of that from your history?" I asked. "As I assume you did. There was nothing about the fifties, and I certainly didn't read *that* story."

"You really read that far?" Asa seemed touched. "You read up until the 1950s?"

"Of course," I said. "And I really wondered why that whole decade was omitted."

In the blink of an eye, Asa's mood changed for the worse. "Lillian demanded that I excise the entire scandal from the book," he told me, practically snarling. I couldn't believe how quickly he'd grown angry. "She said most people had forgotten—or never heard—the whole tale. Meanwhile, she'd worked her entire life to restore the family's reputation, through her own good works." He raised his bearded chin. "I told her that was admirable, but that I had a responsibility to tell the truth."

"Just like historian Gertrude Himmelfarb would advise."

He knitted his brows. "You know about her? The cat's name makes sense to you?"

"Yeah, I spent *a lot* of time in grad school." I pointed to my chest. "PhD. Philosophy."

Asa got quiet, and I didn't think it was because I'd

impressed him with my degree. He was trying to figure out how much, exactly, he should tell me.

"I'm sorry that you had to change your history," I told him, speaking in what I hoped was a soothing tone. The last thing I wanted to do was trigger one of his flashes of rage when I ventured, "And you had to do it, right? Because Miss Flynt told you she wouldn't deed the house to the historical society if you didn't take out the part about the scandal."

Asa hesitated, then nodded. "Yes. I let her read the original manuscript, because she *insisted* on knowing how I'd portrayed her family. And when she saw that I'd included the scandal and the speculation about the murder, she threatened to change her will." I saw a shadow of pain and betrayal in Asa's eyes. "And she almost sold the house, anyway. Even though I did as she asked—against my conscience."

Gently placing Himmelfarb the cat on the floor, I stood up, in case I had to run away after I asked my next question, which might provoke him. But I wanted to know the truth. "You and Miss Flynt fought recently, didn't you? And she burned the manuscript the night of her murder."

Asa's eyes widened with alarm. "How did you . . . ? And . . . And it's not like you think . . ." He raised his hands. "We *did* argue about the manuscript and her will, but that happened days before she was killed. I swear."

"I believe you," I said, so he wouldn't get nervous and do something crazy. I also thought he was telling the truth. "I found all those copies of your book, without any mention of Benedict Flynt, right after Lillian's death," I reminded him. "Even though it's self-published, it would've taken a few days, at the very least, to alter and reprint the whole thing, then have it shipped here."

Asa sank down onto one of the boxes, and when he looked up at me, I saw that he was relieved. "You honestly believe me?"

"Yes," I promised. "Your story makes sense."

He fidgeted with one of the artifacts he'd shown me while I'd been struggling to stay awake. I couldn't even recall where the plumed pen and inkwell fit into the story. Then he met my gaze again, and I saw that, in spite of the fact that he probably hadn't killed Lillian, he was still scared—and guilt ridden.

"I . . . I saw her, the day of her death," he confided. "She'd called to tell me that she planned to burn the manuscript I'd loaned her, to obliterate the story forever. But I wanted it back. I'd put so much work into it. I wanted my original copy, just as I'd written it."

I was confused. "Couldn't you just print another copy?"

He seemed almost insulted. "I used a typewriter for the first draft."

"You're kidding!"

His narrow shoulders slumped, as if he also realized that he might've carried the whole "stuck in the past" thing a little too far. Yet he quickly jutted out his chin, defending himself. "I wanted one document that would be forever unique, for the archives. Each typewriter leaves its own footprint, unlike documents created on a computer. And there's a certain *commitment* to a typewritten history. It can't be easily altered—as the computer file obviously was, to suit Lillian's revisionist whim!"

The weird thing was I kind of understood his point. Yet he must've put a lot of extra effort into retyping the whole thing on a computer, so his publisher could print the manuscript, too.

Then again, he'd probably loved rehashing the centuries a second time.

"So, what happened when you asked Miss Flynt to return the original?" I asked.

"It was too late. I hurried over to the mansion, to beg her not to toss the pages into the fireplace, but I didn't get there on time." Asa's face got even whiter than usual as he recounted the memory. "I kept calling to her, but she didn't answer, so I went up the stairs and . . ."

"She was already dead. In the tub."

He nodded numbly. "Yes. And the only *complete* history of Sylvan Creek was in flames. Turning to ashes."

I thought he was still telling the truth. He was a strange man, and desperate to save a society and a manuscript that few other people, if anyone, really cared about, but he wasn't a killer.

"Why didn't you call the police? Why did you just leave her in the tub—for me to find?"

"I was afraid." He hung his head. "Lillian and I *had* been at odds recently. And Martha advised me to stay quiet." He continued to slouch down, folding up. "She and I fought about whether I should tell the truth when we were setting up for the Fur-ever Friends gala."

I'd seen that fight from the window of Flynt Mansion. He'd curled up then, too.

Asa rested one hand on his stomach, like he felt queasy, and his voice dropped to a whisper. "The whole time we were decorating, I knew Lillian was in the tub. And now *you* know. . ."

"It's okay, Asa," I assured him. "I won't go to the police. But I think *you* should tell them everything you just told me. Detective Black is probably going to figure out what happened that night, sooner rather than later. He's pretty sharp. It would probably be better for you to come clean on your own. And I would back you up. I'm kind of friends with Jonathan Black."

The raw gratitude on Asa's face was almost painful to see. He'd clearly been living with a big burden, with no support from Martha. "Thank you, so much. I'll consider that."

I moved toward the thick door of the vault, ready to leave, even if the space didn't terrify me quite so much anymore. But before I crossed the threshold, I remembered something that I wanted to ask him.

"The woman in the painting," I said. "Do you know her name?"

He nodded. "Of course. Her name was Violet Baumgartner. And her illegitimate daughter—as you might have already guessed—*wasn't* murdered. She was *threatened* into a lifetime of silence and hiding by the cruel father who abandoned her."

It only took me a moment to put the pieces together.

"Oh, my gosh!" I gasped. "Bea was telling the truth! She *is* Lillian's sister!"

Chapter 54

"I can definitely see the resemblance between mother and daughter," I told Socrates and Tinkleston, who lay on opposite sides of the fireplace, about three feet apart from each other. I wouldn't have called them friends—I hadn't seen Socrates look directly at Tinks yet—but it was difficult to maintain much distance in a cottage the size of a postage stamp. Not if they both wanted to enjoy the crackling fire. Stabbing a butcher knife into the large, oblong pumpkin that I was carving, I glanced again at the painting. Violet Baumgartner's stern face, illuminated only by the fire and the room's two small lamps, looked more intimidating than ever. "The wide jaw, the thick eyebrows . . . I can definitely see Bea in her mother," I added. Then I frowned. "If Bea wore makeup. And combed her hair. And didn't dress like she pulled her entire wardrobe from a discount supermarket lost-and-found bin . . ."

"Mrrow!"

I was interrupted by Tinkleston, who growled in a throaty, menacing way. Looking over, I saw him flex his claws and narrow his eyes at the portrait.

"You see hints of Bea, too, don't you?" I asked him,

resuming my attempt to give the uncooperative gourd a jagged grin. "And you remember how she kept you stuck in that crate."

Retracting his claws, Tinks blinked at me, as if he'd understood everything I'd just said. I was starting to believe that he was a particularly perceptive cat. He and Socrates might eventually come to realize that they had quite a bit in common.

"Don't worry," I told Tinkleston. "You're not going back to Whiskered Away Home. You live here now."

Tinks's sourpuss expression didn't change, but he curled up more tightly on the rug, while Socrates *thunked* his head down onto his paws and sighed.

I smiled at him, convinced that he'd come around soon enough. Then the cottage grew very quiet as I focused on my annual arts and crafts project. I was leaving for Moxie's soon, to help her hand out candy to trick-or-treaters, and I always took a poorly carved pumpkin, as well as homemade apple cider donuts for us and Doggy Donuts for the many pups who would go door to door, too. It sometimes seemed like as many pets as humans trick-or-treated in Sylvan Creek.

No wonder Elyse Hunter-Black wants to film here.

But what will she do now that Flynt Mansion isn't for sale?

Or will my mother prove that her listing agreement preempts the will . . . ?

I was so preoccupied with my thoughts—and my jack-o'-lantern's lopsided, crossed eyes—that I hardly noticed a soft rapping at my door.

In fact, at first I mistook the sound for the light tap of the plum tree's branches against the window, which I'd strung with tiny orange lights. The night was breezy, with a promise of rain later, and the tree was knocking now and then, as if it wanted to come inside before the storm.

Then I heard the faint noise again, and I untwisted myself from my lotus position on the floor. "Hold on!" I called, rising awkwardly. "I'm coming!"

I assumed that Jonathan, who wouldn't get any trick-or-treaters at his remote house, was oblivious to the holiday and making good on his promise to install more locks.

"Just a second," I told him, as I used my forearms to twist the doorknob, because my hands were goopy, and I still held the knife.

But when I managed to open the door, I didn't find a tall, handsome detective standing there, tool kit in hand.

No, I was greeted by a short, nervous *ghost*, who held what looked like a *gun* under a white, trembling sheet, and who greeted me with a shaky, "T-t-t-trick or t-t-t-treat!"

I took a moment to look my visitor up and down, noting that the sheet was way too long, and Charlie Brown would've been embarrassed by the ragged attempt at eye holes.

Glancing quickly over my shoulder, I saw that Tinkleston still slept, while Socrates stretched and yawned.

Then I turned back to my visitor, who continued to threaten me with a twitching, concealed firearm, and said, "Would you like to come in for something warm to drink and a homemade donut?"

Chapter 55

"Fidelia is a very unusual name," I noted, setting a mug of steaming white hot chocolate in front of my guest, who'd taken off her sheet to reveal that the gun—as I'd suspected—was actually a carrot. Well, I hadn't guessed it was a carrot, but I'd been pretty sure that Davis Tuttweiler's late-in-life, insecure, largely abandoned daughter hadn't really been packing a pistol. Placing a plate of still warm apple cider donuts on the kitchen table, too, I sat down across from her. "Are you named after your grandmother? Or an aunt?"

Fidelia's hair was shapeless to begin with, and the sheet hadn't done her limp locks any favors. She pushed some flattened, brown curls out of her hazel eyes with a hand that was still shaking a little. "No, I'm named after Fidelia Bridges." My ignorance must've been apparent, because she added, "The nineteenth-century painter."

"Oh, *that* Fidelia!"

Socrates, who sat at my feet, eating a Doggy Donut from an antique ceramic plate shaped like a pumpkin, knew that I'd never heard of the artist in question. He shot me a disapproving look, challenging me for so long that I admitted to Fidelia, "I have no idea who that is."

She slouched on the chair. "Nobody does."

"Fidelia," I prompted gently, through a mouthful of donut. I could taste the little bit of cardamom I'd added to the batter, along with cinnamon, allspice, and two cups of tangy cider pressed at the Twisted Branch Orchard. "Why have you been following me?"

Dipping her head with shame, Fidelia cupped her hands around her mug and stared into the decadent, thick brew of cream, white-chocolate chips, and vanilla, all topped with more cream—whipped—and a sprig of mint from my windowsill garden. "I wanted to confront you several times, but I just couldn't get up the nerve. I was going to demand that you give me the painting, which should've been *my* inheritance. But I just couldn't do it."

I took a sip from my mug and wiped whipped cream from my lips with the back of my hand. "What do you mean, *your* inheritance?"

"I knew that one of my father's paintings was at Flynt Mansion," she explained, raising her face again. She had hollow cheeks and dark circles under her eyes. "I didn't see my dad much, but he liked to tell the story about how one of his portraits had been cursed by a minister. Dad said that, if anyone removed the painting from the Flynt's property, the subject would haunt the house forever." She smiled wanly. "Davis Tuttweiler was an eccentric man. The tale amused him."

I was confused. "But why would you think the painting is *your* legacy?"

"I didn't, really," Fidelia admitted, fidgeting with some buttons on a cardigan that aged her about ten years. "But my father left me *nothing* when he died. I got tired of struggling, so I reached out to Lillian Flynt, asking her to have pity on me and give me the painting, or at least leave it to me in her will. I knew that the Flynt family loathed the portrait, and I'd done some research, too. I also knew that Lillian had no real heirs. I came to Sylvan Creek, hat in hand, and—to my surprise—she said she would consider my request."

"When did all this happen?"

"I arrived in town about two weeks ago," Fidelia said. The corners of her mouth drooped. "I really thought I had convinced her that *I* deserved the portrait."

"So what went wrong?"

Fidelia suddenly glowered at me. "Right before she died, Miss Flynt told me that she'd changed her mind. That I needed to 'fend for myself in this world,' and that *you* would inherit the painting—because its monetary value would mean nothing to you."

Had I just been handed a clue to the mystery of Lillian's bequest to me?

And had Fidelia positioned herself as a suspect in Lillian's murder? I could picture her the night of the Fur-ever Friends gala, standing alone in the yard. At what point had she arrived at the property?

I watched her closely. "Why were you at Miss Flynt's house the night of the fund-raiser?"

Fidelia grew even more pale. "I wanted to ask her, one more time, to reconsider. I waited for her to join the party. But she never came out of the house. And then the ambulance and the police arrived, and I learned that I'd never have the chance to speak with her again."

Her story made sense.

"So, what do you want from me?" I asked, as if I didn't already know. She'd tried to threaten me with a root vegetable.

"I want you to give me the painting," she said, looking

around at the cottage. "You *do* seem to live simply, but everything is just perfect. You don't need the portrait, like I do."

I took a moment to consider her request. I didn't like the painting, and I didn't care about the money. Then I realized that, if Lillian had wanted Fidelia to have the portrait, *she* would've given it to her.

"I'm sorry." I reached over and clasped Fidelia's thin wrist, giving it a squeeze. "I can't do that. At least, not right now. I have to figure out what Lillian wanted me to do with the painting."

Fidelia hung her head again. "I knew you'd say that."

I looked down at Socrates, who had finished his donut and was licking his chops. He had no sympathy for Fidelia, either. He believed in self-reliance. Shaking his big head, just slightly, he wandered back to the fireplace.

Tinkleston didn't seem to find Fidelia spunky enough, either. He was on the icebox, clearly trying to decide whether to pounce and shake her up a bit.

"Fidelia?" I ventured. "Were you in Flynt Mansion when I took the painting? And the other day, when my sister, my friend, and I were there?"

"I don't have a lot of money, and I have nowhere to go," she said in a whisper. "I knew the house was empty, so I moved out of my expensive hotel and into the mansion the minute the police took the tape down. I've been staying there until I figure out what to do next."

"You could've just stolen the painting," I pointed out, reaching for another donut. "It was right there, in a house with a broken lock. Why stalk me, then show up here wearing a sheet and wielding a carrot?"

Fidelia shrugged. "I kept thinking I'd ask you for the painting, if I could just get up the nerve and find the right words. Then I'd have it legally. But when you removed it from the house, I realized you probably planned to keep it—or sell it. Maybe quickly, if you'd learned its value. I couldn't be sure Miss Flynt was right about your lack of interest in money. I got a little desperate."

"Yeah, I guess you did," I agreed.

Her gaze flicked to the sheet, which I'd hung on a peg near the door. The carrot was in the icebox. "I suppose my plan was flawed."

"Well, you tried," I said encouragingly. "Your approach was definitely original."

Socrates groaned, and Fidelia didn't take much comfort from my words, either. Her head thudded to the table, and I barely heard her mumble, "I never think things through."

I didn't know what to say, so I ate my second donut while I waited for her to lift her head. When she finally sat up again, she sighed heavily. "I suppose you think I'm lying about the night of the gala, and that I killed Lillian Flynt."

I shook my head. "No, I do *not* think that. You couldn't even steal a work of art worth thousands—"

"*Hundreds* of thousands."

"Worth hundreds of thousands of dollars," I continued, with a quick peek at the *Woman in Red*. Impasto or no impasto, I still didn't understand what the fuss was about. "You're not a killer."

Fidelia drooped lower in the chair. "I'm not an *anything*. As my father often told me."

I watched as she finally took a sip of her drink. And, while I agreed in theory with Miss Flynt's assertion that Fidelia needed to pull her life together, I also felt sorry for the young woman who sat across from me, feeling completely worthless.

"I have a lousy father, too, you know," I told her. "And my mother can also be a handful, to say the least. But you can't let your parents define your life. As the French philosopher Voltaire once said, *Each player must accept the cards life deals him or her. But once they are in hand, he or she alone must decide how to play them.*"

Fidelia blinked at me. "Wow. Are you a philosopher, or something?"

"More like a perpetual student of philosophy."

Fidelia observed me for a moment, then said, "I think I might understand why Lillian left the painting to you."

That was reassuring, because I still had no clue.

"So, what are you going to do now?" I asked, checking the old clock on the oven. I needed to get to Moxie's soon. "You can't stay in Flynt Mansion forever. It's going to be a museum someday."

"I moved out already, tonight," Fidelia said. "That place was too spooky. I'm staying at the hotel in town again. Although I don't know how I'll pay off the credit card bill."

"You must be good at *something*," I said, rising and taking my mug to the sink. "Have some way to make a living?"

"Well, I really love accounting."

I turned around to see that Fidelia's eyes were actually alight.

"Really?" I struggled to hide my disbelief. I couldn't imagine loving accounting, but to each her own. "Do you have a degree?"

Fidelia's cheeks flushed. "Yes. But it's from an online school. The course only took ten weeks."

That didn't inspire much confidence, but I kept thinking about how Jonathan Black had taken a similarly woebegone orphan under his wing, and after a moment's hesitation, I suggested, "Why don't you keep the books for my business, Lucky Paws Pet Sitting? They're a mess. Because I don't really keep books. But maybe you could help me start."

Fidelia beamed. "Really? You'd *hire* me?"

I didn't have extra money to pay salaries, but I nodded. "Sure. Although I can't pay you much. You'd mainly get some experience to put on your resume."

That wasn't a very good offer, but it was apparently the best one Fidelia Tuttweiler had right then. My new employee rose, came over to the sink, and hugged me. "Thank you so much!"

Returning the awkward embrace, I patted her back. "You're welcome." Then, when she pulled away, I asked, "Do you want to come with me to my friend's house tonight? We're going to hand out candy to trick-or-treaters. It's pretty fun."

"Thanks, that's a nice invitation." Fidelia swiped a finger under her eyes. Was she crying? "But I think I'll just go back to the hotel. I want to brush up on my accounting. I might still be able to log on to the SUA website and access some course materials. I *just* graduated."

I cocked my head. "What is SUA?"

"Soaring Upward Academy," Fidelia informed me.

The name was more suitable for a preschool than an institution of higher learning, and I hoped I wouldn't regret my decision to hire one of the academy's graduates.

I could also picture the school's logo, which would probably include a bird, soaring skyward, perhaps off a book. . . .

"They didn't send you a jacket when you enrolled, did they?" I asked, picturing the symbol I'd seen on the windbreaker and the Casita Burrito cart. I doubted that an online university had reached out to Sylvan Creek's Howl-o-Ween Parade organizers to raise money, but some schools were technically nonprofits. "Like, a promotional windbreaker?"

Fidelia was clearly puzzled. "No . . ."

"Never mind," I said, just as my telephone rang. "And hang on a minute, okay? I need to get this."

Not waiting for her response, I hurried upstairs to my loft, lifted the receiver, and said, "Hello?"

"When are you getting a new cell phone?" my mother demanded, without greeting me. "It's time to admit that the old one will never work correctly, and I need to get in touch with you at times!"

"What is so urgent?" I asked, leaning over the railing to watch Fidelia don her sheet and rip one eyehole until it was big enough for her head to fit through, creating a makeshift poncho.

Was I really going to trust her with what little money I had . . . ?

"Daphne, listen to me!"

"I'm listening," I promised Mom. "What is wrong?"

"There *was* blood on that ugly jacket!" My mother sounded uncharacteristically shaken. "*Lillian's* blood. And the police were able to lift one set of fingerprints from the cheap fabric."

I didn't want to ask, but I had to do it. "Whose prints were they?"

There was a moment of suitably dramatic silence, then my mother announced, "Mine, of course!"

Chapter 56

"Do you think your mom's really in trouble?" Moxie asked, dumping a big bag of chocolate skulls into a bowl that featured a clawlike hand sticking out of the center. Whenever a trick-or-treater would reach for a piece of candy, the hand would clamp down. Moxie went all out for Halloween. Her tiny garret apartment was strung from its creaking wooden floors to its exposed rafters with strands of lights shaped like witches and ghosts and skeletons, and she had carved about ten artful jack-o'-lanterns, which grinned at me from the nooks formed by the turrets and sharply peaked eaves of the old Victorian house. Socrates, who lay on a Turkish rug I'd brought Moxie from Istanbul, kept one eye on a huge, fuzzy spider that lurked in a web stretched across the apartment's darkest corner. "I mean, your mother admitted to picking up the jacket, and it was in her tote bag," Moxie added. "Just because her fingerprints are on the fabric doesn't mean she killed Miss Flynt."

Even as Moxie reminded me of that, we exchanged skeptical looks, silently agreeing that Jonathan and Detective Doebler probably wouldn't rule out the possibility. If Lillian Flynt had told Realtor Maeve Templeton that she'd changed her mind about selling the mansion and planned to honor her earlier promise to leave the property to the historical society . . .

"I think Mom will be all right," I said, shaking off the image of my mother wearing an orange prison jumpsuit. The shapeless design and unflattering color would kill her, even before she got into an inevitable fight with her cell mate over who deserved the best bunk. I was positive that my mom would go for "prime real estate" under even the most dire circumstances. "I'm not going to worry yet," I added, plucking a skull from the bowl and narrowly escaping the hand. I unwrapped the foil and popped the candy into my mouth. "In fact, I almost feel sorry for Jonathan, who'll have to question Mom again."

"Yeah, I kind of feel bad, too," Moxie agreed.

Although I'd liked her Kim Novak look, I was glad to see that my best friend was dressed as one of the Pink Ladies from *Grease*, in a satin jacket, shiny black pedal pushers, and black heels. In truth, the outfit was hardly a costume by Moxie's standards.

"Hey, how come you're not wearing your witch cape?" Moxie asked, seeming to read my mind, as I thought she often did. Talk about spooky, but in a good way. "Or the clown suit?"

"I am never wearing that cape again after getting humiliated at the gala." I bent to pick up my jack-o'-lantern, which I'd set on the floor near the door. "And the clown costume is downstairs in my van. It reminds me of the awful night I found Pastor Pete, and I'm going to return it to Lighthouse Fellowship tonight."

"You must've been terrified," Moxie sympathized, opening yet another bag of candy. Sylvan Creek drew a lot of trick-or-treaters. "I can't believe you got chased through a lonely orchard, then found *another* body."

I pulled off my pumpkin's ill-fitting lid. "Yeah, Jonathan seemed unhappy about that, too."

"Do you think the same person who murdered Miss Flynt also killed the minister?" Moxie mused aloud. "Is there a connection?"

"I keep trying to find one. But I can't. And, to be honest, for a while I thought Pastor Pete killed *Lillian*. She was treasurer of Lighthouse Fellowship, and he was misusing funds. I have a feeling she found out the truth at some point. I saw a note on his calendar about meeting someone with the initials *LF* the day Miss Flynt was murdered."

Moxie's eyes lit up at the prospect of juicy gossip. "So those rumors were true? He was really stealing from his parishioners?"

I recalled my promise to Jonathan about keeping the investigation into Pastor Kishbaugh's finances quiet. "Maybe," I conceded. "But you can't say a word. It's all speculation at this point, and I promised Jonathan I wouldn't spread any stories. He told me a few things in confidence."

Moxie got a different kind of gleam in her eye. "So, you had some sort of secret discussion with Detective Black, huh?"

"Moxie . . ."

"Oh, fine." My tone must've been sufficiently discouraging, because she sighed. "I'll drop it."

"Thanks," I said, lighting a small candle and sticking that into my pumpkin, which didn't look nearly as nice as Moxie's jack-o'-lanterns.

"Where's Piper?" Moxie asked, as I carried my glowing creation to the balcony that overlooked the street. A pair of arched French doors was flung open to let in a pleasantly warm, pre-rain breeze, as well as a lot of leaves from a pair of tall, matched oaks that made the apartment feel like a tree house.

"I have no idea where my sister is," I said, setting my jack-o'-lantern on the railing so the kids passing below would see it. "I stopped by the farmhouse, hoping to convince her to get out of those sweatpants she's been wearing lately and come with me, but she wasn't there. . . ."

My voice trailed off, because as I looked down at the street, I saw none other than Piper, who was strolling along the sidewalk with the guy who'd bought her cider at the Howl-o-Ween Parade. She was gazing up at the man, who was fairly tall, and smiling as they both talked animatedly.

She obviously didn't see me, and I started to call out to her.

Then, in a rare moment of self-control, I stopped myself.

Something told me to just leave my sister, and whomever she was with, alone.

Turning around, I went back inside and found that Moxie had put the Doggy Donuts—made with eggs, flour, yogurt, and honey—into a bone-shaped bowl. She'd also piled several of my apple cider donuts onto an olive green Melmac plate shaped like the *Star Trek* officers' insignia. She didn't have much of a kitchen, let alone a dining room, and she set the plate on a pile of colorful, vintage suitcases that served as her coffee table. She'd already placed two glass bottles filled with cold, white milk on the makeshift table, too.

"Let's have a snack before we go downstairs to greet the little hobgoblins," she suggested, sitting cross-legged on the floor. "I'm starving."

I joined her, but said, "I'm actually pretty full. I ate

two of these donuts with Davis Tuttweiler's daughter, Fidelia, after she showed up on my doorstep dressed as a ghost and threatened to kill me with a carrot."

Wow, that sounded weird when I said it out loud, and Moxie, who uttered a lot of crazy things herself, seemed to agree. She choked on her donut and had to smack her hand against her chest, then take a sip of milk through a very cute black-and-orange-striped paper straw. When she composed herself, she asked incredulously, "Davis Tuttweiler's daughter tried to *kill you with a carrot*?" She coughed, still clearing her throat, then added, "How did *that* happen? And *why*?"

"Fidelia thinks—or thought—that the portrait of the woman in red should've been rightfully hers," I explained. "She's been following me around, trying to get up the nerve to ask me for the painting." I really wasn't hungry, but I picked up a donut anyhow and broke off a piece. "She finally worked up the courage tonight—and went a little overboard." I shrugged. "We ended up talking, and I'm keeping the portrait for now."

"Poor Fidelia." Moxie made a sad face. "It sounds like she embarrassed herself."

Over on the rug, Socrates snorted and fell over sideways, like he couldn't agree more.

"Yes, Fidelia's sort of a lost soul," I noted. "She had hoped Miss Flynt would bequeath her the painting since Lillian didn't have any heirs. But Miss Flynt changed her mind, right before she was killed."

"Jeez, maybe Fidelia's the killer," Moxie suggested.

I took a sip of milk, too, then said, "I really don't think so."

Moxie helped herself to the donut I hadn't finished. "So? Are you ever going to give her the painting?"

I shook my head. "I don't think so. That clearly wasn't Miss Flynt's intent. I'm giving Fidelia a job, instead.

She's a newly graduated accountant, and she's going to straighten out my books."

Or destroy my business.

"This whole murder gets crazier and crazier," Moxie observed, wiping her sugary fingers on her pedal pushers. "I don't think Hitchcock could've come up with all these weird characters. And you still have no idea what you're supposed to do with the portrait, do you?"

"Not a clue," I admitted, as Moxie rose to clear away the plate and her empty bottle.

I stayed seated for a moment, reflecting on what she'd just said about the murder, the "characters" who'd been at odds with Miss Flynt before her death, and Hitchcock's movies, in which no one was ever really trustworthy.

Pastor Pete had certainly pulled the wool over a lot of people's eyes.

And Bea Baumgartner's whole life was a lie, in a way.

How could I be so sure that Fidelia Tuttweiler, whom I'd just met, was as meek as she seemed?

Or that Asa Whitaker's fragile, needy persona wasn't just an act?

Taking another sip of milk, I thought about the video footage of Martha Whitaker, from the library's security cameras.

Could even *that* be trusted?

People tampered with technology all the time.

I swallowed hard.

All joking aside, was I *positive* that my own mother was innocent, given how badly she'd wanted that sale?

"Daphne?"

Moxie's voice brought me back to reality, and I looked over to see her checking a watch with a pink face and the silhouette of a black poodle, right in the center.

"Did you say something?" I asked.

"I was just reminding you that, if you want to return your clown suit before the trick-or-treaters arrive, you should probably go now. It's getting late."

Untwisting my legs, I stood up. "Yeah, I do want to get rid of the *new* ugly mask I had to buy and those stupid, oversized shoes. . . ."

All at once, as I mentioned the way too big footwear that was waiting in my VW, my mind flashed back to the night I'd discovered Miss Flynt's body in her bathtub, after I'd first found Tinkleston under her bed.

He'd looked adorable, sitting in a slipper.

Then I pictured the note I'd taken from the kitchen, too.

The unusual, loopy initials, *LF* . . .

My heart started pounding, and I told Moxie, "I'm sorry, but you're going to have to hand out the candy this year. I can't help you."

"What's wrong?" she asked, as I hurried toward the door, with Socrates close on my heels, like he knew what was happening. "Where are you going?"

"I actually have *three* stops to make," I told her, pausing to grab a few doggy and people donuts, which I stuck into two sacks. "And, hopefully, at the last one, I'll unmask *another* killer!"

Chapter 57

Socrates and I first dropped off the clown costume, hanging it on the coatrack at Lighthouse Fellowship, where Tamara Fox had left it for me. Although the new mask I'd purchased wasn't quite as creepy as the one I'd lost, the outfit still gave me the willies, and I hurried out of the church, looking back once at the oversized red shoes I'd tucked under the droopy, nylon suit.

As I helped Socrates into the VW and buckled his harness, I asked, "Do you really think I might be onto something?"

He gave me a level stare. He clearly believed I shouldn't even think about solving Miss Flynt's murder.

"I don't plan on doing this alone," I assured him, sliding behind the wheel and turning the key, so the engine sputtered to life. Then I checked the gas gauge. I did *not* want to run out of fuel, where I was going. Luckily, the tank was slightly over half full, assuming that the gauge could be trusted, and I put the VW in gear, driving slowly out of Sylvan Creek, because the streets were filling up with trick-or-treaters.

Stopping at a corner, I waited as a ninja, a black cat, and a classic toilet-paper mummy ran across the intersection, their plastic pumpkins swinging in their hands.

When they were safely on the sidewalk, I accelerated again, and we were soon on a familiar narrow, country road, which grew more lonely and heavily forested with each mile that passed.

Spotting the turn to Jonathan Black's house, I steered the old bus onto the bumpy lane.

A minute later, I helped Socrates out of his seat and smoothed my curls, which were getting wilder as the rain drew closer. Then I marched up onto Jonathan's dark, not exactly welcoming porch. But I could see lights on inside the A-frame house and smell burning firewood, so I raised my hand and knocked, my heart thudding with excitement over the news I had to share.

No one answered for what felt like ages, and I was just about to tell Socrates that we would come back some other time, when the door swung open.

I was a visitor who hadn't called in advance, so I probably had no right to ask any questions, let alone the nosy one that popped out of my mouth.

"What are *you* doing here?"

"I'm picking up Paris and Milan," Elyse Hunter-Black politely replied. "I had to run back to the city today, and Jon was nice enough to watch the dogs for me." She slipped out onto the porch, followed by her greyhounds, who took their usual positions at her side. "Although, I don't think Paris, especially, enjoyed her time with the yippy little Chihuahua," Elyse added. "She's really on edge!"

I looked down to see that both greyhounds, whom I still couldn't distinguish from one another, wore matching placid expressions. Socrates also seemed baffled by the comment, and disapproving of the dogs' coordinating orange and black sequined collars.

Then I smiled at Elyse. "Everybody gets used to Artie after a while. He's an acquired taste."

Elyse didn't appear convinced.

"So, what brings you here?" she asked, folding a long cardigan more tightly around her small frame. The sweater was black, so she blended into the night, but her blond hair and silver earrings gleamed in the moonlight when she cocked her head. "Can I help you?"

"I actually had something to tell Jonathan, and an invitation to extend." I tried to look past her, into the house. "Is he around?"

I had planned to invite Jonathan to come along with me as I hopefully cracked the case of Miss Flynt's murder. But apparently he was already working toward that goal himself.

"I'm sorry," Elyse said. "But Jon and his dogs went into town about ten minutes ago. He had some sort of revelation about Lillian Flynt's murder, and he wanted to follow up on whatever hunch he had."

"I had a revelation, too!" I said, getting excited again. "In fact, I really think I've solved the case, so if he calls in the next hour or so, could you please tell him that I'm headed over to the mansion?"

"I'm not sure if I'll talk to him again this evening," Elyse informed me, stepping back into the house. "But if I do, I'll be sure to pass along your message." She hesitated. "Or you could text him." She seemed uncertain, but offered, "I suppose I could give you his number, if you need it. . . ."

"Thanks, but I don't have my phone with me," I said, finally recalling that I held two bags, both of which I offered to Elyse before she could close the door. "And, please, take these homemade donuts I brought. One bag is for Axis and Artie." I nodded to the correct sack. "And the other is for Jonathan, to help pay off a debt I owe him. But there are enough to share with you and your dogs, too."

"Thank you, Daphne," Elyse said, accepting the treats and again moving to close the door. "I'll let Jonathan know you stopped by."

A moment later, I heard the latch click into place, and I looked down at Socrates and shrugged. He seemed to agree that, for a woman who helped to run a network that was all about stylish living and entertaining, Elyse hadn't offered us a particularly warm welcome. She hadn't been rude, but she hadn't exactly rolled out the red carpet, either.

"Well, I guess we'll get going," I told Socrates, leading the way to the van. A shiver of anticipation, mingled with a little appropriate for Halloween apprehension, ran down my spine. "We have a haunted house to search!"

Chapter 58

I was becoming pretty familiar with Flynt Mansion, but as Socrates and I stood on the porch on a windy, gloomy Halloween night, facing a tall, forbidding door, I felt like I was a nervous kid in a dinosaur costume again.

Moxie believed the house was haunted, and I thought the place had a strange vibe, too.

And knowing that not one, but likely two, women had been murdered there didn't help calm my nerves.

I glanced down at Socrates, who shuffled on his over-sized paws and looked repeatedly toward the van.

He didn't want to go inside, either.

"Why do I suddenly feel like I'm going to get something worse than a mushy apple?" I whispered to him.

My normally stoic canine friend whined softly in response.

That wasn't encouraging.

And yet, I *had* to know if my memory was correct. Because if I was right about the initials on the note—which, unfortunately, Jonathan had confiscated—and what I'd seen under Miss Flynt's bed, I might have honestly solved my second homicide.

"Here goes," I told Socrates, reaching out and jiggling the doorknob to open the faulty lock.

A moment later, we were both inside, and the door swung shut behind us.

Chapter 59

Even with the electricity flowing, Flynt Mansion was still pretty dark. The few lamps that I was able to find by fumbling around the first floor all looked like they dated back to Thomas Edison's time. Their stained-glass shades blocked most of the light from what must've been, at most, thirty-five-watt bulbs.

"Lillian must've had eyes like an owl to survive in here," I told Socrates, as I led the way up the stairs to the second floor. I kept my hand on the railing, and when we reached the top, I nearly knocked the decorative top off the newel post again. Grabbing the finial with both hands, I tried to twist it back into place. "Miss Flynt should've sold the Tuttweiler to buy some lamps and hire a handyman."

Socrates didn't so much as snicker. His head hung low, his brow was deeply furrowed, and his tail drooped.

I'd only seen him look so apprehensive twice before. Once on the day I'd nearly been murdered, and again at Twisted Branch Orchard, when we'd been chased and found Pastor Pete's body.

Did my normally skeptical sidekick sense a threatening—perhaps ghostly—presence, right then?

"Even if ghosts exist, as I suspect, I don't really think they can harm you," I quietly reminded him and myself. I couldn't find a light in the hallway, so I dragged one hand along the wall, feeling closed doors, then bumpy plaster as we passed down the corridor. When we reached the bathroom where I'd found Lillian's body, I swore the air got colder, and I could imagine her spectral, misty form hovering in the tub. "I've never heard of anyone getting killed by a spirit," I added. "Never!"

I doubted that Socrates really believed in ghosts. But he continued to seem uneasy, like me, and I was glad when we reached Miss Flynt's room. The hinges creaked as I pushed the door open, and I went inside first, followed closely by Socrates. Groping blindly, I made my way to the nightstand, where I switched on yet another small, weak lamp.

But the light would be enough to let me see everything I hoped to find, and I bent down next to the bed, lifting the lacy skirt.

And there they were.

Two pairs of slippers, tucked under either side of the bed.

One set was pink, ratty, and small, designed to fit a woman's feet.

And the other pair—Tinkleston's former hiding spot—was plaid, less worn, and definitely made for a *man*.

Chapter 60

"Miss Flynt had a secret boyfriend!" I told Socrates, who didn't seem half as excited as I was. He sat near the bed, watching as I opened the closet door. Pushing aside Miss Flynt's extensive collection of dowdy blouses and skirts, I found two men's dress shirts, a tie, and a pair of slacks. The clothes were hidden, hung at the very end of the rod, but when I sniffed them—which could've proven to be a mistake—they smelled freshly laundered. I backed out of the closet. "He kept some stuff here!"

Socrates exhaled loudly, a canine sigh, like he thought we should get out of there.

"I'm done," I promised, moving to the nightstand again. I planned to switch off the lamp, but right before I pulled the old-fashioned chain, I opened the drawer, hoping to find some proof that my hunch was correct. I was pretty sure I knew who Miss Flynt had been seeing, and why the relationship had to be kept secret. And sure enough, I found a small picture in a gilt frame. The photo was black and white and very old, but I recognized Miss Flynt, who wore a fancy dress and stood in a young man's embrace. "It looks like they were at a prom," I said softly. "And, although he's *really* changed, I recognize him, too." I glanced at the edgy basset hound, who'd moved closer to me. "And he signed the fake instructions for Tinkleston's care with those distinctive initials. I *knew* that somebody who didn't care about animals wrote that message. . . ."

"Very clever," someone noted, in a deep, masculine voice.

For a split second, I thought Socrates had finally spoken. I sometimes believed it was only a matter of time before he couldn't keep his opinions to himself.

Then I realized that Socrates wasn't talking. He was *growling*. A low, rumbling sound from deep within his broad, dappled chest.

I turned slowly around, and although my voice shook, I asked Larry Fox, "Why did you kill Miss Flynt—whom you've clearly loved since *high school*?"

Chapter 61

"How fortunate that I came back tonight to clear my clothes out of the closet," Larry said, leaning against the door frame. Apparently, we were going to chat for a while. "I thought no one would come near this house on Halloween night, but I was wrong. *Someone* was foolish enough."

"Detective Black knows that I'm here," I bluffed. I doubted that Elyse had passed along my message. Still, I added, "He'll arrive here soon."

I was a terrible liar. Socrates hung and shook his head, while Larry just laughed.

"Really?"

"Yes." I jutted out my chin, acting far more defiant than I felt. "So don't even think about killing me. You'll never get away with *two* murders."

"I don't know about that," Larry said. "I'm on the verge of getting away with one. I don't think I'm even on the list of suspects." He'd been smugly boastful, but he suddenly grew melancholy. "Lillian and I were *very* discreet. Never together outside this house. . . ."

"Why did you kill her?" I asked softly. I was buying time, and I was incredibly curious about what had gone wrong. I held up the photo, which was still in my hand. "You clearly loved each other for years."

"Yes, I've always loved Lillian," he admitted, growing quiet, too. I could tell that, although he'd taken her life, seeing Lillian's image affected him. His eyes softened. "I was a fool to let her go, years ago, when I went to law school. But she refused to come with me. And when I came back to Sylvan Creek, after years away, she wanted nothing to do with me." He smiled faintly at a memory. "Eventually, though, neither one of us could resist what we felt."

"Did Tamara know?"

I couldn't help asking.

"Of course," Larry snapped. His gaze had been trained inward, but he looked at me again. "She's no fool! She arrived early on the evening of the big 'gala'— hoping, as always, to take charge—and she found me with Lillian, right after I'd pushed her into the tub."

"What?" I couldn't believe my ears. Tamara hadn't seemed overly agitated the night of the fund-raiser. In fact, she'd seemed primarily irritated by Tinkleston. I blinked at Larry, confused. "Why didn't she call the police?"

Larry laughed, a short, disdainful snort. "Tamara would never do that. She cares too much about her 'image.' She would've ruined her own life if my affair with an older woman became public knowledge. Not to mention the shame she would've suffered, if anyone knew she was married to a *murderer*. Tamara walked out the door like nothing had happened and continued setting up her big party. I never worried for a moment that she'd turn me in."

"I should've known that someone very close to Lillian was the killer," I muttered, with a glance at Socrates, who watched everything intently. "She was wearing a robe! But I thought somebody—maybe Asa Whitaker or Bea Baumgartner—had come upstairs, following her after an argument. It never occurred to me that she had a *romantic* side."

"And you will be the last to know that," Larry warned me, taking a step into the room. "This love story will die with you."

Socrates growled again, but—like most people did—Larry underestimated a basset hound's power when angered. Larry's gaze continued to bore into mine, and I saw that his eyes were nearly as cold and lifeless as Miss Flynt's had been on the night I'd found her body.

How strange that Larry had clearly been capable of great passion.

"You never told me why you killed her," I reminded him, taking a step backward. Unless I planned to escape up the chimney like Santa Claus, I was boxing myself farther into the room, but I had no choice. My gaze darted around, but the only weapons in sight were the little picture I held, the lamp, and some pillows. Shaking off the image of Larry and I getting into a pillow fight to the death, I asked, "Why? Why would you murder the woman you'd finally won back?"

"I wanted to divorce Tamara and leave town with Lillian to start a new life," he said, his voice dropping lower. He balled his fists at his side, getting agitated. "She was going to do it, too. Sell this old house and go someplace new, with me. But on the day your mother was to show the property to a buyer who seemed intent on making an offer, Lillian got cold feet. Said what we were doing was wrong, and that she couldn't leave Sylvan Creek. 'Her town' needed her." His chest, under a dress shirt that was a lot like the ones in the closet, heaved as he grew increasingly upset. "She always put this stupid community ahead of me!"

I didn't blame her. Larry Fox was a lying, cheating, murderous jerk.

I dared to take my eyes off him for just a moment to steal a glance at the smiling, young couple in the photo.

Larry's hair had been dark and even thicker when the picture had been taken. He'd been scrawny, too, with no hint of the muscular, barrel chest he'd developed over time. And his skin looked like it had been pale, while he now had a perpetual golfer's tan.

Had his personality been different, too, years ago? Better? Kinder? Less *devious*?

And how had Lillian, who'd been in the local newspaper nearly every week of her life, kept so many secrets about her love life, her unacknowledged sister, and . . . who knew what else?

All at once, I thought of another person who had quietly deceived an entire congregation.

"You've *already* committed two murders, haven't you?" I asked Larry. "You killed Pastor Pete, too, didn't you?"

The sickening, self-satisfied look on his face gave the truth away. He didn't even have to answer.

"Why?" I searched again for a weapon, because our conversation had to be coming to a close. "Why murder *him*?"

Larry seemed almost eager to explain. He probably thought this was his one chance to brag about what he'd done, with no fear of the story spreading, because he planned to kill me, too.

"Kishbaugh caught me leaving the house after I killed Lillian," Larry explained. "He'd come for a meeting with her."

The one I'd seen on Pastor Pete's calendar.

"I didn't know about their appointment," Larry continued. "He walked in to find me standing in the kitchen in my wet, bloodstained jacket—with blood on my hand, too—and writing a note that would hopefully deter people from snooping around."

"Why not kill *him* right then . . . ?"

Larry actually grinned. "I didn't need to. Lillian had told me everything that 'Pastor Pete' was doing with his 'flock's' money. The trips to Europe when he was supposed to be building hospitals in Haiti. The embezzlement. The falsified books. I warned him that I'd go to the police and spill the whole story if he didn't stay quiet about what *I'd* done.

"Let's face it," Larry added, with a grunt. "Lillian's death benefited him, too. He was in no rush to run to the police and have them start asking questions. I told him that I'd tried to make it look like an accident, pushing her into the tub, so it would appear that she fell, and dropped in the CD player she always kept in the bathroom."

"Why did she do that?" I asked, as Socrates moved closer to me. A protective gesture. I was worried about him, too, and hoped that he would run if anything happened to me. "Why keep a CD player in the *bathroom*?"

Larry frowned, growing reflective again. "She liked to listen to classical music while she relaxed in the tub. It was one of her few indulgences." He paused, losing himself in memories again. Then he shook his head sadly. "She truly appreciated culture. I can't even understand the music Tamara listens to. . . ."

Just when I thought Socrates and I might be able to push past him and run for our lives, he snapped back to the present again.

"Unfortunately for Kishbaugh, investigators began to close in on his scams," Larry continued. "I saw an article in the *Gazette* that said he'd likely be arrested soon."

I was afraid for my life, but I couldn't help wondering again, *Who was this new reporter who actually covered news in Sylvan Creek?*

Then I forced myself to focus on the conversation, to keep Larry talking and buy more time. "You were afraid that, if Pastor Pete got arrested, he'd take you down with him, right?"

"Yes." Larry nodded, solemnly. "I had to shut him up. The sooner the better."

Just like he'd silence me—and maybe Socrates—soon.

I suddenly felt a different prickle of fear in my stomach. Over a memory. "You chased me at the orchard, didn't you?"

"I thought your dog saw me trying to sneak off after killing Kishbaugh," he said, with a glance at Socrates. "I followed you, thinking I had to stop the thing from tattling." Larry smiled wryly. "Then, when we were all running—risking making a scene that would attract some of Tamara's other ghouls—I remembered that I was chasing down a stupid *dog*! A beast that couldn't talk! I turned back and left you to deal with the body."

I dared to look down at Socrates. The ridge of fur along his back stood straight up with anger in response to the insult. But he wisely remained quiet. I felt sure that he was trying to figure out how to leverage the fact that Larry underestimated him. And I was fairly confident that he'd find a way.

I returned my attention to Larry. "What's the deal with the jacket?" I noted. "Why'd you leave it behind after killing Miss Flynt? And what does the symbol mean?"

Larry finally seemed less than proud of himself, because he'd made a mistake. "I had to ditch it. By the time I was done convincing Kishbaugh to keep his mouth shut, all you animal lovers were starting to show up on the lawn. I couldn't leave in a wet, bloodstained jacket. I finished the note, making it look like Lillian had gone away for a while, then ditched the jacket—fast—and slipped out the back door. If your mother hadn't 'tidied up,' nobody would've found that thing until long after the crime had been forgotten."

"You changed the will, didn't you?" I asked. "Lillian never deeded the house back to the historical society, did she?"

"No," Larry admitted. "When she died, the house was still to be sold privately by your mother. But I thought it would be best if the mansion went to Asa, who thinks he knows all of the town's secrets, but who would never *really* dig into this particular tale. He wanted the house too much to ask questions."

Socrates moved to stand in front of me, like he realized that time was running short. Larry would make a move soon. He'd taken another step farther into the bedroom.

"What does the symbol on the jacket mean?" I asked again. I could hear the hint of desperation in my voice, and Larry found my fear amusing, too. "What do the flames, the bird, and the book represent?"

"I am a member of the Munificent Order of the

Phoenix," he explained, grinning. "A *very* secret benevolent society." The smile died on his lips, and the laughter in his eyes faded, replaced by malice. "Although, some of us are less benevolent than others."

Both Socrates and I took one more step backward, but there was nowhere to go, and I flinched as Larry grabbed my arm.

Chapter 62

"Where are you taking me?" I demanded, struggling as Larry dragged me out of the bedroom and down the dark corridor. I wished he'd never acquired that barrel chest or his biceps. I also didn't understand why Socrates wasn't helping more. He trotted along with us, but he wasn't attacking Larry's ankles, or even growling. I had to assume that he had a plan, but I hoped he'd put it into action soon. In the meantime, I continued to fight against Larry's formidable grip. "Let me go!"

"I'll let you go—down the stairs," Larry informed me, huffing slightly with exertion. I dug in my heels but, as usual, I'd worn my oversized cowboy boots, and one of them flew right off. "I might not have managed to make Lillian's death look like an accident," he added, "but no one will question how a klutz fell down a flight of old stairs in the dark!"

Was my clumsiness becoming the stuff of local legend?

"Socrates, do something!" I begged, because we'd reached the staircase. I was out of time. I glanced down at the basset hound, who'd never failed me, and urged, "Run! Get help!"

But Socrates didn't move. He lifted his head, raising his nose in the air, and *barked*, louder than I'd ever heard him bark. The deep, resounding "WOOF" seemed to fill the whole mansion. And just as Larry Fox hauled me backward, the better to toss me *forward*, I understood what Socrates was trying to tell me. He wasn't sniffing, he was *pointing*.

Using every last ounce of strength I possessed—plus a move from a martial arts discipline I'd tried, briefly, in Israel—I twisted my arms free, lunged, and grabbed the broken, decorative top of the newel post, clutching it tightly. Then, although I despised violence, I smacked that old piece of Victoriana into Larry Fox's thick skull, just hard enough to send him reeling.

I would never be sure if Socrates, a peacenik himself, purposely positioned his long, low body so Larry pitched over him and narrowly missed tumbling down the stairs himself. I suspected that Socrates *might* have suspended his principles for just a moment to save me. And with a rush of adrenaline still coursing through me, I bent down to offer him an impulsive, grateful hug, forgetting for a second that he didn't like displays of affection.

Unfortunately, I was already off balance and only wearing one boot, and the next thing I knew, I lost my footing and launched myself down the old staircase, if less violently than Larry would've done. I felt each riser smack my rear end as I bumped all the way to the landing. And when I managed to stop my momentum, I lay for a moment with my eyes closed, trying to make sure I hadn't broken anything—only to feel a drop of drool on my nose, followed by a wet, slobbery tongue licking my face.

I cautiously opened one eye to discover that a

one-eared Chihuahua with a severe overbite was dancing around me on worried little paws.

"I'm okay," I promised Artie. "Nothing's broken. I mainly bounced down on my butt."

Then I accepted the hand up that Jonathan Black offered me while noting drily, "You *really* need to buy shoes that fit."

Chapter 63

"Are you sure he's going to be okay?" I asked Jonathan, who stood with me in Flynt Mansion's parlor, both of us watching uniformed officers lead Larry Fox out the door to a waiting squad car that illuminated the dark night with bursts of red and blue. "I hit him pretty hard."

"He'll be fine," Jonathan assured me. "He's walking out on his own. And why are you so worried about a man who attempted to toss you down a flight of stairs?"

I shrugged. "As the Dalai Lama once said, *Our prime purpose in this life is to help others. And if you can't help them, at least don't hurt them.* I don't know who could've helped Larry Fox—he made some huge mistakes—but I didn't want to harm him more than was necessary for me to survive."

Jonathan watched the door close behind Larry, who'd trudged out, his head hanging down. "He's lucky he tried to kill a student of philosophy. I wouldn't have shown quite as much mercy if he'd tried to break my neck."

I wasn't sure about that, especially when he turned

to me again and asked, with genuine concern, "Are you all right, Daphne?"

"My butt will survive," I said, resisting the urge to rub the wounded spot, which was starting to bruise. "I've endured worse falls."

Apparently, I hadn't quite understood the question. "I was asking about more than your . . . posterior," Jonathan clarified. "You nearly got killed—again."

"I'm fine," I promised him, just as Artie, Axis, and Socrates ran past us. Of course, Socrates slowed to a lope when he passed me, lest I think he was having fun. Then, when he thought he was out of sight, he picked up the pace again. I smiled at Jonathan. "I knew Socrates would have a plan and save the day."

Jonathan wasn't amused. "Daphne, you can't trust a dog to take care of you."

I disagreed, and I was sure *he'd* relied on Herod, but I let him continue.

"Why did you come here alone?" he asked. "If you *had* to snoop, why couldn't you at least wait until Elyse could tell me where you were going? Or, better yet, find a working cell phone and tell me yourself?"

"I decided to make sure the slippers really existed, before I took any more steps to get you involved," I said. "Plus I couldn't imagine why Larry would return to the scene of a crime he'd committed. I had no idea he kept a bunch of incriminating clothes here. I assumed the house would be empty—discounting a possible ghost."

Jonathan shook his head. "You don't really believe—"

I spoke right over him, before we could get into a debate about spirits. "Regardless," I said, grinning, "you have to admit that I did catch another killer for you."

Jonathan was ready to admit nothing of the sort.

"I already knew Larry Fox committed the murder," he informed me. "I matched the unusual *LF* on the note you took from the kitchen with his signature on the will."

"You saw that?"

He nodded. "Yes. I noted the signature when your mother was contesting the will, at Fox's office. I'd also identified Fox as a member of the Munificent Order of the Phoenix and knew the windbreaker belonged to him."

The news that Jonathan had also solved the crime was somewhat deflating. "So, what were you waiting for? Why didn't you arrest him?"

"Those of us who are actually *authorized and paid to solve homicides* like to wait until we build what's called a 'solid case,'" he advised me. I could see a welcome glimmer of amusement in his blue eyes. "We don't bumble our way into dark mansions and risk getting tossed down staircases—only to fall ourselves."

"Okay, you made your point," I said, hurrying after him, because he was walking away, toward the door. "But I did solve the crime simultaneous to you. You have to at least concede that."

"I'm not conceding anything," he said, as on some silent cue that I hadn't caught, Axis—and, to my shock, Artie—came running out of nowhere and fell in step with him. Artie actually pranced with pride, presumably over his success in obeying a command.

"How did you train Artie to do that?" I asked, forgetting all about murder for a moment. "I didn't think that was possible!"

Jonathan didn't share his secret to training the

world's most exuberant, independent Chihuahua. He merely looked over his shoulder at me and grinned. "Happy Halloween, Daphne. I hope you figure out what to do with your painting."

I stopped in my tracks.

How had I forgotten about *that* thing?

Chapter 64

The rain moved in with a vengeance around midnight. Normally, I found the patter of raindrops on the cottage's roof soothing, but that night the torrential downpour hammered against the tin so loudly that I couldn't sleep. I also kept thinking about the painting downstairs.

I wasn't sure if the spirit of Violet Baumgartner really roamed around Flynt Mansion, but now that I no longer had a murder to preoccupy my thoughts, the *Woman in Red* was starting to haunt *me*.

Sitting up and swinging my legs over the side of my bed, I pulled my soft flannel robe around myself, stood up, and tiptoed past Socrates, who was exhausted from the evening's adventures and snoring in his bed. Quietly making my way to the kitchen, I brewed a cup of chamomile tea, then sat down on the love seat to contemplate the portrait by the light of the dying fire.

"How can I figure out what Miss Flynt wants me to do with this?" I whispered, tucking my feet under myself to warm them. "I obviously didn't know her at all!"

Violet Baumgartner glared back at me, offering no answers.

My eyes still trained on the painting, I took a sip of tea, nearly spilling hot liquid all over myself when, to my surprise, Tinkleston hopped lightly onto the cushion right next to me. I hadn't even seen him prowling around the room.

"Hey, you," I said softly, not wanting to scare him off. Outside, the wind roared, and the branches of the plum tree scratched at the window. "Is the rain keeping you awake, too?"

Tinkleston meowed, which I took for a "yes." Then he blinked at me, and for the first time since I'd brought him to my home, I really had a chance to look into his big, orange eyes.

Maybe it was wishful thinking, but I swore I saw gratitude there.

"It's my pleasure to take care of you," I told him, as he settled behind my knees, curling into a ball.

I knew that I was pushing things, but I dared to stroke his soft, black fur, earning a swipe from his little pom-pom paw. But the gesture seemed halfhearted, and he didn't run away or even open his eyes.

I studied Tinks's sourpuss face while he slept, and all at once I realized that, while Lillian Flynt had certainly kept her share of secrets, I *did* know some things about her.

She'd loved Tinkleston enough to bequeath him to me, knowing that—not to blow my own horn—I would give him a chance and not dump him in a shelter the first time he unsheathed his claws.

Miss Flynt had also hated the way Bea ran Whiskered Away Home. I was sure that's why she'd refused to support the "rescue."

And, although she'd lived in a mansion and never labored for *money*, Miss Flynt had believed in the value of hard work. That was why she hadn't just given Fidelia the portrait. And why she always encouraged me to use my talents.

My eyes had been fluttering shut, but I jolted and sat up straight, nearly dislodging Tinks, who growled in his sleep. I didn't mean to disturb him, but I suddenly knew what I was supposed to do with the painting.

Maybe my plans weren't exactly what Lillian had in mind when she left the portrait to me, but I was pretty confident that I would at least come close to fulfilling her wishes.

Or maybe Miss Flynt hadn't ever had a specific plan of her own and had just trusted me to do something worthwhile with a despised piece of her family's history.

Either way, I felt happy with my decision, and after a few minutes, I pulled a warm, fringed throw over myself and Tinkleston, being careful to keep his pushed-in nose exposed. Then I drifted off to sleep to the sound of the waning storm.

And when I awoke on a sunny, crisp November day, the first thing I did was go upstairs and call my mother, who wasn't even fully awake—until I brought up her favorite topic, asking, "Can you meet me in town to talk about a property?"

Chapter 65

"This is a really nice party, for something you threw together in five minutes," Moxie said, without a hint of insult. She seemed genuinely impressed by my house-warming, most of which took place outside, because the cottage was so small. But my guests appeared happy to linger around the table I'd set up under the plum tree. As the sun set, the votives in the Moroccan lanterns I'd hung from the branches glowed like fire-flies, and the chilly air was warmed by a small bonfire burning in a circle of stones. "Don't forget that my present is a mural," Moxie added, pulling her hands out from under a 1960s striped poncho and holding them over the fire to warm them. "I'll paint it whenever you want."

"I will keep that in mind," I promised her, filing that reminder way, way in the back of my brain. *Way* back. "And I'm glad you're having a good time."

I thought the open house was nice, too, for a last minute affair. The farmhouse table, which I'd found in Piper's barn, was covered with spice-colored linens and practically buckling under the weight of two crock-pots filled with mulled wine and cider, three maple-apple upside-down cakes, a gingerbread-pear loaf, and some plum *crostatas*, as a nod to my cottage's nickname. Anticipating that dogs would visit, I'd also whipped up some Honey, I'm Home cookies, cut into the shape of dog houses. The little honey-and-rolled-oat treats were going fast, as were the snacks for humans. My tiny home was overflowing with friends and family—and a few strangers, too. I didn't recognize one tall man with longish, dark hair and a scruffy beard, who was helping himself to a *crostata*. When he bent over, I saw a notebook poking out of the back pocket of his worn jeans.

"Who is that guy?" I asked Moxie.

"Oh, that's Gabriel Graham," she told me. "He bought the *Weekly Gazette*. And he's actually trying to fill it with news!"

I narrowed my eyes, not sure if I wanted a journalist crashing my party. "So he's the new reporter I've been hearing about . . . ?"

I was just about to approach him when someone else drew my attention.

My sister, who was talking with the man I knew only as "Roger."

Piper must've sensed me observing her, because she glanced in my direction, then lightly touched her date's arm, excusing herself and walking toward me and Moxie.

"So, who's your new friend?" I asked, when she'd joined us by the fire. "And how'd you meet him?"

"He's a cutie," Moxie added. "I like his naturally wavy hair—and his sweater vest!"

Piper gave Moxie an uncertain look, but I was pretty sure the comment was meant as a compliment. Moxie liked all things argyle.

"Not that it's your business," Piper told us both, "but his name is Dr. Roger Berendt, and he's a new professor at Wynton. I met him when he brought his dog, Seymour, in for an emergency procedure. We've seen each other a few times since then."

For a person who hadn't wanted to share much, Piper had spilled a lot. And her cheeks weren't just rosy because there was a nip in the air or wine in her pretty, beveled-glass cup.

She *liked* Dr. Berendt, but she wasn't about to admit it yet.

She'd also spoken somewhat sharply because she was genuinely upset with me.

"Not to change the subject, but I can't believe you almost got yourself killed again, Daphne," she said, crossing her arms, like she needed to keep herself from waggling a finger at me. "What were you thinking, sneaking into that house alone, at night?"

"I had to know if I'd really seen men's slippers under Miss Flynt's bed, the night she was murdered," I explained. "I was returning my oversized shoes to Lighthouse Fellowship, and I remembered that when I found Tinkleston, he was sitting in a big, plaid slipper. That didn't strike me as strange at the time, because so much was happening. But when I had a chance to reflect, I thought it seemed odd." I looked at the cottage and saw Tinks perched in a window, his black body silhouetted and his orange eyes glowing. I turned back to Piper. "I swear, he was trying to point out the killer. I just had to figure out what he was trying to say."

"So Lillian Flynt and Larry Fox really were in love, huh?" Moxie shook her head. "Who knew?"

"Not me," Piper said grimly. "I'm shocked that it was a crime of passion."

"Yes," I agreed. "The whole time I was trying to solve the murder, I thought the motive would be money, given that Miss Flynt had a fortune. But it was about a rekindled teenage romance."

Moxie rested one hand on her chest, tilted her head, and pouted. "Aw, that's sweet."

Piper shot her a weird look. "No. It's really not."

"Speaking of the Flynt estate, where's Mom?" I asked my sister. "Is she still sulking about losing the sale of the mansion?"

Piper knitted her brows. "Didn't you hear?"

"Hear what?"

"When Larry Fox admitted that he'd changed the will, Elyse Hunter-Black swooped in with a team of lawyers and successfully argued that the previous version should stand. Mom's with her now, closing on the property."

"Oh." Why hadn't I expected that? Larry had said, point blank, that he'd changed that crucial provision. I thought about Asa Whitaker, who probably couldn't afford to hire his own squad of high-priced attorneys. "Poor Asa must be depressed."

"According to Mom, he didn't even try to put up a fight," Piper said. "Apparently, once he realized that his dream of a museum was about to become an overwhelming reality—and almost certainly a flop—he got cold feet. He's supposedly happy to stay hidden away in his old bank."

"Hey, whatever happened to your inheritance?" Moxie asked me. "What are you doing with the painting?"

"You should either sell it or find somewhere safe to keep it," Piper added. "If you're right about its value, it shouldn't sit around in an *unlocked* cottage."

She sounded like Jonathan, who hadn't shown up at my party yet, although I'd invited him. At least I knew why my two other missing guests—Mom and Elyse— were running late.

"Daph?" Piper prompted, when I didn't respond right away. "The painting?"

"Oh, yeah." I snapped back to reality. "I sold the Tuttweiler, in a bidding war. Apparently, *a lot* of people like impasto."

Moxie beamed. "Congrats!"

Piper, of course, was interested in the bottom line. "How much did you get for it?"

I shrugged, like the sum was no big deal, then told them, "About two hundred thousand dollars."

Moxie was adjusting a wide-brimmed hat, and she nearly knocked it into the fire, which would've been a blessing in disguise. Between the hat and the poncho, she looked a little bit like Clint Eastwood in one of his old westerns.

"Daph, you're rich!" she cried.

I shook my head. "No, I'm not. Most of the money is going to charity." I waved to Bea Baumgartner, who was loading a plate with cake and bending poor Roger's ear. She smiled and waved back. Returning my attention to Piper and Moxie, I told them, "I put a lot of the money into a trust for Whiskered Away Home, which will now be an official, licensed charity, run by a board of directors. I also set aside money to renovate the barn, and cats will actually be adopted once everything's in place. No more hoarding."

Piper nearly reeled headlong into the fire pit. I reached out a hand to steady her.

"*You* set that up?" she asked incredulously. "You?"

"With the help of a lawyer—and Mom, who, I have to admit, has a mind for that sort of thing."

Moxie continued to struggle with her hat. "How'd you get Bea to agree to all that?"

"She really does love cats," I reminded them. "And

she was desperate for funding. She didn't have much choice."

Piper still seemed shocked, but she managed to ask, "What's happening with the rest of the money?"

"I gave some to Fur-ever Friends, because I'm pretty sure that was Lillian's favorite charity. They won't have to worry about fund-raising for a long, long time. A *lot* of dogs will be rescued."

Moxie frowned. "Is that it? Did you really give it all away?" She seemed to realize that didn't sound very charitable. "Not that I think supporting good causes is a bad thing!"

I smiled. "Actually, I did keep a *tiny* bit for myself, some of which I'll use to pay Fidelia Tuttweiler to keep my books and do the accounting for Whiskered Away Home, too, if she proves competent." We all looked over at Fidelia, who was feeding Socrates a Honey, I'm Home treat. She wasn't bad with animals, and I was starting to believe that she'd be a decent accountant, too. She certainly loved her chosen profession and had agreed to take some classes at an actual business school. "I think Lillian would approve of me helping a lost soul like Fidelia get established in a career," I said. "Miss Flynt believed in the value of hard work."

"That sounds like a good plan," Moxie agreed.

"Is that it?" Piper asked, with a glance at the cottage. "You have no intention of *finally* paying all the rent you owe me for this place and the time you spent in my farmhouse?"

I grinned more broadly. "As a matter of fact, I did set aside some money for rent. . . ."

I was just about to reveal my master plan for the small sum I'd put aside for myself when someone lightly touched my elbow. Yet another latecomer to the party who didn't even greet any of us.

"Daph," Dylan said seriously. Almost *sadly*. "We have to talk. Now."

"Why?" I asked, my heart sinking, as Moxie and Piper politely excused themselves. "Why right now?"

I supposed I already knew what he was going to say and had avoided the discussion because I didn't want to hear the truth, which nevertheless caught up to me.

"Because," he said, "I'm leaving Sylvan Creek."

Chapter 66

The evening was getting cold but, as always, Dylan was dressed for the beach in shorts, a sweatshirt, and flip-flops. And it wasn't just his clothes that reminded me of sand and surf. It was . . . Dylan, from his blond, sun-streaked hair to his ocean-blue eyes, to the mellow way he rolled through life, just waiting to catch the next wave—which was carrying him out of Sylvan Creek.

We'd retreated to the tiny, screened porch off the cottage's kitchen to get some privacy, but as we stood looking out over the party outside, it seemed as if there was nothing to say. Or maybe way too much.

"I hate good-byes," I finally said. "I guess that's why I kept avoiding talking to you. I knew, when I saw the *help wanted* sign in Piper's practice, that you were leaving, but I wouldn't let myself believe it."

Dylan smiled. "That's not like you, Daph. You're good with change."

"Maybe not so much lately," I admitted. "I kind of like things just the way they are right now."

Dylan's smile faded away. "I guess that means you won't come with me?"

I reared back, not sure I'd heard him right. "What?"

"You could come along," he suggested. "Not that I know exactly where I'm going. Aside from somewhere near the ocean."

There was a time when I would've jumped at the chance to simply wander without any clear destination, and I took a moment to consider Dylan's offer, my attention torn between the choice I needed to make and the party I needed to rejoin soon.

Outside, my sister was laughing with Roger Berendt, and my best friend had somehow gotten tangled in her poncho. She kept twisting around, trying to find her way out.

Jonathan Black had arrived at some point, too. He was deep in conversation with Gabriel Graham. As I watched, Jonathan pointed toward the cottage, then made a spiraling motion with one finger, near his head, which could've been a reference to my curls—or an indication that he thought I was crazy.

Looking past the two men, I saw Artie and Axis running circles with Socrates, who wasn't even trying to feign indifference.

Could I really uproot him now that he had friends?

Then I felt something rub against my ankle, and I glanced down to discover that Tinkleston was winding around my legs.

He'd just found a real home, after losing his person. . . .

"What do you think, Daphne?" Dylan asked, nudging me out of my reverie. His eyes gleamed, like he'd already started on his adventure. "Don't you want to see the wide world again? We could end up in Tahiti. Or Argentina. Who knows?"

That was tempting. I'd never been to either of those places. There would be new people to meet, and new things to see.

My mouth kept opening and closing as I tried to find an answer for Dylan. I knew that once he was gone, the offer to join him wouldn't come again. He was a now or never, leap of faith kind of guy, and he'd drift out of my life, trusting that the universe would bring us together again someday. But he'd never actively try to make that happen.

"Well, Daph?" he asked again.

I was just about to make my decision when I heard the click of high heels on my wooden kitchen floor, and my mother burst onto the screened porch, fanning herself with papers and saying, "I'm sorry I'm so late, Daphne. I just closed on Flynt Mansion, and I'm running behind schedule. But I've brought the lease for the Espresso Pronto property, so you can sign tonight."

I hesitated one more second, looking between Dylan, who represented the freedom I'd always prized, and the papers in my mother's hands, which—if I signed them—would commit me to opening a bakery for pets and tie me to Sylvan Creek for at least three years.

I could feel my feet getting figuratively—and literally— cold. Then I looked outside one more time at the people and pets I cared about, and down at the cat with the terrible name, who was starting to seem happy in his new place.

Lillian had trusted me to give Tinks a home, and I'd accepted that responsibility.

"I'm really sorry," I told Dylan, who probably wasn't exactly sure what was going on. I'd never told him, or anyone but my mother, about the bakery plan yet. "Part of me would love to travel the world with you, but I just can't leave Sylvan Creek right now."

Then, before I could back out, I accepted the documents from Realtor Maeve Templeton, went inside my snug little cottage, and signed my name to the lease agreement, with a very serious, but approving, black Persian cat as a witness.

Recipes

Liverin' It Up Treats

I would never tell Socrates, but the secret to his very favorite snack is . . . baby food! He would be so appalled. I actually hide the jar when I make these little crackers. I also can't believe anyone would feed a baby pureed liver—and I don't just say that as a vegetarian. It just smells bad, to a human nose!

¾ cup wheat germ
¾ cup nonfat dry milk powder
1 egg
1 tbs. brewer's yeast
1 (3.5 oz.) jar pureed liver baby food
¼ cup water, or more if needed

Preheat your oven to 350 degrees. (You may need to guesstimate if your oven is from the mid-twentieth century, like mine.)

Mix all the ingredients together in a bowl. Add a little more water if the dough isn't coming together.

Drop the dough by teaspoonfuls onto a greased cookie sheet—or, better yet, use parchment paper. Less mess, less chance of things sticking.

Bake the snacks for about 20 minutes, then remove them from the oven and cool them before Socrates . . . er, your dog . . . gets hold of them!

Store leftovers—there won't be any—in the fridge.

Pumpkin-Peanut-Butter Ghosts

Nothing says Halloween quite like pumpkins and ghosts. This recipe combines the two—plus lip-smacking peanut butter—for a pup-friendly snack that's always a big hit. Your four-legged friends will be haunting you until you make them again!

> 2½ cups whole wheat flour
> 2 eggs
> ½ cup canned pumpkin puree
> 2 tbs. peanut butter
> ½ tsp. salt
> ½ tsp. ground cinnamon (It's a pet friendly
> spice, but I don't overuse it.)

Preheat your oven to 350 degrees, or thereabouts.

Whisk all of the ingredients in a bowl, going light on the water at first. Add water gradually to make a workable dough. You want the dough to be stiff enough to cut into shapes.

Roll out dough and use a cookie cutter to create ghosts. Or create them with a knife. They don't have to be perfect!

Bake 40 minutes, cool and serve.

Batty-for-Turkey Treats

Cats are notoriously finicky, so it's easy to forget that they might enjoy a nice homemade treat, too. And I promise you that even the pickiest feline eater will come running for these snacks, which also happen to be healthy. I love to see the look on Tinkleston's face when he eats these. He is at least 50 percent less dour than usual.

    ½ pound ground turkey
    1 egg
    ½ cup grated carrots
    ¼ cup Parmesan cheese—or more!
    ½ cup crackers, finely crushed
    Pinch of salt

You guessed it . . . Preheat your oven to about 350 degrees.

Mix all the ingredients by hand. The texture should remind you of a meat loaf. If things are too soggy, add more cheese and crackers.

Smoosh the mixture onto a baking tray, until it's about a half-inch thick.

Using a cookie cutter, create bat shapes.

Bake for about twenty minutes, let them cool—and watch them fly away, as your cat chows down!

    (These *may* look only remotely like bats, once
    cooked, but sometimes they turn out great!)

Honey, I'm Home Cookies

These cookies are sure to appeal to your favorite dog's sweet tooth. You can make them into any shape you like, but I love the idea of little dog houses. I like to wrap them up in cute containers and send them along with my fosters when they get their "fur-ever" families. I think it's a nice way to wish them happiness in their new homes, and thank their adopters, too!

½ cup peanut butter, creamy or crunchy
¼ cup honey
1 tbs. olive oil
1 cup chicken broth
1 cup whole wheat flour
1 cup all-purpose flour
1 cup rolled oats

Get that oven going at 350!

Mix together the peanut butter, oil, honey, and broth.

Use a separate bowl to whisk together the two flours and the oatmeal.

Add your dry ingredients to your wet ones.

Roll out your dough on a floured surface and use your preferred cookie cutter. Reroll any scraps to make as many cookies as possible.

Bake on a greased or parchment-lined baking sheet for about 15 minutes.

Cool and share your sweet treats!

Read on for a preview of the next Lucky Paws
Petsitting Mystery,
starring Daphne Templeton, Ph.D.,
and Socrates, her long-suffering basset hound . . .

PAWPRINTS & PREDICAMENTS

By Bethany Blake

Available in spring 2018!

"A doggone charming read from start to finish!"
—Cleo Coyle, *New York Times* bestselling author,
on *Death by Chocolate Lab*

For more information
about *Pawprints & Predicaments* by Bethany Blake,
go to www.kensingtonbooks.com

Chapter 1

The thirtieth annual Sylvan Creek Tail Waggin' Winterfest promised to be even bigger and better than the festivals of years past, which was saying something, because the pet-friendly, week-long event had long been *the* highlight of January for many folks in the Pocono Mountains.

And this year, the little village of temporary huts that was always erected at wooded Bear Tooth State Park, on the shore of Lake Wallapawakee, had been completely refurbished, each tiny, heated shack painted a pretty, but wintry, shade of robin's egg blue. There were more vendors, too, selling things like gourmet hot chocolate, s'mores and cold-weather gear for dogs and cats. For the first time ever, a polar bear plunge would kick off the festivities later that evening, and the bonfire that burned at the center of the ephemeral town crackled in a bigger ring of stones, while the paths through the festival were lit by new glass lanterns. There were even moonlit walks through the woods, led by old Max Pottinger, who told the tale of a legendary spectral St. Bernard that supposedly patrolled the vast network of cross-country ski trails, guiding those who lost their way.

Strolling through the heart of the festival on a night that threatened snow, I couldn't help thinking the scene was picture perfect. And yet, something didn't seem quite right.

"It's almost *too* nice, this year," I complained to my sister, Piper, and my best friend, Moxie Bloom. Slipping on some ice in my favorite flea-market cowboy boots, I nearly dropped my third s'more. Then I righted myself and added, "Don't you think it's kind of odd?"

"The festival's definitely different," Piper agreed, kicking through the snow in her sensible, waterproof boots, which matched her rated-for-the-Arctic down parka. My sister was a veterinarian who often saw patients literally in the field, and she was always suitably dressed for the weather. And, as someone who'd restored an 1800s farm, called Winding Hill, Piper wasn't necessarily opposed to updating shabby structures. "I like the fresh paint," she noted, with a glance at a booth selling hand-knit sweaters for dogs. "And the vendors are better this year. I think it's nice to have more than just the VFW selling hot dogs." She frowned, still staring at the hut, which was strung with clotheslines that sagged under the weight of small cardigans and pullovers. "Although, while I'm a fan of Arlo Finch's crafts, I'm not too fond of his practice."

"You're just too rational," I said, waving to Arlo, a lanky, bearded, graying hippie throwback who practiced holistic "pet healing and energy therapy" when not knitting *adorable* canine garb. I'd already stopped by Arlo's booth and purchased an argyle cardigan for a one-eared, drooling Chihuahua that I used to foster, even though I had trouble picturing the man who'd adopted Artie buttoning the little dog into a sweater.

Especially one knitted from free-range yak yarn and delivered in a bag that advertised Arlo's practice, Peaceable Pets. I made a mental note *not* to mention the yarn when I dropped off the present. "I'm definitely open to the idea of alternative medicine," I added. "Some therapies have been time-tested over centuries."

"I agree with Daphne," Moxie said, tucking her hands deeper into a fluffy, white, fake-fur muff. "I would totally get acupuncture, if I wasn't scared of needles."

Piper gave Moxie a funny look, then told us both, "New Age medicine is all mumbo jumbo." She zipped her parka right up to her chin as we all walked on, past ice sculptures that were also new to the festival. The frozen artwork glittered in the moonlight. "And I don't know why you wouldn't like an *improved* Winterfest, Daphne."

"Because even the people look like actors," I complained, sidestepping a twenty-something couple who might've walked directly off the pages of an L.L. Bean catalog. The woman had a tiny, perfectly groomed Yorkie tucked under her arm, and the man sipped cocoa from a commemorative mug. I couldn't ever recall Winterfest having a logo before, but the ceramic cups featured a cartoon image of the legendary Lake Wallapawakee Saint Bernard, who was romping in a snow pile. I watched for a moment as the man and woman stopped to check out the dog sweaters, the woman holding up an even *cuter* cardigan than the one I'd bought. Darn it. Then I returned my attention to Piper and Moxie. "Don't you think the whole thing is kind of . . . *Stepford Wives*-ish?"

"Ooh, I love that movie!" Moxie cried, missing the

point. "Although, the festival reminds me more of *White Christmas* than robot wives."

Moxie, of course, knew both movies by heart. She loved all things vintage, and—along with the muff— wore a 1940s wool coat that nipped in at the waist, a pair of leather boots with fur trim around the ankles, and a turban-style hat that hid one of her few concessions to modernity, her spiky red hair.

All at once, as I studied my friend's attire, I realized that her outfit, like the too-flawless setting, was a little . . . off.

"Umm, you know you have to ditch all your clothes on the lakeshore, right?" I asked Moxie, with a glance down at my old barn coat, tattered wool mittens, and oversized boots. My long, unruly, dirty-blond curls were tucked under a knit ski cap I'd found on the floor of the pink 1970s VW bus that served as headquarters for my business, Daphne Templeton's Lucky Paws Pet Sitting. In short, I looked like I was about to muck out stalls, while Moxie could've gone shopping on Park Avenue—circa 1945. "Aren't you a little overdressed?" I suggested. "You look awfully nice to jump in a lake."

Moxie stopped in her tracks and pulled the muff back close to her chest. Her green eyes were wide with surprise. "Why would I jump in a lake? In January?"

I looked at Piper, who was rolling her eyes, as if to say, *"I knew this would happen."*

Then I turned back to Moxie. "Because we're doing the polar bear plunge this year!" I reminded her. My s'more was oozing, but I hardly noticed the gooey marshmallow dripping onto my mitten. "You're the one who suggested it!"

Moxie shook her head. "Oh, no. I said we should *go to the* plunge. I didn't say we should *do* it."

As I tried to recall a conversation Moxie and I'd had a few weeks before, I heard a soft snuffling sound, almost like laughter, and looked down to see that my canine sidekick, a normally taciturn, introspective basset hound named Socrates, was struggling to contain a rare show of amusement.

"This is not funny," I told him, which didn't stop his tail from twitching, just a tiny bit. His usually baleful brown eyes also twinkled with amusement—until I gave him a warning look, and he hung his head, his long ears dragging in the snow. Needless to say, Socrates had refused to wear a hat, and he'd turned up his freckled nose at the insulated jacket I'd offered him, too. Canine apparel appalled him. "I'm already registered," I added, addressing Moxie again. "I have a number. I have to do the plunge!"

"Moxie is smart to sit the event out," Piper said. "From what I've seen, the organizers slapped the whole thing together at the last minute. I don't think there are even plans to restrict the number of people who enter the lake at one time. It could be a mess."

"I'll be careful," I promised, thinking she was worrying too much. "And it's for a good cause. All the proceeds go to feed the rescue cats at Breard's Big Cats of the World."

"I don't know if I support that 'charity,'" Piper said, continuing to be critical. "Is it a zoo? A shelter? A nonprofit, even? Because you have to pay to tour the place."

I honestly wasn't sure how to classify Big Cats of the World, either. But I knew that Victor Breard, a native of France, had a good reputation for taking in exotic animals that were rescued from bad situations—say, the tiger cub someone illegally adopted, then couldn't handle—and giving them safe, secure homes on his licensed two-hundred acre preserve, just outside Sylvan Creek.

"Well, regardless, I'm doing the plunge," I said, shooting Moxie a dark look. I was ninety percent sure *she* had misunderstood our earlier conversation.

"I'm sorry, Daph," she apologized. "I'd register now, but I'm not wearing a bathing suit." Then she raised her muff. "Besides, what would I do with Sebastian while I was swimming?"

"What?" Piper seemed puzzled. "What are you talking about?"

I was also confused. "You've *named* that fake fur thing?"

I was starting to think Moxie had gone over the edge when all at once, a tiny, white head popped out of the muff; a small, twitching nose sniffed the cold air; and a pair of intelligent pink eyes blinked at me. I jumped, and Socrates, normally unflappable, took a few steps backward, nearly bumping into one of the ice sculptures.

I had to force myself not to pull away, too. "You adopted a *rat?*"

Moxie raised her hands to let Sebastian brush his little cheek against hers. "Yes! It turns out small pets are allowed in my apartment. And he's *adorable*, don't you think?"

I loved animals, and I'd taken care of everything from pythons to tarantulas, but something about rats spooked me, as Piper knew, all too well. She grinned at me. "You look awfully taken aback for somebody who often quotes the Dalai Lama about the importance of loving all living creatures."

My pragmatic, successful sister loved to mock my admittedly impractical Ph.D. in philosophy.

"I'm sure Sebastian and I will end up being friends," I told Piper and Moxie. I forced myself to meet those pink eyes again, and Sebastian blinked up at me, then squirmed and returned to the warmth of his mobile den. I caught a glimpse of his naked tail slithering away and fought back a shudder, even as I said, "I promise, we'll be buddies, soon."

When the rat was out of sight, Socrates exhaled softly, like he was also relieved.

"I guess you're right about the plunge, Moxie," I added glumly. "You can't take a rat into freezing water." Then I looked hopefully at Piper. "Unless . . ."

"Moxie doesn't have a bathing suit," my sister reminded me. "And I'm afraid I can't hold Sebastian. I'm here on official, if unsanctioned, business, looking out for any dogs that might follow their owners into the water, then get panicked or hurt in the crowd."

"Sorry," Moxie apologized again, as we passed by a hut selling mulled cider and warm donuts. I'd finished my s'more and briefly debated buying yet another treat, in an attempt to fatten myself up, like a walrus insulated with blubber, then decided it was too late. "I wouldn't take part this year, anyhow," Moxie noted. "Not when the whole thing will probably be filmed!"

I grew even more concerned. "What do you mean by *that?*"

"Everybody from the media is here," Moxie explained. Her hands were trapped, so she nodded over at the bonfire, where kids were roasting hot dogs and marshmallows on sticks, while listening to old Max Pottinger spin the tale of the mysterious Saint Bernard, prelude to leading another walk in the woods. Max, wizened, bent and seemingly oblivious to the cold in a flannel shirt and ball cap, spoke in hushed tones, but his listeners were wide-eyed and rapt. The only exception was the new owner of, and only reporter at, the Sylvan Creek *Weekly Gazette,* who was in constant motion, snapping photos of Max and his audience. "I do not want Gabriel Graham putting my frozen, screaming face on the front page of a paper that people are actually starting to read now," Moxie said. "And you know he'll pick the most unflattering picture for page one!"

"Yes, he probably will," I muttered, as Gabriel—thirty-something, good looking, and perhaps *too* charming—crouched down and snapped away. The flames roared up behind him, and I couldn't help thinking that, with his dark, wavy hair, goatee and gleaming white teeth, he looked a little bit like the devil.

Gabriel must've sensed that he was being observed, because all at once, he straightened, slipped the distinctive red plaid strap on his hefty Nikon camera around his neck, and began to walk in our direction.

"Hey, everyone," he greeted us, with a nod to Socrates. I wasn't sure if I liked Gabriel, but I appreciated that he included the shortest member of our party, who sometimes got overlooked. Although I couldn't understand how. Socrates had a certain gravitas. Then Gabriel smiled at Piper. "Nice to see you." Before she even replied, he looked me and Moxie up and down and added, ambiguously, "You two look *interesting*, tonight."

"Why, thank you," Moxie said, taking the comment as a compliment. "My outfit is vintage forties. And Daphne's dressed to jump in the lake."

Gabriel's brown eyes glittered with amusement. "Always up to something, aren't you, Miss Templeton?" he observed. "The last time I spoke to you, you'd just solved a murder."

"Yes." I crossed my arms over my chest. "I read your article—in which you gave Jonathan Black most of the credit for solving the case."

I'd actually helped handsome, enigmatic Detective Jonathan Black solve *two* homicides during his brief

time in Sylvan Creek, but nobody ever seemed to want
to acknowledge my contributions. Least of all, Jonathan.

"I'll try to feature you prominently in my story on
the plunge," Gabriel promised. "I'll be sure to seek
you out when I'm taking pictures. And maybe someday I can do a feature on the pet sitter with the Ph.D.
in philosophy, who is also opening a bakery for dogs
and cats?"

Everybody knew that I was a pet sitter. My van announced my profession and featured a pretty eye-
catching painting of a misshapen dog that was often
mistaken for a misshapen pony. That was Moxie's
handiwork. The fact that I'd rented a small storefront on Sylvan Creek's main street and planned to—
hopefully—soon open a bakery for pets was also
common knowledge. But I wasn't sure how Gabriel
knew about my degree. And I didn't know if I liked his
mildly flirtatious, if mocking, tone, either.

"No, please don't feature me . . ." I started to protest,
my ears getting warm under my cap.

Piper was clearly amused. And Moxie was oblivious
to my discomfort. On the contrary, she seemed increasingly excited about the prospect of seeing *my* "frozen,
screaming" face on the front page, and she interrupted
me, noting, "Wow, a photo and a feature story!" Her
eyes were fairly glowing. "And maybe you'll be filmed
by Stylish Life Network, too, when you run into the
water!"

I looked down at my barn coat again, then caught
Gabriel smirking at me. "I think we've all established
that I'm not very 'stylish' tonight," I reminded everyone, while Socrates snuffled again.

Gabriel, meanwhile, surveyed the candlelit village,
which had been updated with support from the network, for a show called *America's Most Pet Friendly Towns*.

Sylvan Creek had been chosen—some preferred the word "targeted"—for the program the previous year, and a crew had been filming—some said "terrorizing"—the community for nearly six weeks, with no sign of packing up and leaving.

"Stylish Life did help to make this place look pretty nice," Gabriel observed. "Not too shabby, for a festival in a forest."

"Actually, I was just complaining that everything looks *too* perfect," I said, stepping back so two adorable Samoyed puppies could dart past me. I watched the pair tumble in the snow, thinking I'd never seen the dogs before. Was it possible that they'd been planted by the crew, to add even more "atmosphere"? "I sort of miss the shabby, rustic touches Winterfest used to have," I added. "Like the *old* luminarias, made from plastic milk jugs, with candles that kept burning out."

Piper knitted her brows, as if she wasn't quite up to speed. "You're saying Stylish Life funded the improvements?" She suddenly seemed less impressed by the changes. Like pretty much everyone in town who dealt with animals, Piper had suffered some run-ins with the film crew. "I didn't know that."

"Oh, yes, Stylish Life paid for a lot of the updates," Moxie said. As the owner of Sylvan Creek's unique salon for humans and pets, Spa and Paw, Moxie heard all of the local gossip. "Apparently, people who watch that network don't want to see plastic jugs stuck in the snow. From what I hear, some of the older festival organizers were kind of insulted to be told their event was 'tacky.'"

I could believe that feathers had been ruffled. I'd also had a few encounters with the Stylish Life team, and they weren't exactly tactful. But for once I held my tongue, not trusting Gabriel to keep any tales I told off the record. Piper was wisely staying quiet, too, although I knew she could've gone on for hours about the crew.

"Yes, I've heard that some of the Winterfest folks are unhappy," Gabriel said. "And there's also a rumor that someone at Stylish Life made up the legend about the Saint Bernard, just to make this already pet-centric town even more intriguing for animal-loving viewers." He slipped his hands into the pockets of a rust-colored down vest, and his teeth flashed white when he smiled more broadly. He really was the epitome of "devilishly handsome." "I have to admit, that wouldn't be a bad idea. Everything I print about the 'ghost dog' sells papers."

Socrates whined softly and shook his large head, presumably at the folly of humans. He did not believe in Bigfoot, yetis, monsters that lurked in lakes, or especially spectral Saint Bernards.

"There have definitely been more 'sightings,' lately," my equally skeptical sibling agreed, air-quoting "sightings." "But that tale has been around forever."

"Oh, yes," Moxie concurred. "The story, which *I* happen to believe, is older than Mr. Pottinger." She frowned. "But I wouldn't put it past Lauren Savidge to make stuff up. She's horrible!"

Moxie had finally invoked a name that the rest of us had probably subconsciously avoided speaking, just like one might not utter the name of a demon out loud, for fear of summoning the evil spirit.

Small, loud, forceful and sometimes conniving, in my opinion, "field producer" Lauren Savidge was the brash leader, and most despised member, of the small TV crew.

Gabriel Graham certainly knew all about Lauren, but he cocked his head, all–deceptive–innocence. "How so?" he asked Moxie. "What did Lauren do to *you?*"

Piper and I exchanged concerned glances, but Moxie took the bait. "Well, the other day, she barged into Spa and Paw and ordered her crew to start filming, without even asking if I minded. Then I swear, she nudged my arm while I was clipping my landlord's poodle, Marzipan, so his tail lost its little puffball, and I nearly cried—"

"Umm . . . Moxie . . ." There was warning in Piper's voice. Obviously, she'd noticed that Gabriel's eyes were lighting up at the prospect of yet another juicy story about Lauren's heavy handed attempt to create TV-worthy drama in our sleepy town. One of Gabriel's hands had slipped out of his vest pocket, and he was reaching for something in the back pocket of his worn, faded jeans. Probably a notebook.

Forgetting for a moment that I wasn't eager to touch Moxie's arm, lest I encounter a pink, twitching nose, I also tried to silence my friend by reaching out to squeeze her wrist.

But before I could interrupt, someone who'd obviously been eavesdropping barged into our conversation, uninvited, and confronted us all, saying, "If you've got complaints about me, please tell me to my face."

Although I hadn't said a word about Lauren Savidge, I turned around to discover that she was pointing an accusing finger at *me*. Then she announced, in a tone that was almost threatening, "In the meantime, I would like to speak to you, Daphne." And, although she was flanked by her assistant, Joy Doolittle, and her cameraman, Kevin Drucker, she added, ominously, "*In private.*"